For our great and necessary libraries everywhere! Many thanks for the continued dedication and hard work of everyone who works in them.

CHAPTER ONE

Acting Detective Chief Inspector Hillary Greene leaned forward slightly in her chair, heard the skirt of her best dress uniform creak ominously and hastily sat upright again. The skirt still dug spitefully into her waist, but she managed to smile nevertheless as the assistant chief constable up on the stage spoke her name, and began to clap.

All around her, the applause was politely amplified by the guests and she stood up slowly, not sure whether to feel relieved because the pinching of her waist had now come to an end, or feel downright panic-stricken because now the full force of the media was focused upon her.

The venue was the Olde Station Hotel, a mere stone's throw from Oxford's railway station, and at this particular moment in time, its large dining room was bedecked with white and near-black flowers; some PR assistant's brilliant idea, no doubt. Certainly Hillary's uniform (which she'd last worn, what, nearly ten years ago?) was the traditional black and white, and a good percentage of the guests at this medal awards ceremony were similarly dressed, or had adorned black dinner jackets.

Hillary took a slow breath as she wound her way through the tables to the small makeshift stage where she walked carefully up two wooden steps and wondered, with just a tinge of hysteria, what the hell she'd do if her skirt popped a button and pooled around her ankles just as she accepted her award for bravery. No doubt the resultant photograph appearing in Oxford's papers the next morning would have a pithy comment to go with it. She managed to keep her face straight (and her stomach sucked in) as she approached a smiling ACC, and took his hand.

As he spoke, once more outlining her 'outstanding' bravery during the Luke Fletcher case, he pinned the tiny piece of metal on to the lapel of her uniform jacket, which strained somewhat over her generous breasts. She noticed him noticing, and bit back a sigh. So much for the two-week diet she'd been on that had guaranteed the shedding of at least six pounds. Six ounces, more like. Still, at nearly forty-four, her middle-aged spread wasn't nearly as wide as some of those around her. She stood stiff, feeling equal measures of embarrassment and unease as he pinned the medal on to her, aware of flashbulbs going off throughout the room. Some of the photographers, she knew, belonged to the gang of her family members who'd descended on the hotel that morning en masse. She knew that her mother, for one, would have the scrapbook all ready to accept this latest proof of her daughter's glorious career, and would drag it out for unwitting visitors for years to come. She wanted to shout out that this was way over the top for what she'd actually done, but, of course, kept her mouth firmly shut.

She smiled and shook the mayor's hand, accepting his congratulations and wondering if the big shining metal chain around his neck was genuine gold and, if so, which one of her colleagues would be likely to get the shout should it ever get stolen.

She shot a surreptitious glance at the clock on the wall as she turned to leave the stage. Lunch was going to be served early, at twelve, then she had a half hour or so of gladhanding to get through, which meant, with a bit of luck, she could be back in the office (and out of her bloody uniform) by two.

At the bottom of the stage she was obliged to pause for yet more photographs, and was aware of Acting Superintendent Philip 'Mel' Mallow coming up to stand beside her. Hillary groaned audibly as the reporters thrust out microphones towards her face and Mel, her friend of the last twenty-odd years, pinched her arm warningly, and whispered, 'Be nice,' before beaming urbanely.

'Detective Chief Inspector, how does it feel to be a hero? I mean, officially? To receive this medal must be the highlight of your career.' The reporter wasn't one she recognised, and she forced a smile on to her face. It felt stiff and unnatural and she only hoped she wasn't baring her teeth like a terrier about to bite.

'Well, I don't know that I'm a hero,' she said, and meant it. 'There were other officers present at the same raid. I was the only one unlucky enough to get shot.' And almost in the bum, too, she might have added, but luckily the bullet had entered just above and to the left, creasing her hip instead. Thus saving her from a lifetime of teasing by workmates and villains alike.

'But you saved the life of your fellow officer, didn't you?' somebody who'd actually read the police press liaison officer's report suddenly chirped up from the back. There was always one conscientious one, Hillary mused glumly. Mostly though, she could rely on journalists to be interested only in the free booze.

'Yes, she did,' she heard Mel say smoothly, with a smile in his voice. 'And I'm the officer she saved,' he oiled on, drawing the pack off her as he launched into a sanitized and newspaper-friendly version of the night in question. He hadn't earned his nickname of Mellow

Mallow for nothing. Hillary gave him a grateful smile and slipped away. As she did so, she wondered, with just a hint of justifiable malice, what Mel would say if anyone should ask him why the senior officer that night, Superintendent Jerome Raleigh, wasn't here today. But with luck, nobody would. Jerome Raleigh had officially resigned and gone to live abroad. Which was as good a story as any, after all.

As a steady stream of reporters abandoned Mel and headed for the bar, she could already feel herself becoming yesterday's news and smiled with relief. The Great British public might like to acknowledge its heroes in uniform, but scandal still sold more papers — and was far more interesting.

She dodged into the nearest ladies' loo and instantly unpopped the button on her skirt, looking at herself in the full-length mirror as she did so. The black-and-white uniform, with its old-fashioned black-and-white checkerboard effect, suited her long bell-shaped mass of dark brown, chestnut-streaked hair and dark brown eyes. Her figure could best be described as Junoesque: she was fairly tall and big-boned, and supported one of those curvy, hourglass shapes that were out of fashion with everyone but the average man.

Hillary noticed that her skirt managed to stay up even without the button holding it in place. Oh well. When lunch finally got served, the salad option it would have to be. Pretty damned pathetic really, for the heroine of the hour.

She frowned at the medal reflected in the mirror. What the hell was she supposed to do with it exactly? She was plain clothes normally, so she could hardly wear it after she'd changed. Did she frame it? Leave it pinned on to the uniform until the next official occasion when she'd be forced into wearing it again? Or did she put it in her desk drawer and drag it out whenever a subordinate got antsy?

* * *

One and a half hours later, and with a heartfelt sigh of relief to be getting back to normal, Hillary pulled Puff the Tragic Wagon, her fifteen-year-old Volkswagen, into the car park at Kidlington's Thames Valley Police Headquarters and spotted an empty space beneath a huge flowering horse chestnut tree. She parked and got out, and stood for a moment or two, peering up at the cones of white and pink flowers above her with her first genuine smile of the day. May had always been her favourite month. Everything was in blossom (including her waistline) and even the scent of hot tarmac and exhaust fumes was overlaid by the scent of spring flowers and lilacs in bloom.

She pushed through the revolving door into the lobby and got the usual good-natured barracking from the desk sergeant and took the lift to the big open-plan office where she'd worked for the last ten years. It was still a novelty for her to then walk on to one of the small cubicle-like side offices and shut the door behind her. For years this had been Mel's domain, but for the last six weeks it had been hers. She carefully closed the Venetian blinds that blocked her view of the office, then, with a sigh of pure bliss, began to disrobe. Within minutes she was back in her loose-flowing linen trouser suit. Yesterday, the first of May and a bank holiday to boot, had stunned everyone by starting off blisteringly hot, and the weathermen were promising a week more of such weather still to come.

Once seated behind her desk, she reached for a file from her towering in-tray and sighed. Budget projections. She hated budget projections. She hated the number of subcommittee meetings she now had to attend as well, not to mention the mountains of paperwork that seemed to grow exponentially. She resented having to schmooze with the brass, and keep an overview of all the cases her team were involved in, but never offering any input herself. In fact, she was fast coming to the conclusion that being a chief inspector was a bigger pain in the arse than being shot.

With the abrupt and unexpected departure of Superintendent Jerome Raleigh a few months ago, Mel had been bumped upstairs into his slot, and Hillary had jumped at the chance to slide into Mel's. The only thing was, she was having to reluctantly admit, if only to herself, that the working life of a chief inspector just wasn't for her. She couldn't remember the last time she'd interviewed a suspect or a witness. Couldn't even pinpoint the last time she'd got out of this damned private office. Considering the fact that she'd been champing at the bit for the last few years to gain a promotion, Hillary was feeling absurdly disappointed.

The phone burped at her and she picked it up grumpily, expecting the civilian assistant she shared with two other DCIs to inform her that she had forgotten yet another meeting with a Neighbourhood Watch aficionado or some such thing. Instead, the rich baritone of Chief Superintendent Marcus Donleavy came down the wire.

'Hillary, congratulations. Sorry I couldn't be at the ceremony. Everything went smoothly, I hope?'

'Yes, sir, thank you.'

'If you've got a moment?'

'I'll be right up, sir.'

As she hung up, Hillary felt her heart plummet. She had a horrible feeling that Donleavy was going to make her promotion permanent. She opened the blinds again and, as she stepped through the door, glanced across the large open space to the far right-hand side, where her old desk stood empty. She could see the blonde head of her sergeant, Janine Tyler, bent over a report on her desk, and DC Tommy Lynch on the phone. Of DS Frank Ross there was, of course, no sign. A circumstance that was guaranteed to make everyone's day.

Hillary sighed as she made her way to the lift. As much as it irked her to say it, she missed the daily routine with her staff. The cases coming in, the delegation, the piecing together of a case. The arrests. Just how unprofessional would it be for her to turn down a promotion? And would it ever be offered again if she did so? After all, by the time she was fifty or so, she might be in the mood to relish the idea of a desk job. And the money was definitely better. Not that money was an issue right now. She'd just sold her old marital home for a healthy profit, and had finally taken the plunge and bought from her uncle his narrowboat (on which she'd been living for the last few years), so she was unusually flush at the moment.

She was ushered through the small outer room of DCS Donleavy's office by his smiling PA, and into the boss's inner sanctum. As she entered, Mel rose from one of the chairs opposite Donleavy's desk. His smile, she noticed at once, was somewhat strained, and instantly Hillary sensed the tension in the atmosphere. Something was definitely up.

'Hillary, please sit down.' Marcus Donleavy was wearing one of his trademark silver-grey suits, which went so well with his silver-grey hair and silver-grey eyes. But he too looked unusually ill at ease. In the past, she and Donleavy had always got on very well. She knew that the super rated her as a detective, and their personalities had always been compatible. True, that relationship had been strained somewhat over the Jerome Raleigh affair, but she still thought of the super as a friend. Now, wondering just what the hell was going on, Hillary slowly sat down. She cast Mel a quick questioning glance, but he was already re-seated, legs elegantly crossed, and was inspecting the tassels on one of his expensive Italian loafers. (His second marriage had been to a wealthy woman, and he'd done well in the subsequent divorce.) He was so careful not to meet her eyes that Hillary felt her stomach clench.

'Needless to say, the PR people are very pleased with how the award ceremony went,' Donleavy began. 'And, naturally, everybody here feels the same. It makes what I have to say now doubly hard. Hillary, I want you to understand that I, we all, that is, feel that you've done an excellent job as acting DCI these past few months . . .'

Hillary blinked and felt her jaw begin to sag as she suddenly twigged what was going on. Bloody hell, they weren't going to make her promotion permanent! The cheeky buggers had given it to someone else. Had to be, with a build-up like that. She clamped her lips firmly together and for a second felt like spitting tin tacks. Then her own innate sense of fair play reluctantly kicked in, making her want to grin ruefully instead. Well, she didn't have the problem of turning down a promotion any more, did she? Still, she couldn't see why she should make it any easier on them by letting them know that she would hardly be crying into her coffee over it.

'I'm glad to hear it, sir,' she said blandly. 'I like to think I've given it my best.'

Mel uncrossed his legs and began to inspect his fingernails. Hillary bit back a smile and looked blandly on at her super.

'Oh, no doubt about it,' Marcus said smoothly. But even though he was beginning to suspect that she might not exactly be broken-hearted at having to move back to her old desk, he was very much aware that there was far worse news to come. And because he respected and liked DI Greene, he resented having to be the one to give it. 'However, to be blunt, the brass don't yet think you're quite ready to stay at that level.'

Hillary nodded. 'I daresay the long shadow cast by my husband had a lot to do with that, sir,' she said flatly. She'd been separated from Ronnie Greene for some time before he'd been killed in a car accident, and allegations of corruption had come tumbling out of the closet like so many grinning skeletons. Allegations that had then been investigated and thoroughly substantiated. Ronnie had been bent as a corkscrew, running, amongst other things, an illegal animal-parts smuggling operation. And his old mate, Frank Ross, had been just as bent, but rather more lucky, because none of the mud had been made to stick to him. And although nobody believed Hillary had been involved, memories were long.

Marcus opened his mouth to deny it, then shut it again. What could he say? He knew Hillary was a realist, as he was himself. 'I had hoped that this award for bravery would level the playing field somewhat,' he began, then shrugged.

Hillary, having had her fun, decided to let it go. 'I'll move my things out of the office right away,' she said, getting up. 'Who's the new DCI? Do I know him?'

It was at this point that Mel went pale, and Donleavy took a deep breath. And Hillary, for the first time, felt something dark and nasty crawl up her spine. Her mouth had gone suddenly dry, but she managed to work up some saliva and ask casually, 'Have they promoted in-house, or is it someone from another force?'

Now that the evil moment had arrived, Donleavy's face went completely blank. It was yet another indication that Hillary wasn't going to like the answer to this question one little bit.

'Oh no, it's in-house,' Donleavy said. 'In fact you know him. That is, you've had some dealings with him before,' he amended awkwardly. 'He applied for the job as soon as the situation became vacant, and impressed the selection committee unanimously.' Then, aware that he was waffling and merely postponing the inevitable, he added quickly and firmly, 'It's Paul Danvers.'

Hillary turned without another word and walked across the carpet to the door. She couldn't quite feel her feet. She slammed the door behind her — hard — as she left and barely acknowledged the startled glance of the PA as she marched towards the exit.

* * *

She felt numb — and childish — as she clattered down the stairs towards the central office. But, in truth, she'd had to get out of there fast, before she could make an utter fool of herself. She was sure she could still hear a scream piling up in the back of her head, even now.

Paul Danvers. They'd given Mel's job to Paul Danvers. The man who'd investigated her for corruption. The man who might fancy her. The man who was younger and prettier than herself. They'd made him her boss!

It had to be a joke, right?

She staggered to a stop at the bottom of the stairs and clung to the newel post. First they gave her a medal and a pat on the head, then they put her under the charge of Paul bloody Danvers. What was that quote she always remembered from her days as an English lit. major at Radcliffe College? *Those whom the gods wish to destroy, they first call promising.*

Yeah. That just about covered it.

She stiffened as young voices rang out beneath her, and before the two uniformed constables could pass her on the steps, she used her key card to gain access to the office and stepped inside.

At least she couldn't possibly look as wild-eyed and raving as she felt, for hardly anybody gave her a second look. She'd run the gamut of congratulations and ribbing on her way in, and now everybody's nose was back to the grindstone.

Hillary took a deep breath and marched grimly to her — no, to *Paul Danvers*'s office — and went inside. She quickly began to empty the desk of her files and personal items, upending them into an empty cardboard box that had once held copying paper. Luckily, she hadn't been in the job long enough to accrue too much stuff. As she opened the door, the box firmly under her arm, she felt the eyes turn to her at last as she walked the long walk across the floor, back towards her old desk.

At least she didn't have to make any specific announcements. That action alone told everybody watching what had happened. She'd been booted back to DI again.

There was a sudden buzz of conversation, and she knew that most of it was sympathetic to her cause. It made her chest feel warm and some of the numbness began to wear off. OK, so she'd been dealt a shitty deal, but that was life, and there'd be plenty who'd be in her corner. Danvers, as a cop who'd investigated another cop, had never been popular, and now he'd be even less so. She supposed it was petty of her to be glad about that, but she was only human, after all.

She dumped her stuff noisily on to her empty desk and Janine looked up in surprise, then watched as her grim-faced boss settled herself back in. She shot a glance across to Tommy Lynch, who looked dismayed by this latest event, and then bent back over her report. She wasn't going to ask. She had more sense. Everybody knew that something weird had gone on during the Fletcher bust, and Raleigh's abrupt departure was still a mystery, although everyone suspected that Hillary knew more about it than she was saying. So if her boss not getting the permanent promotion to DCI was some kind of payback, she didn't want to get involved.

Frank Ross, who'd sneaked in sometime during her interview with Donleavy, grinned hugely, but had enough sense — just — to keep his mouth shut as well. A fifty-something, slovenly fat man, with a surprisingly endearing Winnie-the-Pooh type face, Frank was loathed by one and all, but nobody could call him stupid. Besides, he too was keeping his head well down for the moment. He was lucky to still be employed with an intact pension after what that bastard Raleigh had tried to pull. And the fact that he owed his saved skin to DI Hillary Greene still rankled.

It was Tommy, of course, the youngest and most straightforward of her team, who asked the question. 'Guv, what's going on?' He was a tall, athletically built black man, who'd passed his sergeant's Boards some time ago and was just waiting for a position to become vacant, and he, of all the team, had been the most pleased to see Hillary get Mel's job. He'd been secretly half in love with her since joining her team, and the fact that he was getting married in a month's time to his long-time girlfriend, Jean, didn't stop him from still feeling protective of his boss.

Hillary shrugged. 'Just what it looks like, Tommy,' she said flatly. 'Donleavy just told me they've appointed a new and permanent DCI.' She pushed the last of her personal stuff, a somewhat unhappy-looking African violet (a gift from her mother) to one corner of her desk and looked across at Janine. 'So, what's happening? Anything interesting?'

Janine shrugged. 'Sorry about the promotion, boss,' she said quietly, and truthfully. She'd enjoyed working as top dog on the small team for the last few months, and was genuinely appalled that Hillary Greene hadn't got the promotion. She'd worked hard for it and deserved it. Even more significantly, if she'd got it, it would have meant that she, Janine, could have petitioned Mel for Hillary's old job.

Janine had just sat her Inspector's Boards, and was sure that she'd aced them. But now, with Hillary back in her old slot, Janine felt aggrieved. She didn't particularly like working for a woman, although she had nothing against Hillary personally.

'Anything good been happening, besides the McKinley bust?' Hillary prompted. Now she was back in harness again, she might as well go out and get cracking. Interview somebody. Put the wind up a snout. Drag some pervert in for questioning. Something, anything, besides sitting here, having people feel sorry for her.

'Not really, boss,' Janine said. 'I've got McKinley sewn up. There's an alleged rape—'

The telephone on her desk shrilled and Hillary snatched it up. 'Yes?' she barked.

'Hill, it's me,' Mel said. 'Look, sorry, I didn't know what was happening until a few minutes before you arrived. Donleavy didn't warn me, or I'd have told you.'

'Sure,' Hillary said flatly. 'By the way, is your promotion to superintendent confirmed yet?'

The long silence on the other end spoke volumes. 'I see,' Hillary said, glancing across at Janine, who was staring at her avidly. 'Of course it is.'

Not three months ago, Mel and Janine had been an item, and had been for some time. It was the main reason, or so the station gossip had it, that Mel hadn't been promoted to superintendent the first time around. And look what that had led to — the appointment of Jerome Raleigh. But now that the man from the Met had legged it, and Mel had shown his penitence by dumping Janine, his promotion had been a sure thing.

Janine looked quickly down at the file she was reading and tried to look uninterested. But Hillary knew that her mind must be racing. Her pretty blonde sergeant believed that being dumped by Mel gave her an edge, and who could blame her? Mel was riddled with guilt, and wide open in the do-me-a-favour-or-else department. If Janine didn't eventually get a promotion to DI out of the situation, Hillary was a Dutchman's uncle.

'Look, Hill, the reason I called you,' Mel said in her ear, interrupting her dire musings, 'I've just had a suspicious death come in. Almost certainly homicide by the sounds of it. It's right up your alley. You need to get over to some place called Aston Lea. It's a hamlet, I think, near Steeple Aston. You know it?'

Hillary didn't, but knew she would find it. 'Fine, I'm on my way,' she said flatly. But although her heart leapt at the thought of getting her teeth stuck into something worthwhile, she was not about to offer her old boss any olive branches just yet. She'd just been right royally shafted, and wasn't in any mood to be magnanimous. Still, having Mel owe her a favour or two didn't exactly hurt.

She hung up and reached for her bag. 'Come on, everyone.' Her gaze reluctantly included Frank Ross as she spoke. 'We've got a suspicious death.'

Janine was up before she'd even finished speaking. 'What about the new DCI?' she said. 'Won't he or she want to brief you first? You know, get settled in to the new office, get acquainted and all the rest of it?' What she really meant, of course, was that Hillary should stay here and play office politics, leaving her to grab some glory out at the murder site.

Hillary, reading her like a book as always, smiled with all the panache of a great white shark spotting a disabled seal. 'Oh, I'm sure Detective Chief Inspector Danvers can find his way around without me holding his hand,' she said softly. And, as she looked at the stunned faces of her team, she added softly, 'After all, if he gets lost, I'm sure some kind soul will show him to his new office.'

CHAPTER TWO

Hillary tossed her car keys to Tommy in the car park and checked her watch, making a mental note of the time she had remaining before nightfall. 'We'll take my car. You can drive. I need to check the map.'

'Right, guv.'

Hillary slid into the passenger seat and raided the car's glove compartment for its road atlas. The page was already opened at Oxfordshire, and she quickly found the village of Steeple Aston. The single unnamed black dot on the map about a mile away was, she hoped, Aston Lea. 'Right, we need the main Banbury road,' she said to Tommy as she thrust the atlas back into the glove compartment and checked the rear mirror. Already Janine's sporty little 'new' Mini was waiting behind to follow. Of Frank's latest rustbucket there was no sign, but since nobody cared whether he made it to the crime scene or not, Tommy quickly pulled out and sped away.

Hillary rolled down the window, for the sun was blazing away through the windshield, and admired the rows of flowering laburnum trees in the gardens skirting Kidlington's main thoroughfare. Already the women walking through the pedestrianized shopping precinct were wearing their summer togs. Legs in shorts and shoulders in skimpy tops might look white and pasty, but who cared when the sun shone and the cherry blossom cast pink petals into a slight breeze?

It was not the kind of day that most people would associate with murder, and Hillary hoped that, for most of them, it would stay that way. But she couldn't help but wonder whose life had just been wrecked. Who would forever afterwards associate a lovely May day with loss and misery. So far she knew nothing about the victim, his or her family, or the circumstances. But in the next few hours, all that would change. And for the next few weeks, maybe months to come, her life was going to revolve around this moment in time.

'Guv, I thought I should let you know,' Tommy began diffidently, indicating to pass a slow-moving car and wondering if now was really the right time to bring this up. 'I got a letter in the post this morning. There's a sergeant's spot opened up at Headington nick. They've offered it to me.'

Hillary smiled widely. At least there was some good news today. 'Tommy, that's great,' she said, and meant it. 'I worked out of Headington for a while, in my WPC days. It's a nice billet. You'll enjoy it there. And haven't you and Jean just got a mortgage on a small semi out that way?' And when Tommy nodded, she turned back to the passing scenery and said placidly, 'Well then, it looks like you've finally got things sorted.'

Tommy sighed a little wistfully, but was smiling nevertheless. 'I guess so. But they don't expect me to start for another two weeks, so I won't be leaving you shorthanded. At least, not yet.'

Hillary nodded and wondered who her next green and eager newly promoted detective constable would be. Mel and Donleavy, she knew, rated her in-house training, and a clerk in records had once admitted that Hillary had gained something of a rep for being a safe pair of hands for 'problem' children. Not that Tommy had ever been a problem, but being big and black and ambitious, he'd no doubt worried somebody in the higher ranks, and she hadn't been surprised when she'd been appointed his senior officer. She only hoped whoever she got next would turn out to be as quick a learner as Tommy, and, if she was really lucky, would be as easy to get along with. She was going to be sorry to see him go, but he deserved the promotion.

Seven miles later, she nodded towards the crossroads up ahead and said, 'Keep going past the lights at Hopcrofts Holt, then take the next turning on the right.'

The road to the hamlet turned out to be single-car access only, with the odd passing spot carved out on the grass verge. Out of her window, towering ranks of white cow parsley — or ladies' needlework as her grandmother had always insisted on calling it — flashed by, then Tommy slowed the car to a crawl as first one bungalow and then, on the opposite side of the lane, another bungalow, hove into view. 'Is this it?' he muttered doubtfully. Down the road he could see the roofs of maybe one or two more houses, and that was it.

'See any patrol cars?' Hillary asked, just as doubtfully.

'No, guv.'

Hell, perhaps this wasn't the place, Hillary mused, and was reaching for the glove compartment again when a uniformed constable suddenly popped up out of a hedge to take a look at them. Tommy pulled over, and when Hillary opened the car door and got out, she could see that there was, in fact, a concealed entrance in the flowering hawthorn bushes. As Tommy parked up on the grass verge, Janine's Mini pulling in behind him, Hillary walked towards the uniform. A traditional five-barred country gate of rather rickety parentage gave way to a surprisingly thriving set of single-chain allotments.

'You can't park here, madam,' he began, and Hillary reached instinctively for her badge. The constable was probably new, or maybe from Bicester or Banbury, since most of the Kidlington rank-and-file knew her by sight. 'Sorry, ma'am,' he added respectfully as he read her name on the card. It still, she noticed with a brief and short-lived shaft of fury, listed her as an acting chief inspector.

'Where's the crime scene?' she asked, glancing back at the bungalows on either side of the road. They looked like typical members of their species, with good paintwork, neat walling, and lavishly flowering gardens. Probably both occupied by retired people. She hoped the murder victim wasn't old. There was something particularly harrowing about murdered seventy or eighty year olds.

'Through here, ma'am,' the constable said, pointing past the gate and taking her by surprise. At first glance, she'd seen nothing out of place on the productive allotments.

The constable was a fairly fit forty-something, with the weathered skin of a dedicated outdoorsman. 'A young lad found dead in his father's allotment shed,' he added, guessing from her start of surprise that she hadn't been briefed yet. 'He was found by his younger sister at roughly two forty-five p.m. She ran home to tell her parents, and her father came and confirmed it. He phoned us. He's in the car now,' he added, pushing the gate open and standing aside to let her pass. He nodded at Tommy and Janine who'd arrived on the scene to listen to his initial statement.

Once inside, Hillary could see that a patrol car had pulled into the allotments themselves, and was parked up on a wide grass road, which followed the line of the hedge around the perimeter of the lots. Inside the car, she could see two heads: one in front, one in back. 'Janine, perhaps you can go and get an initial statement from him. Tommy, with me. Has the medical examiner arrived yet, Constable?'

'Not yet, ma'am.'

'Thank you. You'd better stay here and look out for him, and SOCO. It's an easy spot to miss.'

'Ma'am,' he said placidly. For a man who couldn't have been called upon to attend the scene of many homicides, he was reassuringly calm and matter-of-fact. Hillary appreciated the type — content not to make promotion, but do the job well, collect his pay cheque, and go home to his wife and kids and garden — or whatever hobby he favoured. She wished there were more like him.

It was not hard to spot the actual crime scene now, for it had been efficiently sealed off with blue-and-white POLICE — DO NOT CROSS tape. There were seven allotments in all, five of which had sheds. The strips of land all looked to be thriving, with rows of about-to-be-dug new potatoes, and cheerfully flowering scarlet runner beans running up wigwams or rows of staked sticks, depending on the owner's preference. The allotments, she noticed gloomily, were tucked well out of sight, being bordered on the roadside by the thick hawthorn hedge, and down at the bottom, by a more straggling row of native trees. Witnesses were probably going to be non-existent in this isolated and well-hidden spot. It was the allotment tucked in the far right-hand corner that drew her eye.

A young lad was dead inside there, or so the constable had said. How young? She felt her stomach clench at the thought of a dead child. Of all the nightmares coppers faced in their careers, dead children were the worst.

Tommy stood beside her, worriedly chewing on his lower lip, no doubt thinking the same. Hillary gave a mental shrug and told herself to get on with it. She glanced at the ground and sighed. It was dry and hard, no doubt due to the recent two days of bright sunshine. So, probably no chance of footprints or other useful evidence. The wide grass road led straight down to the allotment, but she could see no signs of a vehicle passing this way. So the killer didn't arrive by car. Or if he or she did, they parked on the road. She made a mental note to ask the uniforms to appeal for witnesses to any car parked nearby at the relevant time.

She walked to the edge of the pathway, brushing up against the hawthorn, and indicated to Tommy to do the same. 'We'll walk down there and take a peek. Careful — SOCO won't appreciate too much disturbance.'

'Guv,' Tommy said, carefully placing his big, heavily clad feet in her own smaller footsteps. The hedge behind him was a mass of white flowers that gave off a rather sickly smell, and Tommy felt his gorge rise. He swallowed hastily and told himself not to be a muffin. Since working with Hillary Greene this would be his fifth murder case, and he was not about to blot his copybook now by upchucking on the broad bean plants.

Hillary paused a little way from the shed and regarded it carefully before going inside. Most of the other sheds were the standard tiny wooden shells that you either bought flatpacked and put up yourself, or had delivered more or less ready-made and simply plonked down wherever it was required. But this shed was different. It was bigger and more raggedy somehow. It had the look of being cobbled together from odd planks of wood. Definitely a Heath Robinson sort of affair, it smacked of parsimony. Couldn't they afford a proper shed? Was the victim's family that hard-up? There was one small window, covered in grime and set slightly off-kilter. There was no door facing her, which meant she'd have to go around the side. She glanced once more at the ground in front of her, bending down to check the grass more thoroughly. Although she could make out flattened areas where someone had trod — probably the father, and maybe even one or both of the uniformed officers responding to the call — she could make out no tread patterns that might prove useful, and satisfied that she wouldn't be causing any damage, carefully stepped out to the opposite side of the path and made her way around the far side of the shed.

The entrance stood open. She wouldn't call it a door, as such, for there was no handle or latch, and it comprised barely two planks of wood crudely nailed together. A piece of string had been looped through a natural hole in the wood, and she could just make out a rusted hook screwed into the other side of the entrance, where it could be tied off. The gap between was very narrow and, as she suspected, it looked dark and gloomy inside. She moved forward, careful to keep her hands in her pockets (the policeman's mantra at any crime scene) and peered inside. To enter, she'd probably have to turn sideways and edge in like a crab.

She could smell dust and compost, and a not unpleasant aroma of antiquity, and at first could see only the usual junk associated with such places. Wheelbarrows, old and disused, the latest and newest model to the fore. Standing around the walls, long, tall, poking things: rakes, hoes, spades, forks. On the uneven flooring, bags of fertilizer, a big bale of string and . . . with a start, she suddenly saw him. He was sitting on a sack stuffed with something hefty.

Hillary took a deep breath, and waited for the usual wave of pity to pass over her. She blinked as her eyes accommodated themselves to the gloom. He was a big lad, but not fat, with dark hair and what she thought might be blue eyes. He might be as old as an under-developed sixteen, or as young as a well-developed thirteen, it was hard to tell. He was dressed in dark blue tracksuit bottoms and a T-shirt. The logo was hard to make out, mostly due to the fact that he had a pair of garden shears sticking out of his chest. The dark stain of blood had pooled into his lap, but very little had made it to the floor. And from that alone she surmised that his heart must have stopped beating almost instantaneously. She hoped so anyway, the poor little bugger.

He looked . . . surprised, Hillary thought. At least there was no sign of horror or awareness on that young face, still filled out with puppy fat. She backed out of the opening, motioned Tommy to take a preliminary look as well, and glanced around.

Directly behind her was the straggly line of trees. Mock orange blossom, she thought. The usual ubiquitous elder. No thorn trees though. Through the gaps in the branches, she caught sight of a scruffy paddock, more thistles and dock than grass. And another stand of rough trees just beyond that. It had the look of derelict land; a real rarity in this day and age, when any piece of land going to waste was promptly built upon.

'I can hear a car, guv,' Tommy said, dragging his gaze away from the murdered boy and looking back towards the gate.

'Let's go,' Hillary agreed, taking the same careful route back. Back at the barred gate, she smiled as a slight and dignified figure stepped carefully on to the grass path. Dr Steven Partridge must be approaching his mid-fifties by now, but he looked and dressed like a thirty-something reject from Howard's End. Today he was wearing impeccable cream-coloured trousers with a crease that could slice bread, and a white, probably silk, shirt. Gold glinted discreetly from cuffs and the watch on his wrist. His hair was carefully dyed a becoming dark brown, and was smoothed back with some kind of aromatic hair oil.

He looked up and spotted her, and smiled with genuine pleasure. 'Hillary. So it's one of yours.'

'Yes, 'fraid so,' she agreed ruefully, and, as he passed, she held out a hand in warning. 'He's young,' she said softly, and saw his face tighten. Then he nodded, sighed and moved on past her. Hillary watched him go, then approached the phlegmatic constable at the gate.

'Constable . . . ?'

'Wright, ma'am.'

'Constable Wright. What else can you tell me?'

'Victim's name is William Davies, ma'am, aged fifteen. His family live in the last bungalow as you carry on down the road. Aston Lea's all bungalows, ma'am, built in the thirties by the then estate owner for his workers. Father's name,' he checked his notebook, 'is George Davies. Works as a mechanic up at the garage on the main road. Nothing known,' he added, the usual shorthand for letting her know he had no criminal record. 'Mother is Marilyn Davies. She works in the shop at the petrol station. Lad was found by his sister.' Constable Wright's face began to darken now, as he carried on. 'One Celia Davies. She's eleven.'

Hillary gave a little grunt of distress, then nodded at him to carry on. 'Seems she's not at school because of one of those teacher training days or what have you. Anyway, her mum sent her down to the allotment to remind William that she wanted him back in time for tea. Apparently the lad wasn't well, which was why he was home from his school. Some sort of tummy bug. He hadn't eaten any lunch, or not been able to keep it down, and his mum wanted him to have his tea early. A boiled egg,' he added flatly.

Hillary took another deep breath and let him get on with it. It was the little details that could sometimes break your heart, and you just had to pretend they didn't.

'Anyway.' Constable Wright sighed heavily, and went back to his notebook. 'She couldn't see him from the gate so called to him, but when he didn't come out of the shed, she went in and . . . found him. She ran home and told her mother, and her father hot-footed it up here to see for himself.'

'Her father wasn't at work either?' she asked sharply.

'No, ma'am.'

Hillary nodded but instantly wondered why not. And was the fact that the whole Davies family seemed to have been at home today somehow significant? She made a mental note to find out and then nodded at him to continue.

Wright shrugged, as if to say there wasn't much else to come. 'Father finds his son and staggers back home to call us.'

'Did he touch the body?'

'He says not, ma'am.'

Hillary's eyes narrowed. She found that hard to believe. Surely a father finding his son in that state would instinctively touch him? Hold him, try to pull the blade out. Cry over him, rock him — something. But then, she knew shock took people in different ways. Perhaps the horror of that scene had frozen him on the spot, and then all he wanted to do was turn away from it. Blot it out. It could as easily have happened that way.

'What time did the call come in?'

Wright checked the notebook again. 'Dispatch has it at two fifty-three p.m., ma'am. The timing seems to be right, but I didn't question the little girl closely, or the father either, come to that. Most of this is just what he blurted out when we arrived.'

'He came back to the allotments then?'

'Yes, ma'am. He was in the road when we arrived, and motioned us in. He was white and shaking, but seemed coherent enough.'

'Right. Well, I'd best have a word,' she murmured. 'I take it the little girl is with her mother back at the house?'

'Yes, ma'am. I asked her, the mother that is, if she had a friend or wanted a neighbour round, but she said no.'

Hillary frowned. Another strange reaction. But then again, perhaps the Davies weren't close to their neighbours. And in a tiny hamlet like this one, that factor alone might be significant.

Hillary moved up to the patrol car and Janine, spotting her, got out to give her a quick rundown on what she'd picked up from George Davies. Most of it tallied exactly with the report given to her by DC Wright.

Hillary opened the back door and slid inside. Beside her a man sat slumped forward, his hands dangling listlessly between his spread knees. He smelt, oddly, of paint. He was wearing old trousers with a small hole in one knee, and a shirt that was fraying at the cuffs. Probably his old working-around-the-house clothes, donned for mowing the lawn or cleaning out the gutters. But again, Hillary wondered if money was tight in the Davies family.

'Mr Davies, my name's Detective Inspector Hillary Greene. I'm going to be heading up your son's murder inquiry.' She tried to say the blunt, harsh facts as gently as she could, but as she spoke, she saw his head rear up. He was thickset, like his son, and with the same dark hair, but in his case it was now going thin on top. He had bright blue eyes.

'You're a woman,' he said. It wasn't an accusation, or a wonderment, simply a statement. Hillary didn't take offence, but said simply, 'Yes,' and waited. After a moment George Davies nodded.

'You'll find whoever did it?'

Hillary hesitated for a scant second, then said again, and simply, 'Yes.'

Of course, she'd been on so-called management courses where officers were advised never to make promises of that sort. But Hillary knew what George Davies needed to hear, and after seeing that poor dead boy in his dad's allotment shed, she meant exactly what she said.

George Davies let out a long shuddering sigh and leaned back against the upholstery. 'I can't believe it.'

'No.' Hillary didn't suppose he could. Best just to get straight on with it. 'Mr Davies, why weren't you at work today? Yesterday was a bank holiday, isn't today a working day for you?'

Davies nodded. 'Yeah. But the boss likes me to work of a Sunday. Lots of folks bring in their cars for fixing then, because of the weekend see. So I always have a day off in the week instead. Whichever looks less busy, the boss doesn't mind. Except for Fridays. I never have a

Friday off. And yesterday, as you said, was a bank holiday, so I thought I'd take today off as well and make it two days in a row. Weather was going to be good, like, and my wife wanted me to redecorate the loo. So . . .' he shrugged.

So that was one small mystery solved. And also explained the smell of paint.

'Your wife wasn't at work either?'

'No, we only got the one car, see, so whenever I have my day off, she has it too. Besides, our Celia didn't have school today, so it made sense to stay home for her, like. The garage where I work is attached to the petrol station where my wife works. The boss's wife always minds the shop and sees to the pumps when Mari's off,' he explained.

And again Hillary wondered. Only one car then. The Davies definitely weren't well-off. But they seemed to be good parents — timing their work around the needs of their children.

'And William was ill, I understand?'

'Who?' George asked blankly.

'William. Your son.'

George Davies managed a smile. 'Oh. No. Billy. He's always been Billy.'

'Sorry. I understand he had a tummy bug.'

'Hmmm. So he said,' George agreed. 'Didn't seem much wrong with him to my mind. But his mum said he was off his food, and there's been some sort of tummy bug about. One of these twenty-four hour diarrhoea things.' But he didn't sound convinced, and Hillary got the distinct impression that his father thought that young Billy had been swinging the lead. Still, who didn't try and get off school once in a while? She had, when she'd been his age. And she'd bet George Davies had too.

'But if he wasn't well, why was he on the allotment at all?' she asked carefully. 'Was he a keen gardener?'

George grunted a laugh, then abruptly bit it off, as if expecting to be hit by lightning for such an offence. 'No,' he said, after a long and heavy moment, having obviously fought off the threat of imminent tears. 'No, he was a lazy little sod, really. Like all boys his age. But he liked the allotments. Always hanging around, doing nothing much. You know what kids are like. And he liked to take photographs and stuff. Besides, I think his mum sent him up here for some taters.'

For a moment Hillary was lost, then suddenly twigged. Taters was the old Oxonian country word for potatoes. 'You keep the winter crop in the shed?' she asked. So the bag Billy had been found sitting on might have been filled with his dad's potatoes.

'Yeah. They need chitting, I 'spect,' George Davies added vaguely, but the thought of having to do it at some point seemed to exhaust him. She could almost see him wilting. Finally, reaction was setting in, and she quickly folded her notebook away.

'I'm going to ask the constable here to take you back home,' she said, nodding to DC Wright's partner, who was sat behind the wheel, and hadn't said a word during the entire interview. 'I think it might be a good idea to have the doctor out,' she added to the man behind the wheel, a youngster with a shock of very pale hair and a faceful of freckles. He nodded instant understanding, and started the engine as Hillary slipped out.

Janine stood beside her and watched the patrol car head through the gates. DC Wright began to close the gate behind them, then quickly opened it up again. 'Looks like SOCO have got here,' Janine muttered, as the first of several mid-range cars began to pull up on the road outside.

Hillary nodded. 'Best leave them to it.' She headed for the gate and nodded at DC Wright as they passed through. Tommy was leaning against her car, talking on the radio, probably reporting in. With a start she wondered if he was talking to DCI Paul Danvers.

She was about to take a deep breath and go and take over, when, behind her, she heard her name being called. Doc Partridge had finished his initial inspection and had declared the official time of death. There was not a spot of dirt or blood on his clothes as he walked up to her.

'Well, I'm not expecting any surprises,' he began instantly. 'I'm sure the obvious thing killed him. Didn't find any defensive wounds on his hands or arms. I think whoever stuck that blade into him took him by surprise. You noticed the shears were open?' he added, but it was strictly rhetorical. Of course she'd noticed.

Hillary nodded. 'Using just the one blade made it easier to kill with?' she asked sharply.

'I would say so. Shears that are shut up must make a blunter weapon. But the individual blades both look sharp and well maintained. I don't think the killer would have had to use too much strength to stab him.'

'So a female killer can't be ruled out?'

'No.'

Hillary sighed. 'Right-handed?'

'I'd say so, given the angle. And not much taller than the victim, either. Say in the five-eight to five-eleven range. But that's pure speculation, of course,' he added sternly.

'Right, Doc. When can you post-mortem him?'

'I'll try to get to him first thing tomorrow. Got a drowning and a suspicious cot death to do before him though. And you know how cot deaths are,' the pathologist sighed heavily. 'Have to take your time and get it right with them. Make a mistake of one kind, and an innocent mother or father gets jailed for a murder they didn't commit. Get it wrong at the other end of the scale, and the next baby brother or sister dies as well.'

Hillary winced, and realised that the old saying was true: no matter how bad you thought you had it, there was always some other poor sod who had it worse. 'Thanks, Doc, I know you'll do your best.'

Steven Partridge smiled wearily, looking his true age for the first time she'd known him. She watched him leave, then nodded across to Tommy. Of Frank Ross there was still no sign. He'd probably got lost somewhere en route. In the vicinity of a pub, no doubt.

'If a DS Ross shows up, tell him we're at the vic's house,' Hillary said to DC Wright, who nodded amiably.

'Yes, ma'am.'

'And strictly no press allowed inside,' she added darkly. It wouldn't be long before they descended.

'Yes, ma'am.'

Hillary glanced at her car, then mentally vetoed it. 'Let's walk,' she said to Janine. It would give her a chance to get her thoughts in order before she had to talk to the grieving mother and a traumatized little sister.

And in the back of her mind lurked the knowledge that most murders were committed by members of the family.

This had all the hallmarks of being a pig of a case.

CHAPTER THREE

The Davies bungalow was called 'The Lilacs,' and at some point George Davies, or maybe his wife, had taken a red-hot poker and burned the name into a rough piece of timber, before hanging it above a rarely used front door. The rustic tone it set, however, jarred with the building itself, which was a charmless, squat and square, 1950s bungalow. The whitewash had long since faded to a dull grey, and although the garden was neat and tidy enough, and the paintwork on the doors and window frames was fairly fresh, the building seemed unfriendly somehow.

Hillary followed the concrete path to a side entrance and glanced at Janine as she knocked on the door, noting that her sergeant, too, found the family home depressing. The door was quickly opened by a uniformed WPC, who nodded in recognition before Hillary could produce any ID. 'The mother and little girl are in back, ma'am. Little girl's in bed; mother's fussing. She's in shock, obviously, but seems coherent. Doctor's due any minute.'

'Right then, best get on,' Hillary said, stepping through and appreciating the warning. Once the doctor got here and sedated Marilyn and Celia Davies up to the eyeballs, there was no telling when they might get a decent interview out of them.

The door opened on to a tiny kitchen and, following the WPC's pointing finger, Hillary went through to a narrow corridor. The door to a compact lounge stood open on one side, so she moved to the opposite side, listening for voices and finally hearing them at last in the second bedroom on the right. She knocked briefly and pushed open the door.

Celia Davies's bedroom was obviously the smallest, little more than a box room, into which had been crammed a single bed and a small set of drawers. Dresses hung from hooks attached to the wall above. The decor in here was at least bright and cheerful, and a lemon-coloured wallpaper gave way to marching bands of daisies, cornflowers and poppies. White curtains hung at a small window, overlooking the narrow lane outside.

In the bed, a small girl with mouse-coloured hair, and the now-familiar big blue eyes, peered up at her. She clutched a small and battered stuffed white dog a little closer to her in a protective gesture, and Hillary felt her heart plummet. Interviewing distraught children was not how she liked to spend her days. Already she felt like the Wicked Witch of the West. Or was it East?

'Hello, you must be Celia,' Hillary said gently, smiling down and then turning to meet the eyes of Marilyn Davies as she rose from the bed. 'I'm DI Hillary Greene, Mrs Davies. I just need a few quick words with your daughter, then we'll chat in the kitchen, shall we? Have a nice cup of tea.' How trite, how meaningless the words sounded. They made her wince internally even as she spoke them, but in all the years she'd been doing this job, she'd never found words that fit an occasion like this.

'I don't want our Ceel upset,' Marilyn Davies said at once. She was one of those stick-thin women, with wispy mouse-coloured hair, that looked as if the next decent wind would bowl her over. Like her husband, her eyes were a vivid blue, but right now they looked watery and dazed. Her hands were obviously cold, for she kept putting them under her armpits as if to warm them, then would catch herself doing it and yank them back down again to her sides. All signs of agitation and shock, Hillary knew. They were going to have to make this quick.

'Oh, I'll be quick and gentle,' she said firmly. 'Now, Celia.' Hillary crouched down quickly beside the bed and smiled. 'I want you to think carefully. When you went to fetch Billy, did you see anyone on the allotments?'

The little girl shook her head and began to suck on the ear of the stuffed dog. Her mother moved, as if to take it out of her mouth, then thought better of it. Obviously, for once, this childish habit wouldn't be admonished.

'Do you know who has allotments as well as your dad? I bet you do, and all their names.'

The little girl nodded solemnly.

'But you didn't see anybody there today, when you went to get Billy?'

'No.' The word was whispered, as if it had been a great secret.

Hillary nodded as solemnly, the keeper of the secret. 'And no strangers either? No,' she echoed, as Celia Davies shook her head. 'How about a car then? Did you notice a car parked on the road, by the allotment gates?'

The girl thought about it, briefly raising Janine's hopes, but she quickly lowered her notebook again when the little girl shook her head.

'All right, Celia, that's all for now. But we might talk again in a few days' time, when you're feeling better. All right?'

The little girl nodded solemnly, and gave the dog's ear a particularly ferocious suck. It had one time been a standard poodle, but the nylon material it was made out of had long since lost its shape. It must be years old, and taste terrible.

Hillary rose, feeling her knee joints wince, and vowed once more to stick to a diet. Then she opened the door and looked wordlessly at Marilyn Davies, all but willing her to follow her out. The other woman sighed, gently pulled the hair back from her daughter's head and whispered something to her, then followed them out. She left the door open, so that she could hear if her child should cry out.

'Do you have any other children?' Hillary asked softly as they walked, single file, down the stingy corridor and into the small lounge. This was papered in woodchip and painted the ubiquitous magnolia. There was a rug rather than a carpet on the floor, and the cupboard standing in one corner was obviously between-the-wars utility. The two-seater sofa and battered reclining chairs looked like charity-shop purchases. A small telly stood in one corner. There was not a piece of artwork on the walls.

'No, all we have is Billy and Celia.'

Hillary took one of the chairs, and felt a spring dangerously close to her posterior shift alarmingly beneath her. 'You own your home, Mrs Davies?'

'Rent. One of those housing association things. Used to be the council, took 'em over from the estate, now it's some place in Banbury. Rent man comes every month.' Marilyn Davies looked around, as if not recognising where she was, then slowly took a seat on the sofa. Janine stayed upright by the door, discreetly jotting down shorthand into her notebook.

'I understand from your husband that you were all at home today, for various reasons. Billy wasn't well?'

'No, he said he felt sick in the night. Didn't eat much breakfast. I thought it best to keep him off school. He'd have gone back tomorrow though . . .' she added firmly, then trailed off, as she realised that her son would never be going back to school again.

Hillary got the feeling that, like her husband, Marilyn Davies didn't really believe in this 'tummy bug' excuse

Billy had given for not going to school. Which prompted an obvious question. Had he skived off school deliberately, or did he just feel lazy? Had he gone to that allotment shed intending to meet someone? Because, having been there and seen it, Hillary was having a hard time believing this could be an opportunistic crime. Some passing pervert spotting a young lad and taking a chance just didn't wash. How much traffic did the narrow country lane ever see? And unless a stranger in a car just happened to see Billy Davies walking the short distance down the road from his home to the allotment gate, nobody would ever know the allotments themselves were there.

'Did Billy often have days off school?' Hillary asked casually and saw Marilyn frown.

'Sometimes. He was bright, like, and liked school well enough, I s'pose. He wasn't no dunce. But he sometimes liked a day off, yeah,' she admitted with a sigh.

Hillary wondered if she was aware that she'd all but admitted that her son was a regular truant, and thought that she probably didn't. And what did it matter now? The thought hung between the two women like a two-edged sword.

'So, what time was it that Billy went out, do you remember?' Hillary asked, after a moment of awkward silence.

'Dunno. About half one. He hadn't wanted any lunch, or so he said. Felt like a walk, maybe over by the folly.'

'Folly?' It was Janine who echoed the word, obviously puzzled.

'Yeah. Three arches, built bang in the middle of a field. They reckon the big house at Rousham had it built, a couple of hundred years ago. A fashion craze or something.' Marilyn spoke in a curious, flat monotone. Was that her usual voice, Janine wondered, or had shock deadened it?

'Oh,' Janine said, and then, aware that she'd interrupted the flow of the interview, shot her boss an apologetic look.

'But when you wanted him to come back for his tea, you sent Celia to the allotments. Is that right?' Hillary asked curiously.

'Well, not really. Yeah, I did, but I didn't know if he'd be there or not. He just used to like hanging around there sometimes. And he'd been gone an hour, so I thought he might have had his walk and popped in there. I wanted him to get something down him — a boiled egg, some soup or summat.'

Once more, Marilyn Davies seemed to realise that she'd never have to cook for her son again, and something in her face shifted. Before she could break down, Hillary took a deep breath and rushed on. 'So you sent Celia to see if he was there. About what time was this?'

Marilyn shrugged. 'Dunno.'

'And after a while, Celia came back? What, five minutes later?'

'Dunno. Could have been. Not that long. I dunno, it didn't feel that long.'

Hillary could feel the woman slipping away, and hoped the doctor wouldn't be long now. 'What did she say exactly? Can you remember?'

'She said someone had killed Billy. I told her not to be so daft. Her dad was in by then, washing up at the sink. He'd got paint all under his nails. He went haring off.'

Hillary nodded. Marilyn Davies hadn't believed her daughter's wild tale and didn't want to believe it now. Perhaps she felt that, if she could just keep believing that it was just a little girl's wild imagination, she could stop her son from actually being dead.

'I need to go and see Billy's room now, Mrs Davies,' Hillary said gently, catching Janine's eye and then nodding towards the kitchen. Janine slipped away and came back a few seconds later with the WPC who took one look at her charge, then went over and sat beside her on the sofa.

Hillary left them, the WPC hugging the now stiff and unresponsive Marilyn Davies and rocking her on the sofa. Out in the narrow corridor once more, she felt Janine roll her shoulders and realised how tense the situation had become.

'I know, it's not nice, you feel like a right cow, but it has to be done,' Hillary murmured. If Janine was going to advance in her career, she'd have to start doing the dirty jobs herself soon.

The first door she pushed open was obviously the master bedroom. The bed was a double, and a big wardrobe stood beside the single window. Again it was woodchip and paint — this time in a pale mint green. The floorboards were wooden and bare. Again no carpet. 'I get the idea money is tight around here,' Hillary mused. 'Check out their finances and make sure.' Although she didn't think money was going to be a motive in this case, every avenue had to be checked.

'Boss,' Janine grunted, silently congratulating herself on remaining single and unencumbered. And not living in a dump like this. She couldn't understand why her boss was still living on a narrowboat when she could have lived in a house, but at least the *Mollern* was better than here. This place gave her the willies.

'This must be his room,' Hillary said, opening a door, only to find a cramped bathroom instead. There was no bath, only a narrow shower cubicle, growing a little green mould in the grouting.

Billy Davies's room turned out to be directly opposite his sister's, and was only a little bigger. It held a single bed squashed into one corner, and a tiny wardrobe. No drawers. She opened the wardrobe and saw several neatly folded shirts on a single shelf above the coat hangers. The Davies might be strapped for cash, but the boy had had clean clothes to wear.

On the walls were photographs — lots and lots of photographs. They surprised Hillary, who'd expected football posters, or girl bands. Then she remembered that George Davies had said his son's hobby had been photography, and decided to take a closer look.

'Let's have a full inventory,' she said to Janine, who sighed and rolled her eyes, but began to work. As she moved around, carefully cataloguing and documenting, Hillary gazed around her, trying to get a feel for the life their victim had led here. The woodchip in this room had been painted a pale aqua, the bare floorboards underneath disrupted by a single dark green mat, placed beside the bed. So the boy wouldn't have cold floorboards to stand on in the winter? There was no sign of a radiator in this room. She hadn't seen any in the other rooms either. Somehow, this small example of the human desire for comfort made her throat clog and she walked quickly to the window and gazed out. This side, the bungalow overlooked a field of barley; farmland right up to the narrow privet hedge that bordered the property.

Slowly, Hillary circumnavigated the walls, looking at the photographs. The boy had been good. He'd captured landscapes in both black and white and in colour, and in all seasons. Some shots of farm machinery, obviously abandoned and growing through with weeds. A few urban shots. Shots of what could only be his school, a big, faceless comprehensive by the look of it. And here and there framed pieces of paper. Reading them, she realised they were all prizes for photography — local papers, local galleries. Nothing big, but obviously a source of pride.

Why had somebody killed a fifteen-year-old schoolboy from an impoverished family, with a love of photography and the desire to skive off school now and then? It didn't make sense.

'Boss,' Janine said, nodding to a small item on the bedside table. Hillary looked at it and nodded. It was a small digital camera.

'We got him that for last Christmas,' George Davies said from the doorway, making them both jump. 'We saved up all year to get it for him, because it was what he wanted most in the world. We told him if he had that, he couldn't have anything else. Not another single present. But that's what he wanted, so that's what he got. Our Ceel, now, she likes lots of presents to open, so we buy her colouring books and paints, stuffed toys, you know. But Billy was right chuffed with that.'

Hillary nodded. 'I don't see a computer.'

George Davies barked a harsh laugh. 'You won't, either.'

'But don't you need a computer with a digital camera? You know, to print off photographs,' she added, indicating the walls.

'Oh, that best pal of his had a computer,' George Davies said. 'He'd go over to Middleton Stoney whenever he wanted something printed off. Thick as thieves those two.' Davies spoke glumly, as if he didn't approve of the friendship. As if he'd read her thoughts, he added, 'Lester's dad owns his own company. Used to show off his computer and all those video games and whatnot, just to make Billy jealous. I reckoned he looked down his nose at our Billy too, on the sly, but Billy wouldn't have it. Kids, they think they know everything.' He shrugged helplessly.

Hillary glanced once more at the photographs. 'He had talent,' she said softly.

'Ah. He reckoned he could make a living at it too. I told him, there ain't no money in arty-farty stuff. But Billy had it all worked out. He wanted to be one of those daft sods that hang around trying to get pictures of so-called celebrities.'

'Paparazzi?' Hillary said, somewhat surprised. George Davies shrugged again, then shook his head and turned away. Like his wife before him, he was probably wondering what it all mattered now. Pie-in-the-sky dreams or not, Billy Davies wasn't going to be taking any more photographs now.

* * *

Hillary and Janine stepped outside, and let out slow, long breaths. The doctor had arrived and, with the WPC, had put Marilyn Davies to bed.

Outside the back door, Hillary noticed a shed and converted coalhouse, and peered inside. Mostly garden tools and the usual paraphernalia: ladders, tins of half-used paint. The odd cardboard box filled with who-knew what. And there, standing against one wall, gleaming dark blue and new-looking in the gloom, the lines of a powerful racing bike. The dead boy's bike. His pride and joy no doubt. Something else that was now obsolete. Hillary thought back to that allotment shed and that thickset boy with the blue eyes and thatch of dark hair, and could almost see him racing along the country lanes, legs pumping hard, working up all those fancy gears, revelling in the speed and oblivious, as all children were, to any danger.

But in this case, Billy Davies had been right to scorn the thought of getting run over by a car. Billy's bike had been safely tucked away in the shed when its owner had died.

'I don't understand this,' Hillary said, as she slowly walked back down the lane towards the allotments. By now SOCO should be well ensconced. 'Who would want to kill Billy Davies. And why?'

Janine frowned. 'Early days yet, boss,' she reminded her. She never called Hillary 'guv.' But she longed for the day when someone would call *her* by that sobriquet.

At the allotment gates, Tommy saw them coming and quickly moved out to greet them. 'They're going to be here hours yet, but they reckon they can get the bulk of it done before dark. We'll have to set up lights though,' Tommy said. 'That shed is a tip. All sorts in there and it looks like it hasn't been cleaned out since before the war. The first one.'

Hillary grinned, knowing the words had come out of Tommy's mouth, but hearing behind them a disgruntled techie. 'Well, you're in for a long night then aren't you, DC Lynch,' Hillary said with a grin, and Tommy groaned good-naturedly.

'Still no sign of Frank?' she asked, but barely listened for the negative response. 'OK, Tommy, start interviewing the neighbours and see if anybody heard anything or saw anyone.' She glanced at her watch and saw that it was just gone 4:30 p.m. 'You'll probably find most of them still out at work, so hang around and go back after five. Janine, you'd better hang around here. I'm surprised the press hasn't got here already. When they do show, give them the usual line. I'll go talk to SOCO, see what they've got.'

As the three peeled off to go their separate ways, a blackbird that was nesting in the hawthorn hedge by the gate shrilled angrily.

Hillary knew how it felt.

* * *

As Tommy expected, the entire hamlet of Aston Lea seemed to be elsewhere. Apart from the Davies bungalow, there was one two-storey cottage that looked as if it had been prettified for weekenders, and seven small, squat bungalows. As he knocked on the door of the second-to-last bungalow on the road, he was already anticipating an echoing silence. So when he heard a faint voice calling, 'I'm coming, hold your horses,' it had him reaching into his pocket for his ID.

The door opened to reveal a little old lady no more than four feet six. She had a near electric-blue rinse to a tightly permed mop, and was wearing a flowered apron and battered slippers. The old woman looked up at the big constable and smiled. 'Hello, what's all the excitement then? Nobody ill over at George and Marilyn's, I hope. I saw the doctor. No good holding that thing up there, I can't see it. Hang on, let me get me glasses on.' As she reached for a pair of thick-glassed reading spectacles, which were hanging on her flat chest by a chain, she was still rabbiting on. 'I was pretty sure I saw the doctor's car. Nothing serious I hope. Oh, police is it? What's going on? That Billy in trouble?'

Tommy, trying to keep from grinning, gave up a brief prayer of gratitude for garrulous, curious old ladies, and said softly, 'I'm Detective Constable Lynch, ma'am. May I come in?'

* * *

Hillary coughed loudly a few yards from the shed door, and a white-hooded head popped out. She vaguely recognised the boffin inside. His speciality, if she remembered rightly, was clothing. Or was it blood-spatter patterning? 'Any chance of an update?' she asked.

'Not a cat in hell's,' was the cheerful response, and the white-coated figure disappeared again. Hillary blew out her lips. Great.

* * *

'Do you want digestives or rich tea?' The old woman, who'd introduced herself as Millie Verne, poured the boiling water into the teapot and reached for the sugar basin. 'Only teabags, I'm afraid. Milk?'

Tommy, sitting at a tiny Formica table, nodded to both the milk and digestives, and spread his notebook on the table. 'Is that Miss or Mrs Verne?'

'Mrs, love, though I've been a widow now for nigh on twenty years. Reckon I'll be widowed longer than I was married afore long. Husband drove the buses. Good man he was, but liked his drink.' Tommy gulped, and was glad he'd never been a passenger on one of Mr Verne's charabancs. 'So, what's going on then? I hope everything's all right. George and Marilyn are friends, like. Well, Marilyn sometimes gets me some shopping in.'

'I'm afraid I can't say just yet, ma'am,' Tommy temporized. He hadn't been given the official go-ahead from Hillary yet to release information to the public. 'Have you been here all day?' he asked gently, mentally crossing his fingers. The Verne bungalow was well situated to see any comings and goings.

'Nowhere else to go, have I, love?' Millie Verne said without rancour, sitting herself down opposite her unexpected visitor and dunking a rich tea. 'Course I was here all day. Waddya wanna know?'

'Have you seen any strange cars hanging around lately? And specifically today?'

'No. This place isn't exactly on the beaten track is it? Most people wanting to get to Steeple Aston, the bigger village down the road a mile, use the other road, the one off the main road; second turning. It's two-lane see, and closer. So only those of us who live here use this lane. Everybody goes off to work in the morning, around eight — you can hear the cars start up — then they all coming dribbling back around half five time. Bit like watching bees set off on the hunt for honey it is. Only me stays behind. And sometimes that Mrs Cooper. She only works part-time.' Tommy realised how lonely the old duck must find it, and took a gulp of tea. 'Right. So, what can you tell me about your neighbours?' he asked, wondering if he was going to wear the nub of his pencil down by the time he'd finished. He had the feeling he was in for a long haul.

'Well, now, where do you want me to start?' Millie Verne asked, eyes twinkling. 'Starting at the top end, there's the Coopers . . .'

* * *

Janine watched the first car arrive, and recognised the man who stepped out of it. He was an all-rounder for the *Oxford Times*, but he liked to specialize in crime. She walked towards him, keeping him from the gate. His passenger was obviously a snapper, and she made sure to keep both men in sight. She knew all their tricks — how the reporter would keep you chatting while his mate tried to dodge off and get some snaps.

She heard a second car and started to curse silently, realising that she could quickly be swamped, then recognised Frank Ross's beat-up jalopy, and managed a wry grin instead. She never thought she'd be pleased to see Frank.

'As I live and breathe,' Frank said, getting out of the car and grinning across at the journo, who gave a not inaudible groan. Everybody, it seemed, knew Frank. And wished they didn't.

'Please, get back in the car, sir,' Janine said firmly to the photographer, who reluctantly slid back inside, but not before taking a crafty shot of her.

As Janine dealt with a steadily growing group of media, she wondered what Mel was doing back at HQ. Or had he gone home already? Mel had a place in the 'Moors' area of Kidlington — the old part of the village, full of big gracious houses and gardens with ponds and weeping willow trees. Mel's place was a particularly fine Cotswold stone house that his wife had let him have in their divorce. It was typical of Mel to marry a wealthy woman. And Janine, until a few months ago, had lived in that house with him. Once, she'd wondered if she might be Mrs Mallow number three. Now she wondered no more. Now she was back in the small semi in Botley that she shared with a librarian and an air hostess.

Mel, newly promoted Mel, owed her. And as she dealt with the press and wondered just how sober Frank Ross actually was, she decided that now was a good time to collect on her debt. She was just contemplating ways to twist Mel around her little finger when there was a sudden stir of interest. A discreet van with blackened windows had just pulled in. They must be ready to move the body.

Leaving Frank and the two uniformed officers to keep the media away, Janine walked to the gate and looked along the pathway. Already the body had been put into a body bag and was being carried along on a stretcher. Her boss walked behind.

When the small cortege reached the gate she could hear the frantic click of cameras snapping behind her and grimaced.

Hillary too, shook her head, and muttered helplessly, 'The poor little sod wanted to be one of those paparazzi. I bet he never guessed he would be the one to get his face in all the papers.'

CHAPTER FOUR

Frank Ross pulled into the forecourt of the garage and headed for the air pump. He couldn't remember the last time he'd checked the tyres, and he might as well get something useful out of the assignment. He doubted he'd get sod all of much use here otherwise. But it was typical of the bitch from Thrupp to give him all the crappy jobs that nobody else wanted, and if he wanted to keep his job, he just had to keep on taking it.

If only he knew where Ronnie Greene had stashed his money before he'd died, he could grab it and swan off to the Seychelles, but he simply hadn't got a clue. So he was stuck at Thames Valley until the first moment he could retire and get a cushy little night-watchman's job somewhere. Give the brass the old two-fingered salute once and for all, and never have to take another order in his life.

'Can I get you anything else?' The voice was female, and Frank straightened up, puffing, from his crouch beside the left front tyre. The speaker wasn't a bad-looking woman — a bit hefty around the middle
— but with genuine fair hair and a nice smile.

'Mrs Wilberforce is it?' he asked, reaching for his ID and showing it to her. 'DS Frank Ross. Your husband owns the garage here, I understand?'

Mandy Wilberforce's smile faltered, and she turned to look over her shoulder. The petrol station boasted a small shop selling all the usual items, and a large, open-ended garage, where she was looking now. Inside, Frank could see an ageing Peugeot up on ramps and a man peering up at its underbelly.

'Gil!' Mandy yelled. 'Better get out here.'

Her husband came quickly, perhaps suspecting somebody of trying to sneak off without paying for petrol, or maybe some randy git coming on to his wife. He was a large but not particularly well-put-together man, with thinning grey hair and filthy hands. 'Yeah?' he asked, then frowned as Frank held up the ID once more. 'What's up? Nothing wrong with my garage,' he said. A shade too quickly for Frank's liking.

'No, sir, I'm sure there isn't,' Frank lied. In his experience there was usually something up with any garage; dealing in spare parts from ripped-off vehicles, turning back the mileage clocks, you name it. And even if they weren't doing anything downright criminal, the charges good mechanics dished out nowadays was daylight robbery anyway. 'But there's been an incident with one of your workers, and I need to ask a few questions,' Frank explained.

'George?' Gil Wilberforce said, obviously taken aback. He had large, boiled-gooseberry eyes and a florid face that now looked comically surprised. Obviously, George Davies was not the sort of man who immediately sprang to mind when trouble was mentioned. A boring plodder then. Not the kind to take a pair of shears to his son. Maybe.

'What makes you think I'm talking about Mr Davies?' Frank asked quickly, and Gil Wilberforce grinned widely.

'Only worker I got,' he said. 'What's up? I can't believe old George has done anything wrong. A good bloke is George. Always on time, and knows his way around cars. Not afraid of a bit of hard work neither.'

'His wife's all right isn't she?' Mandy piped up.

'I can't discuss it at the moment,' Frank said flatly. 'It's his day off today, is it?'

Gil Wilberforce agreed that it was, and confirmed George Davies's account of how they worked the employee's roster.

'So, do you know if he's been having any trouble lately? Maybe someone hassling him for money? Took out a loan with the wrong people?'

'Not George,' Wilberforce flushed with obvious anger. 'He's not the sort to get mixed up in that.'

'Not a gambler then?'

The garage owner snorted.

'Notice anything odd lately? He's been having threatening phone calls? Or maybe grousing about the old wife and kids. The daily grind getting him down? Maybe you've noticed he's been short-tempered or something?'

'No, nothing like that,' Wilberforce denied, and went on to list all of his friend's good points, but by that point, Frank was barely listening. It was just as he'd thought. A dead end. Certainly nobody here was going to come up with any interesting titbits on the Davies family. Still, he might get a free oil job out of it if he played his cards right.

* * *

'So the first thing she says, guv,' Tommy glanced up from his notebook, 'is, "What's Billy got up to now," or words to that effect.'

Hillary nodded thoughtfully. Tommy had come back to her straight away after his chat with Millie, knowing she'd want to be kept updated. 'It's interesting she immediately assumed it was the boy who was the cause of us being here,' she mused. 'Of course, it could just be little-old-lady-versus-teenager syndrome,' she sighed. They tended to mix about as well as oil and water more often

47

than not. It might not be a good idea to place too much credence to Millie Verne's opinions just yet. 'We'll have to see what the other friends and neighbours have to say. See if they confirm that Billy was a bit of a lad.'

'Thing is, she didn't really say much about him after that,' Tommy said, frowning slightly. 'I got the feeling she'd twigged it was something bad and clammed up.'

'Well, leave it a few days, let the news get around and begin to sink in, then do a follow-up. I'm off to Steeple Aston to interview a few of Billy's local friends. I got a list from his dad.' They were talking out on the road, leaning casually against her car. 'Get back to the shed and see how SOCO's doing. You'll be needing to set up the lights soon.'

'Guv.'

'Janine, you can drive.' She tossed the keys to Puff the Tragic Wagon to her junior, and slipped into the passenger seat, pretending not to hear Janine sigh. She knew that the pretty blonde preferred to be seen in her racy new Mini and hid a smile as the DS struggled with a recalcitrant seatbelt. 'There's a knack to it. Let it go all the way in, then give it a hard tug, then pull gently.'

Janine grunted.

* * *

Frank Ross didn't get his free oil job, and he was in a right snit as he drove off. He was supposed to check back at the crime scene, but sod that, it was gone clocking-off time and he never put in unpaid overtime — he left that to the young and the stupid. And the ambitious, like that brown-nose Tommy Lynch. As he drove back towards Kidlington, and his small, smelly flat over a shop, Frank wondered about the new boss.

Paul Danvers.

On the one hand, he knew Hillary Greene must be spitting tin tacks over his appointment, which was enough to cheer him right up. On the other hand, he knew

Danvers had it in for him as well. Had done, ever since he and that other git from York had come down to investigate the corruption charges levelled at the newly deceased Ronnie Greene.

Danvers was nobody's fool, and knew he'd helped his mate Ronnie out on the odd smuggling run. But Frank had spent his end of the money on the horses and trips to the red-light district in Amsterdam. He'd left no paper trail, and nothing had been able to stick. For a while, they'd investigated Hillary too, which had made him chortle into his beer for months afterwards. The thought of Ronnie's uptight, straight-as-a-die missus being put under the microscope must have had his dead friend rolling with laughter in his grave.

Of course, they'd never proved anything against her. They'd have nailed Ronnie, though, if he hadn't died in that car crash first. But they hadn't found his money. That was the one thought that still tormented him. Ronnie had been canny with his finances, and had always planned to retire to the Caribbean when he hit fifty. By Frank's reckoning, he must have stashed away at least a quarter of a million. Maybe even more.

Occasionally, Frank kept an eye on Ronnie's son by his first marriage — a still-green-behind-the-ears PC working out of Witney — but he couldn't see how the nipper had found his old man's stash. Unless he was playing a very clever waiting game. No, much as it galled him, Frank suspected that only Hillary had the nous to find the money. And she probably hadn't even looked, silly cow.

He wondered how she and Danvers were going to get on now. He grinned and lit a fag, hoping that the sparks would fly. He needed some entertainment in his life.

* * *

Detective Superintendent Philip Mallow closed the file on shoplifting statistics for the last quarter and rose stiffly from his chair. He was staring fifty in the face, as his aching back and growing tiredness told him. Once he could have put in twelve-hour shifts standing on his head. Now he walked to the window of his new office, which had a pristine view of the car park, and caught sight of a grey squirrel scampering up the trunk of a flowering horse chestnut.

Suddenly, and the thought took him completely by surprise, he wished that Janine was waiting for him, back at the empty house, like she used to be. It was strange, but he'd never expected to miss her this much. He'd entered into the affair thinking of it as a strictly short-term, no-strings bit of fun. But now that he had the promotion safely in the bag, he found his thoughts kept straying back to her. She'd been young and glorious, and had got him out of his rut. Now he could feel himself slipping back into the same old routine, and it scared him. Useless to hope she'd have him back, of course. He'd dumped her to improve his chances of getting a leg up the ladder, and no woman was ever going to forgive something like that. Not even one as determined to climb that same ladder herself.

Mel was no fool — he knew that at some point he'd be expected to give her a helping hand up to an inspectorship. Maybe then she'd be willing to have a night out, a meal maybe, for old times' sake.

Mel shook his head and turned away from the window. He was pathetic. Like a dirty old man plotting to get his leg over. How long would his libido rule his head? Even now, when he should be thinking of next month's speech on the fight against illegal immigration, which he was due to deliver at a conference in Harrogate, he was thinking instead of Janine's long silken blonde hair on the pillow next to him.

He must need his head examining.

* * *

The Rollinsons lived in a small neat semi in a cul-de-sac not far from Steeple Aston church. Fifteen-year-old Graham Rollinson, according to George Davies, had been his son's best friend at the local primary school, but it was quickly becoming apparent that those days were long over.

As they all sat in the immaculate living room, the slightly built and fair-haired Graham looked both embarrassed and enthralled in equal measure at being questioned by the police. His parents looked merely horrified. To learn that a child had been murdered right on your doorstep, and that that child was also known to your son, was something that would take the wind out of most parents' sails.

'Thing is,' Graham was saying, not for the first time, 'we got put in a different form when we went to Bicester. And we sort of lost touch. I mean we'd chat, like, on the bus sometimes. And in the long summer hols, like, we might go cray fishing, see if we could find any of those American monsters the telly programmes were on about. But not even that, last summer. I haven't really spent much time with him in years. He was all into photographs and stuff. I really can't tell you anything about him now.'

Graham was obviously eager to help, but not much use.

'Do you know why he might have been in the allotment shed this afternoon?'

'Nah.'

'Did he ever say anything to you about somebody bothering him?'

'Nah.'

'Maybe he had something secret, something he swore you not to tell.'

'Nah — and like I said, he wouldn't tell me anyway. Not now. We were best pals when we were little, but I got my own gang now. Billy wasn't our type.'

Hillary's ears pricked up. 'What type was that?'

Graham Rollinson flushed and shot a look at his parents, then shrugged. 'Nothing. I just mean he had his circle of friends, and I had mine. His best mate was Lester Miller. You should speak to him, really.'

And that was pretty much the same story they got from all of the kids on George Davies's list. They'd been close to Billy Davies in primary school, but things had changed once they'd moved schools. And nobody knew what kind of trouble he could possibly have got himself into that would result in such a drastic outcome. Or if they did, they weren't saying.

'A washout,' Janine said in disgust as they got back in the car. 'He seems to be close only to this Miller kid, and gave all his old cronies the elbow.'

Hillary nodded. It was understandable though, in a way. She herself could remember the culture shock she'd felt as an eleven-year-old. She too had gone to a small village primary school of barely thirty pupils, where everybody knew everybody else and friendships were tight, only to be thrust into a three-thousand-pupil or more comprehensive school, which had been like living on a different planet.

'We'll have to hit his school tomorrow,' Hillary agreed, then added curiously, 'Janine, did you pick up on a kind of reluctance in the kids? To talk about Billy, I mean?'

Janine frowned slightly then nodded. 'Yeah, I thought I did. But it was nothing I could put my finger on. I wasn't going to say anything, but I got the feeling they were a bit scared of him. No, maybe not that strong. Wary, somehow.'

Hillary nodded, glad that it wasn't just her. 'It's like they all knew something, but didn't want to tell. Not in front of the parents, anyway. I'm beginning to get the distinct impression that our victim had some kind of a reputation. Maybe he was a bully?'

Janine thought about it. 'He was big-built. And his family's not exactly loaded, so he might have self-esteem issues. Prime bully material. Or drugs,' she added darkly. There was always drugs to be considered.

Hillary sighed heavily. 'Anyway, they all agree this Lester Miller kid is his best buddy. We'll probably know a lot more once we've spoken to him.'

Janine nodded, checking her notebook. 'The kid from Middleton Stoney. Right. George Davies didn't seem too keen on him.'

'I got the feeling that most of those boys' parents tonight weren't too keen on Billy either. None of them were exactly unhappy that their kids weren't tight with him anymore.'

'I noticed. But nobody volunteered why,' Janine added wryly, having met this phenomenon before. Nobody liked to speak ill of the dead. Particularly not the recently murdered dead. And that probably went double if it was a kid.

'You'll have to do follow-ups in a few days' time. See if you can get to the bottom of it.'

Janine sighed. 'Right. Back to HQ, boss?'

Hillary nodded. She was going to have to confront Danvers sooner or later. Might as well be sooner.

'Yeah, then you can get off home. Start fresh tomorrow. Arrange to get Tommy relieved at midnight, yeah?'

* * *

Pulling into the parking lot at HQ half an hour later, Hillary had to queue to get in, and realised that, at nearly 6:30 p.m., she'd hit the changeover in shift. After dropping off Janine, she parked quickly and detoured down to Juvie, where she was relieved to find Melanie Parker still at her desk.

Melanie Parker was approaching sixty, but wasn't about to retire, a fact that most officers gave up prayers of thanks for every night. Melanie had worked the young offenders unit since its inception, and what she didn't know about the local youth scene wasn't worth knowing.

'Well, well, look what the cat dragged in,' Melanie said, leaning back in her chair. She had a moon-shaped face, and a thick thatch of white hair. She never wore make-up, and there'd been rumours hovering around for the last twenty years or so that she was gay. Rumours that never got confirmed or denied.

'Congrats on the gong by the way, and sorry about the promotion. Is it true they put that prat Danvers in Mellow's place?'

Hillary grimaced. She supposed she was going to have to put up with this for some time to come. 'Thanks, and yes, it's true.'

'Bummer, as the Yanks would say,' Melanie said, then added bracingly, 'What can I do you for?' Her time was precious, and a hungry cat and the latest Ian Rankin novel awaited.

'William, or Billy, Davies. Ring any bells?'

Melanie pursed her lips, which showed up her many wrinkles, and began tapping frantically at the computer keyboard. 'Can't say it does,' she admitted. 'Which means he hasn't been hauled in for twocking, vandalism, drugs, rent-boying or any of the other usual fun and games.' She tapped some more, frowned, and shook her head. 'Nope, he's not known to us. Why?'

'Somebody killed him, and I've been getting some curious vibes from the kids I've been interviewing who knew him.'

Melanie scowled. She hated getting news about dead kids — although, in her job, she heard it more often than most. 'What school's he at? Kidlington?'

Hillary shook her head. 'No, Bicester Comp. I think it's that brand-new place they built in the east of the town.'

'Oh, that rat hole,' Melanie said darkly. 'It might be new but it's already got a rep. Drug heaven. Let's see . . . nope. No bites there either. Your boy probably isn't a dealer, because I've got a nice little mole well in there. Give me a bell if you should find you need him.'

Hillary nodded her thanks. 'I might just do that. Thanks.'

She climbed the stairs to the main office thoughtfully, and used her key card to let herself in. The day shift had largely deserted, and the night shift was barely trickling in, so the office was all but empty. She glanced towards her one-time cubicle as she passed by, wondering if anyone was at home. Due to the lengthening nights, there wasn't a light on yet, but that meant nothing. The sun was only just starting to go down.

Putting off the evil moment when she'd have to check in with her new boss, she went to her desk and caught up on messages and her email. A hit-and-run case looked like it was turning sour, with a witness who'd given a number plate now looking as if she was having second thoughts. A spate of burglaries in Woodstock showed no signs of abating and her mother wanted to know if she was coming to dinner on Sunday.

She felt, rather than heard, his approach. She looked up and forced a smile at the handsome blonde man who slipped into the chair opposite Janine's desk and wheeled it the short distance across the floor to face her.

'Hillary.' Paul Danvers smiled genuinely back. He was looking good, if a little tired. 'Congratulations.'

Hillary looked at him blankly. Huh? For what?

Paul's smile widened. 'On the medal.'

'Oh,' Hillary said. That. She'd already forgotten about it — it seemed like a lifetime ago already.

Paul laughed. 'You know, if it had been anyone else, I'd swear that was false modesty.'

Hillary felt her heart plummet. Oh hell, was he flirting with her? Already?

When Danvers and his sidekick had been seconded from York to check out the allegations of corruption about her late and unlamented husband, Hillary hadn't been pleased, naturally. Still it had to be done, and she had to admit that Danvers had done a first-class job and been meticulously fair. Once or twice she'd thought she'd seen admiration in his eyes — the kind that no woman could mistake — but when he'd gone back to York, she hadn't given him a single thought.

Until he'd come back. Barely six months later, he'd accepted a transfer south, and to this very nick. At the time, he'd asked her out for a drink and she'd accepted, understanding that it was necessary. Danvers wasn't a regular at investigating other cops, but he still needed to earn himself some brownie points if he was to be accepted in Kidlington. And the only way he could do that was to get Hillary's official forgiveness. So she'd accepted the drink, let everybody see there was no hard feelings between them, and had once more forgotten about him.

When Danvers had asked her out again a week or so later, she'd been surprised, and had politely turned him down. She had an idea he fancied her, and definitely didn't think it was a good idea. He must have got the message, since he'd never asked her again, and since then, she'd heard he'd kept his head down and his nose clean, and had got a few good results. Slowly and grudgingly, he'd become accepted by the rank and file and top brass alike.

But now that he'd been thrust right under her nose again, there could be no forgetting about the man. He was her immediate superior officer, and she'd have to find a way of working with him, or her life was going to be impossible. And she didn't want to have to transfer to another nick at this stage of her life. With the boat moored at Thrupp, barely a mile down the road, she was well settled here. She could only hope she'd got her wires crossed, and was wrong about him being attracted to her. After all she was not only older than him, she was hardly a glamour puss.

'Tell me about William Davies,' Danvers said, and listened attentively as his SIO outlined her case. He didn't interrupt, and when she was finished, asked a few pertinent questions. Whatever else she might have reservations about, she could tell he knew his job.

'It sounds like it's going to be a tough one,' he added. A dead kid wasn't the easy start to his new position that he'd hoped for. And Hillary was obviously going to be very busy and distracted for some time to come yet. But he could wait. He was good at that.

'You look all in,' he said at last. 'Go home and get some sleep. I'll be here until late, if SOCO calls in with any requests. And, Hillary,' he said, as she nodded gratefully and reached for her bag. 'I know we can work well together. I'm not a bad boss, and what's past is well and truly past as far as I'm concerned. OK?'

Hillary nodded quickly. 'That's how I see it too, sir,' she said firmly. She was not about to slap down any olive branches, even if she didn't think it was going to be as easy as all that. Danvers might not see any trouble ahead, but Hillary saw plenty.

'Please, call me Paul.'

Hillary swallowed hard, but said nothing. Paul smiled and watched her go. She really had a wonderful figure. And great legs. And she was so sharp too, as sharp as he remembered. Just being with her for a few minutes left him feeling stimulated and upbeat.

He began whistling softly as he walked back to his office.

* * *

Outside, Hillary was just crossing the foyer when the desk sergeant nobbled her. 'DI Greene! Here, just a minute, ma'am.'

The respectful 'ma'am' told her that the desk sergeant wasn't alone, and sure enough, when she turned around, there was a member of the public standing by the counter. 'This is Mrs Richardson, ma'am. She wanted to speak to whoever was in charge of the William Davies case.'

Hillary nodded and moved forward at once. 'Mrs Richardson, I'm DI Greene. Would you like to follow me to an interview room?'

'Oh, of course. That is, I realise it's getting late, but I just heard the news on the radio and thought I should speak to you as soon as possible.'

Hillary led her to the first interview room available, and collected a WPC. 'Your full name please.'

'Phyllis Yvonne Richardson. And it's Ms, not Mrs.'

Hillary nodded, making a note. 'And you have something you think might help us?'

'Well, I'm not sure. That is, I know people are supposed to come forward if they knew the murder victim. And I teach Celia Davies at primary school. And I taught her brother before that, but that would be four years ago now, naturally.'

Hillary nodded. They'd have got around to interviewing Ms Richardson at some point — probably a PC already had her on his list. But since she'd taken the time and effort to come in, Hillary wasn't quibbling.

'So you know the Davies children quite well?' she began casually.

'Yes, Celia more than Billy. Girls seem to relate to teachers better, and Celia's quite bright. She's quite a little artist. Of course, she didn't get on with her brother very well, but then I find teenage boys and prepubescent siblings never do get on.'

Hillary smiled and nodded. She and her brother had always fought like cat and dog, too.

'And Celia is definitely the favourite of both the father and mother, which didn't help.'

Hillary made a very careful note of that. Now that might be significant. Had Billy Davies felt isolated from his family? Resentful and jealous maybe. Did he resent his princess of a sister getting all the attention, and sought to find attention of his own, from somebody else?

Paedophiles found such kids irresistible. It sent a cold shiver down her spine.

'What do you remember most about Billy, when he was in your class, Ms Richardson?'

'Well, Billy was one of life's boasters, I'm afraid,' Ms Richardson began. She was a washed-out blonde, with a thin face and very narrow hands, but her pale blue eyes looked shrewd. She was neither too young to be fooled or surprised by kids, but not so old that she'd become jaded. For the first time, Hillary began to hope that she was going to get a clear and unbiased opinion of their victim.

'Sometimes — and it's usually the boys — children tend to see themselves as a hero in their own private Hollywood production, and Billy was one such. Even at ten, he was convinced the world owed him a living, I'm afraid. I didn't see much of him after he left school, but I heard things about him from time to time, sometimes from Celia, sometimes from the parents of other children. I'm afraid Billy became something of an arrogant young man as he grew older.'

'You say Celia shows some talent as an artist. Would it surprise you to hear that Billy had become rather a good photographer?'

Phyllis Richardson thought about that for a moment, then slowly shook her head. 'No. No, can't say as it would. He was always technically minded. Very practical. Some kids are like that, so a camera would suit him very well. I'll bet he didn't have any pretensions about using his talent in any artistic way though,' she added flatly.

Hillary had to smile. 'No. He wanted to be a paparazzo'

Phyllis Richardson sighed and nodded. 'Ah yes, that makes sense. That's our Billy all right. Probably saw himself taking a picture of a VIP in the nude, and making millions from it. It was the kind of way his mind worked, I'm afraid. He was always very avaricious. Once or twice I'm sure he bullied some of the younger children out of their pocket money. He liked his chocolate bars and such. Of course, I kept a sharp eye out, but Billy was crafty.'

Hillary sighed. And going to a big, new comprehensive school that already had a reputation would have presented a lad like that with many more opportunities to get up to mischief.

The kind of mischief that led to his being killed, perhaps.

By the time the interview was over, Hillary was beginning to feel vaguely depressed. Something told her that the Davies family were in for even more heartaches in the months ahead.

CHAPTER FIVE

Hillary woke up when a passing craft rocked her boat, a sensation that would, at one time, have jerked her awake with a pounding heart, but which now felt oddly comforting. She lay still and waited a moment, letting her tiny cabin settle on to an even keel, then sat up on the narrow bed and put her feet to the floor. She could open her sliding-door wardrobe door just by reaching out her hand and, selecting a pair of lightweight beige slacks and a matching jacket with a navy blue trim, she tossed them on to her unmade bed and then headed for the shower.

She'd got a two-minute shower down to a fine art after three years of living on her narrowboat, the *Mollern*, and within ten minutes she was heading along the towpath, HQ-bound.

Even at eight in the morning, the sun was shining hot and strong and, just past her mooring, a row of red hawthorns were beginning to bloom. A pair of moorhens, nesting in the reeds opposite, had produced three fluffy black chicks, and in the farmer's fields skirting the canal, dark green wheat shone with health. A chiffchaff was calling his monotonous but cheerful song, and Hillary heard gruff male laughter from her neighbour's boat,

Willowsands, as she passed. It made her wonder who Nancy Walker had lured into her web this time. The forty-something divorcee had told her a few days ago that she feared her trawl of Oxford students was coming to an end, and that she might chug off to Stratford-upon-Avon to see what the pickings of impoverished actors was like.

Hillary rather hoped she wouldn't go. Although she had no sex life of her own, she'd always been able to live vicariously through Nancy's. And thoughts of her non-existent sex life led her straight to a certain detective inspector in the vice squad, but as she started up Puff the Tragic Wagon she firmly pushed all thoughts of Mike Regis away, which was not easy when she'd heard on the grapevine that his divorce was final, and that he'd begun openly dating again. But, so far, he'd not turned his head her way. Which was her own damned fault, of course. A few months ago, when he'd asked her out, she'd more or less told him to sling his hook.

And slung it, he had.

As she walked across the foyer, the morning-shift desk sergeant greeted her as she passed by, but had nothing of interest to report, be it news of her case, or the latest in station-house gossip. As she keyed her way into the main office, noting that she was the first of her team to arrive, she wondered if Danvers was already at his desk. If it had still been Mel in there, she'd have gone in and chewed over the case, sharing her feeling for how it was beginning to taste and getting his input. But Danvers was still very much uncharted territory, so she went straight to her desk and checked for messages. Her in-tray, as ever, was towering. She gave it a quick trawl through, dealing with the most urgent, scowling to find that a court appearance she had been due to give on a stolen-identity case had been put back yet another week. At this rate, the perpetrator would still be walking around, free and clear, next Christmas.

By 8:30 everyone was in except Frank, and Hillary began dishing out assignments.

'Tommy, I want you and Janine to start off by interviewing every member of Billy's form. I daresay there'll be thirty or so, but it has to be done.'

Janine groaned. Just what she needed. A morning spent talking to resentful teenage girls, who always saw her blonde good looks as a personal challenge or insult, or, even worse, cajoling teenage boys to stop looking at her boobs, bum or legs (depending on preference) and answer her bloody questions.

'I'll talk to all his teachers,' Hillary said, and quickly filled them in on her visit from Billy's former primary school teacher.

At nine, Frank still hadn't arrived, and she was just writing a note on his desk, asking him to question all the allotment holders at Aston Lea, when Janine's dry warning cough had her head shooting up. Walking towards them, dressed in an expensive-looking navy blue suit, crisp white shirt, and pale electric-blue tie, was her new boss. His blonde hair had been freshly washed and cut, and gleamed even more golden in the bright sunlight streaming through the windows. He had the lean look of a regular squash player, and Janine gave a subtle whistle as he approached.

Hillary shot her an appalled look. The last thing she wanted was for Janine to start sleeping with this boss as well. Surely she'd learned her lesson over Mel?

'Hillary, glad to catch you before you go. I know you're busy, so I won't keep you. You can update me when you next get in. I just wanted a quick word with everybody.' He looked around, and chose Janine first. It was probably just protocol — with Frank absent (who had senior status, at least officially), Janine was first in the pecking order; or at least, Hillary hoped that was all it was. To be fair, she could detect nothing lascivious in his manner as Danvers shook her hand. 'DS Tyler, isn't it? We've met before, of course, but not like this. I've been impressed with your CV. You're awaiting the results of Boards, aren't you?'

'Yes, sir,' Janine said, and added at once, 'I'm hoping to get a DI posting soon, of course, but this is a great team to work for.'

Hillary bit back a smile. A typical Janine Tyler remark if ever she'd heard one. She thought she saw a similar cynicism briefly gleam in Danvers' pale blue eyes, but she couldn't be sure, for he'd already turned to Tommy Lynch. 'Tommy, congratulations on the promotion. Headington's a good nick, so I've heard. I'm sure everyone's going to miss you here, though.'

'Er, thanks, sir,' Tommy said. 'I'm sorry to be going, to be honest. Working for DI Greene has been a privilege. I've learned a lot.'

'I'm sure you have,' Danvers said, and although there was nothing even remotely suggestive in his tone, Hillary could feel herself flush. She cursed silently under her breath, and wondered if she was always going to be this sensitive around the walking Moss Bros advert that was her new boss. She hoped not. Life would be intolerable.

'Well, good luck with the case, obviously. I understand it's a bad one, so if anyone has any problems, I hope they won't hesitate to come to me,' Danvers carried on smoothly. 'I'd like to think I was the kind of boss you could come to, if need be. I know this situation isn't ideal, but DI Greene and I have already had a chat and we're both sure things will work out smoothly.'

Hillary, knowing her cue when she heard it, smiled briefly and said, 'I'm sure it will. We're all here to get the job done, after all.' She was glad Frank wasn't here right now. The poisonous little git wouldn't have been able to stop himself from guffawing out loud. As it was there was a brief moment of awkwardness before the DCI nodded and went back to his office.

Janine glanced at Hillary curiously, wondering what it must be like to have to report in to the man who'd once tried to put you behind bars, but her boss was already reaching for her bag. 'Right, we'd better each take our own cars,' Hillary advised. 'And don't forget, it's the brand-new comprehensive we're going to, not to be mistaken for Bicester Community College up near the sports centre in King's End. OK?'

* * *

'I got the feeling he was always bright enough, but like a lot of 'em these days, he had a severe case of idle-itis. Lazy through and through, but get him interested in a subject, and he was like a sponge, lapping it all up.'

The speaker was a Mr Colin Brentwood, and he taught modern history. He was saying pretty much what Mrs Wilkins (sociology), Pat (no Mr for him) Dringle (English literature) and Pam Dawber (mathematics) had all said.

'And what did interest him?'

'The sixties,' Colin Brentwood said shortly, surprising Hillary, who hadn't thought that the sixties was included on the modern history syllabus. When she'd been at school, modern history had meant the Victorians, empire and both world wars.

'He was fascinated by the culture of stardom,' Brentwood went on, which given his ambition, didn't surprise Hillary at all. 'And of course, the sixties was when London ruled the world, pop music and fashion-wise.'

'Were you surprised to hear that he was dead, Mr Brentwood?' Hillary asked, more to shake the man out of his matter-of-fact attitude than anything else. She had talked to several of his teachers so far, and although all had seemed shocked and appalled, none of them had seemed to feel any particular pity. And it was beginning to grate.

'Of course I was. You read about things like this, of course, but they always seem to be happening in the big cities. Manchester, Birmingham and so on. You don't expect it in a small market town in Oxfordshire do you?'

Another thing she'd been hearing a lot that morning.

'Do you know of any reason why anyone would kill Billy Davies, Mr Brentwood?'

'No, I don't,' the history teacher said, a shade huffily now. He was one of those small, sandy-haired men with a little goatee, wire-rimmed glasses, and a tweed jacket with leather elbow patches, who seemed to advertise their profession. She'd almost expected him to start smoking a pipe, but so far he'd shown no signs of this ultimate in academic props. 'He wasn't the nicest kid around, and when he and that Lester Miller got together, they could be a real pain, but to actually kill the poor little blighter . . . no. I don't know why anyone should do that.'

Hillary sighed and nodded. It was all very much as she'd feared. Still, perhaps someone, somewhere, had a little snippet that could get them started on the right track. 'Is there anything you think I should know? I mean, can you remember some small incident that struck you as odd? Something about his personality that made you uneasy. Anything like that?'

Colin Brentwood shrugged his puny shoulders. 'Not really. He was a greedy child, always wanting things. The give-me-more culture that seems to pervade nowadays had a willing acolyte in Billy. And he was a big lad, well able to take care of himself, and he wasn't all that averse to throwing his weight around if he felt like it. The other kids tended to give him a wide berth, but he wasn't an obvious bully. It was more as if he saw school as a necessary evil, and one he didn't have much patience with. He wouldn't have been one to hang around after sixteen in search of a higher education, I can tell you that. He wanted to be out in the world, earning, consuming, getting his hands dirty, impatient to be free and independent. He was that sort of a kid, you know?'

Hillary did know, only too well. They were often the kind she ended up arresting.

'Oh, Billy was definitely the leader,' Viola Grey (her real name, apparently) said a quarter of an hour later. 'Tea? I keep a kettle and illicit chocolate wafers in a cubby hole. Nobody's supposed to know about them.' Viola Grey taught biology, and the scent of acid and the nearness of Bunsen burners and singed wooden desktops, for some reason, put Hillary right off the thought of chocolate. Something she'd previously thought was impossible.

Ms Grey was talking about the close relationship that had existed between their victim and Lester Miller.

'No, thanks,' Hillary waved down the offer of elevenses. 'I understand Lester Miller is well off? That is, his father owns his own company. I'm surprised he didn't put his son into a private school.'

Viola Grey, a plump woman who could only just be out of her teens herself, pushed a strand of long dark hair behind a rather prominent ear, and shrugged. 'Who knows? Perhaps he isn't that rich, or perhaps he's got socialist leanings, or maybe he just doesn't think Lester needs a proper education, since he'll be going straight into the family firm. I think he supplies oil to domestic customers. Or is it anthracite? Or does he just supply the lorries the fuel companies use? I dunno, something like that anyway.' She gave a massive shrug. 'All very lucrative, no doubt, in these days of burgeoning fuel prices, but I don't think you need know the finer details of the reproductive cycle of a herring gull to be an office manager.' She pointed at a poster on the wall, depicting the life cycle of a seagull. 'And Lester doesn't seem to think so either, according to his mock exam results.'

'Is there anything you can tell me about Billy that might shed light on why someone would want to kill him?'

But although Viola Grey could have told her what a two-week-old seagull chick might eat for breakfast, she had no idea who might want to stick a pair of shears into a fifteen-year-old boy's chest.

* * *

'You ask me, that boy was cruising for a bruising sometime, but I can't imagine what he'd done to deserve this.' Christine Bigelow, French.

'He spent most of his time secretly reading photography magazines in class, which didn't worry me, to be perfectly honest. At least it kept him quiet. He sure as hell didn't care how the Cairngorms had been formed.' Jeffrey Palmer, Geography.

'I don't understand it at all.' Maurice Jenkins, Art. 'He was a smashing kid, very enthusiastic. He did a coffee-table book for his special project this year, you know, a mock-up of those expensive illustrated books that nobody ever buys. Its theme was Oxford, rural and academic. Great shots of the colleges, but also of the countryside. One photo in black and white, of a tractor pulling a plough and being followed by this huge flock of black-backed gulls, was superb. I had him put it in for the Collingsworth Prize, and it got an honourable mention. Great kid. He had talent.'

'Did he ever confide in you, Mr Jenkins?' Hillary asked, sensing at last a teacher who actually cared that Billy Davies was dead. Who actually felt some kind of loss. 'Did he ever say anybody was bothering him? Was he depressed or worried recently?'

'No, nothing like that. In fact, the reverse seemed to be true. The last few days he seemed very upbeat. You know, he'd come in whistling through his teeth and grin a hello at you. He was always bored by paints and sculpture, and bookwork was something he loathed, but even the day before yesterday, the last time I saw him now that I come to think of it, he smiled all through my talk on Degas's ballerinas.'

Jenkins was approaching retirement age, Hillary guessed, and had prematurely stooped shoulders and an unfortunate dandruff problem which had no doubt earned him some horrific nickname from his pupils, but he seemed bright enough. Probably after a lifetime in teaching he'd become very observant of the young. Hillary felt her pulse rate accelerate a little. At last, a nibble.

'Very up, how? Did he say anything in particular?' she pressed.

'Oh no. He wouldn't. He didn't confide in teachers, you know, not even me.' Hillary nodded. She'd got the same impression from all the other teachers too.

'But you knew him better than most,' Hillary said flatly. 'Any ideas why he was so chipper?'

Jenkins sighed heavily. 'Billy was a very talented photographer, but a very flawed human being, I'm afraid. If he was excited about something in particular, it would almost certainly have something to do with gain. Billy wanted things. Money, of course, always. The best toys. Power. Knowledge. He was a boy who spent all his time and energy acquiring things for himself. He was probably the most selfish boy I've ever known — and I've known a few. And he was sly. Clever in ways only the sly, as opposed to the truly intelligent, are. You understand?'

Hillary thought that she might. Blackmail. Billy Davies's art teacher, although he would never say so in as many words, suspected Billy was the type to indulge in blackmail.

And everything she'd heard about him so far seemed to fit. He was greedy, clever, sly and hard-headed. His family was obviously living on a tight budget, which had probably fostered his resentment. Yes, he'd have felt no qualms about extorting money. In fact, Hillary could only find one thing wrong with that theory.

What secret worth killing for could a fifteen-year-old boy living in a tiny hamlet possibly uncover?

* * *

'Blackmail sounds a bit iffy to me,' Janine said right away, when the three of them met up at one o'clock by the admin office, as arranged. 'I mean, would any adult really take him seriously? I can't see any man standing for it. Having his arm twisted by a snotty-nosed, working-class yob.' She shook her head.

'Perhaps they didn't,' Tommy said at once. And mimed the stabbing through the chest with a pair of shears. Janine grimaced. 'We'll have to take a close look at all the neighbours,' Tommy mused. 'Although he might have put the bite on somebody here,' he added, looking at the school speculatively.

'Well, let's not get hung up on it,' Hillary advised. 'We'll keep it simmering on the back burner, but that's all.' She knew from bitter experience how one single idea could get a hold of a murder inquiry and screw it up totally. 'We need to keep an open mind, yeah? So far, we don't have any leads worth a damn. Janine, I want you to concentrate on the family. I don't need to tell you what the statistics say about victims and family members.'

Janine nodded. She couldn't see the mother being up for it, but the father maybe. And uncles were always in the frame. 'I'll start digging, boss.'

'So, what do the kids in his form have to say so far?'

She listened to their reports, but they had nothing new. They only served to confirm that if anybody would know what was going on in Billy Davies's life, it was his alter ego, Lester Miller.

'Is Miller in today?' Hillary asked.

'Yes, guv,' Tommy said. 'I hadn't got around to him yet,' he added, guessing that she'd want to be in on it when he did.

Hillary sighed. 'Right. Let's find a pub and have a sandwich, then we'll tackle him.'

* * *

The Fox was a pub she hadn't been in before, but as she ordered a round of ploughman's lunches for everyone and an assortment of soft drinks, she barely paid any attention to the ambience. Something was niggling at her. Something had been niggling at her before she'd gone to bed last night, and it was still niggling at her now. Something she'd seen or heard yesterday, obviously. Something that shouldn't have been there. Or something that should have been there, but wasn't. She didn't think it was something someone had said.

As the barmaid brought their order to the table, she was still replaying her actions yesterday. Something at the death scene, in the shed. Something in his bedroom maybe. But it wouldn't come.

Tommy too was distracted; with the approach of June, his upcoming wedding was an ever-growing presence in his life. He had no real feelings of panic though. He wanted kids, and a home of his own, and a wife to come home to. And Jean was level-headed and hard-working, two traits any copper's wife needed in abundance. He sighed heavily and bit down into a tomato.

Janine wondered if Paul Danvers had a girlfriend.

* * *

Lester Miller had freckles. A lot of freckles. All over his face and on the backs of his hands. There wasn't anything really surprising about that, given his ginger hair and pale complexion, it was just that Hillary had never expected Billy Davies's best friend to be a freckled beanpole of a boy with eyes so pale a blue they were almost white.

'This is about Billy-Boy, right?' he said at once, the moment they walked into the deserted classroom. He'd been due for a session in the language lab, listening to a tape-recorded session of a supposed French housewife doing her morning shopping. But he'd far rather be here.

As Hillary sat down at a desk opposite, turning her chair around to face him, she could detect no redness around the eyes, no fine trembling in his hands. No pinched whiteness around the eyes or mouth. Lester Miller didn't seem that upset that his best friend was dead. Unless he was just very good at hiding it. Some teenage boys liked to take bravado to the nth degree.

'Billy-Boy. Is that his nickname?' Hillary asked, and Lester grinned.

'Nah, not really. It's just what I call him. To make him narked, like.' He was dressed in stonewashed jeans and a green-and-white checked shirt. He wore an expensive wristwatch, and was slumped in his chair like a pile of nutty slack. Perhaps the reality of his friend's death simply hadn't hit him yet.

Hillary smiled. 'You liked to get him narked?'

Lester grinned again, showing a line of uneven teeth. 'Sometimes. He was a mate, wasn't he? He didn't really mind.'

'Sounds like you got on really well. We've been talking to others in his form and they all seem to think that you and he were really tight. He spent a lot of time at your place too, they said.'

'Yeah, well, you can hardly blame him, can you? His place is a right dump. Talk about depressing. Billy couldn't wait to leave. We were going to go halves on some place to live in Oxford. Find some sort of cheap student bedsit, move in, have some fun. The old parents couldn't do much about it, right?'

Hillary said nothing. She didn't ask what these two teenagers were supposed to do for money. That was obvious. Get jobs and some kind of apprenticeship or training which the government pretended was as good as staying on at school. Easy. Earn their way, be free, pull girls, find out about booze and drugs maybe. She could read it all in Lester Miller's open, grinning, unknowing face. And suddenly it hit her how young these boys were.

The one dead, and never to grow any older, and this boy in front of her now, who had no idea what life was all about, but would, in the years to come, soon find out.

It made her feel suddenly very tired.

She opened her notebook and pretended to read a few lines. 'A lot of Billy's friends seemed to think he was a bit of a troublemaker. A bit of a bully. Is that true?'

'Nah,' Lester Miller said at once. 'They're just jealous, see. Billy's smarter than all of 'em, and they know it. And he had balls too, you know?' He said the crude expression with studied calm and insolence, but the quick look he darted at her to see if she was shocked somewhat spoiled it.

Hillary, in no mood to play along, merely nodded and looked bored. 'So, did you bully anyone, Lester? Did Billy-Boy egg you on?'

'Nah, I told you. Billy couldn't give a toss about any of the tossers around here, and neither could I. We'll only be here another year and then we'll be gone. Most of the losers bad-mouthing Billy and me now will still be stuck here, stacking shelves in Tesco or working the tills in Argos, while me and Billy will be long gone. London, eventually.' Hillary noticed all those present tenses and wondered if Lester was aware of them. Time, she thought grimly, for a reality check.

'But Billy won't be joining you in Oxford, or London now, will he, Lester? Billy's dead, and someone killed him. Do you have any idea who?'

Lester's freckled face flushed a dull ugly red, then paled. Then he shrugged. 'No idea.'

'Oh come on,' Hillary said. 'You're his best friend. You and him were like that!' She held up two entwined fingers. 'Don't tell me you didn't know what Billy was doing. Even his art teacher could tell he was excited about something.'

'Oh, "Snowman" Jenkins,' Lester said dismissively. 'He don't know nothing.'

'But you do. So tell me. Don't you want to see whoever killed Billy pay for it? You're his best mate — don't you want to help get his killer?' She used the provocative language on purpose, of course, but Lester Miller didn't bite. Sometimes an appeal to someone's need for vengeance worked where threats or pleas didn't. But for some reason, Lester Miller didn't seem interested in helping to get justice for his friend.

And Hillary found that fact very interesting.

As the silence stretched, and Lester began to shift on his chair but remained stubbornly uncommunicative, Hillary shifted tack. 'A good-looking lad, Billy,' she mused. 'I imagine he had a girlfriend?'

She knew from listening to Janine and Tommy's reports that he'd had several, and had prided himself on having the prettiest girls in school fighting over him. But she wanted to hear it from Lester. From the much less physically attractive Lester.

'Oh yeah, lots. But Heather Soames was his latest,' Lester said casually and apparently without jealousy. 'Though how much longer she would have lasted, I dunno. They'd been going out for, like, nearly eight months.' He said it as if months should mean years. 'And her dad's a bit mental. I reckon Billy was gonna dump her.'

'Was going to, or had?' Hillary asked sharply. When teenage passions were in the frame, and a dumped girlfriend might be in the offing, a stab in the chest took on a whole different significance.

'Nah, he hadn't dumped her yet,' Lester said confidently. 'Heather's, like, really hot, you know, and Billy had been after her for some while. And they were at it, of course. Billy liked that. Getting it regular.' Again he shot her a quick look, hoping for shock or disgust. Again Hillary merely sighed heavily.

'So . . .' she began and felt the phone in the pocket of her blazer vibrate. She took out and read the message, surprised to find an urgent request for a call back from

74

SOCO. 'I might need to talk to you again, Lester,' she said, more as a threat than a warning. She definitely hadn't finished with him yet.

Miller, it had to be said, didn't exactly start quaking in his boots. Another hard-headed boy, Hillary mused. No wonder he and Billy-Boy had been so close.

Hillary stepped outside the classroom and dialled back the number on the message. She was very much aware that she'd let Lester Miller rile her, and gave herself a mental ticking off as she put the phone to her ear and heard it ring. It did no good to feel antagonistic towards witnesses or suspects. It only clouded your judgement and your thinking. Next time she spoke to Lester, she'd have to be careful.

'Hello. This is DI Greene. I've just had a message to contact Dr Fraser. It's the Davies case.'

She heard the usual telephonic clatter, then a surprisingly crisp and loud voice said, 'Yes? Dr Fraser.'

'This is DI Greene. SIO on the William Davies call. You wanted to speak to me urgently?'

'Yes. Davies. Shears.' Fraser was obviously one of those boffins who spoke in shorthand. 'Fingerprints found, matched deceased's sibling, Celia Davies. Thought you might want to know.'

CHAPTER SIX

Hillary thanked the technician and rung off. She leaned slowly back against the cool, white-painted corridor wall and frowned, thinking back.

Had she asked Celia Davies if she'd touched the shears? She wasn't sure, but she didn't think so. It annoyed her that her memory was so sketchy. Had finding out Danvers was her new boss really sent her into such a tailspin that she'd forgotten to ask Celia Davies such a basic question? She didn't think so. The little girl had been in bed, and afraid of her, so she'd deliberately gone easy. But now she'd have to go back, and play the wicked witch again.

From her memories of last evening, she was sure that Celia Davies had not mentioned touching the shears. In fact, the more she thought about it, the more sure she was that she'd got the distinct impression that Celia had simply looked in the shed, seen her brother, and run home. The question was: had she been deliberately manipulated into thinking that way, or was she just guilty of leaping to conclusions? And she rather thought it might be the latter. She simply couldn't see Marilyn Davies as some clever psychological manipulator, and the little girl was surely not so devious. Although spoilt eleven-year-old girls, by their very definition, were probably very good at getting their own way.

No, she was more willing to believe that she'd still been reeling from the angst of the awards ceremony, followed by her demotion back to DI, and finding out that Paul Danvers had been appointed as her new boss. No two ways about it, she must have been well and truly off her form not to ask so basic a question.

And it made her angry.

She pushed open the door of the classroom and smiled briefly at the boy inside. 'You can get off to class now, Lester, but we'll be having another talk soon, all right?' She didn't wait for an answer, but shut the door behind her and made her way down the corridor and out into the open air, with some feelings of relief.

Although she herself had gone to an old-fashioned grammar school, she'd never been overly fond of it, and being back in a school, any school, was giving her a case of nostalgic blues. Unlike some, she'd never thought that childhood had been the happiest years of her life. In fact, thinking about it, she supposed that right now was her happiest time. She was free of her disastrous marriage, was living in an environment that — against the odds — seemed to suit her, and her career was right where she probably wanted it to be.

She felt needed and useful. And right now, that translated into finding Billy-Boy Davies's killer.

She punched in a number as she walked slowly back to her car, getting Doc Partridge's assistant. A few moments later, the pathologist himself was on the line.

'Hillary, nice to hear from you. Problems?'

'The William Davies case.'

'With you. What's up?'

'In your opinion, could an eleven-year-old girl have been capable of delivering the fatal blow?'

Over the line, she heard the medico suck his breath in through his teeth. 'I don't think so. Hold on, let me get my notes, remind myself of the depth of penetration and the angle.'

Hillary reached her car, and opened all the doors and windows to let the heat out. Lilac trees in a nearby garden wafted a giddying scent on the slight breeze and made Hillary wonder what else she might have done with her life; different choices taken that would now have allowed her to spend such a lovely day without thinking about crime and punishment, guilt and innocence. She'd got a good English degree from an unaffiliated Oxford college — she could have been a librarian or a seller of rare books, maybe even a writer of some sort. A biographer maybe.

'Hello, Hill?' Steven Partridge's voice turned off all idle speculation in an instant. 'I take it you're thinking of the younger sister, yeah? How tall would you say she was?'

Of course, Partridge hadn't seen Celia Davies. 'I'd say no more than four feet two. Maybe not that.'

'Then I very much doubt it. Is she stocky?'

'No — a wisp of a thing.'

'Then I'd very seriously doubt it,' Doc Partridge said. 'Why do you ask?'

Strictly speaking, of course, Hillary was not obliged to tell him. The doc had his area of expertise and she had hers. But they'd worked together for many years now, and she was willing to bend the rules to keep up a good working relationship. Besides, she trusted him to keep any and all salient details on an ongoing investigation firmly to himself. 'We found her dabs on the murder weapon. Good solid ones, it seems. Both hands.'

SOCO, on finding so many clear fingerprints on the murder weapon, indicating that someone had taken a firm hold on both handles of the shears, had been quick to follow it up. Naturally, they'd dusted down the boy's bedroom and certain rooms in the family home, and had found an instant match in Celia's dabs.

'Hmm. I still don't think it's likely, Hillary,' Doc Partridge said at last.

'What if she was in a rage?' Hillary had to press it. She knew from several sources that Celia and her brother were not close — in fact, had probably fought bitterly. If Billy had done something to enrage her, she needed to know if Celia could be on the suspect list. 'Doesn't rage give people a boost of strength? You know, like desperation does. You hear about mothers ripping off car doors to get children out of burning cars, that sort of thing. Does it work with a real temper tantrum too?'

'I know what you're talking about,' Partridge said instantly. 'There've been several studies done about how the levels of endor . . . but you don't want details,' he caught himself up before he got into full lecture mode. There was another, longer and more thoughtful silence for a moment, then he said slowly, 'Well, Hillary, I suppose it's just barely possible. If she caught her brother unaware. But he was stabbed from the front, not the back. And he was a big hefty lad. I can't see him being unable to fight off his little sister even if she had turned into a veritable hell cat. Sorry, that's the best I can do. If I were you, I wouldn't be looking at the sister as a serious suspect at this stage. Not unless you get some strong corroborative evidence.'

Hillary sighed, thanked him and hung up. It was all very well for Steven Partridge to dismiss Celia Davies as a killer, but Hillary couldn't afford to be so sure. And there were plenty of cases of killer children to back up her caution. The notorious Mary Bell had probably been overtaken in the public's memory by the two boy killers of little Jamie Bulger, but there were other cases that didn't receive such notoriety where children had committed spine-tingling crimes.

She had to talk to Celia Davies again.

* * *

Frank Ross pulled up outside the dry-cleaning shop in the latest shopping development to hit the market town of Banbury, and climbed out of his car. His jacket — which could definitely have benefited from the services the shop had to offer — was slung on the back seat, and he'd long since ripped off his tie and rolled up his shirtsleeves, which hid his hideously greasy cuffs just right.

He cursed the heat as he walked to the shop door and opened it, a cheerfully tinkling bell above making him wince. He'd tied one on last night, and still had the headache to prove it.

A man appeared from the back and approached the counter that was the single piece of furniture in the tiny store and smiled a greeting. He was, Frank knew from his preliminary notes, forty years old, although he looked older. Tall, thin, fair, he looked at Frank a shade uncertainly. Probably because he wasn't used to seeing people come into the shop without something in need of steam cleaning draped over an arm.

'Can I help you, sir?' he asked cautiously. He knew Frank wasn't a regular, so couldn't be here to pick up some clothes either. And in spite of the Winnie-the-Pooh face and figure, there was something faintly menacing about the man.

Frank showed him his ID and Marty Warrender nodded with relief. 'Oh, right. I was expecting you. This is about Billy, yeah?'

Frank nodded. 'You live next door to the Davies on the right, as you go into the village from the main road?'

Marty Warrender nodded gloomily. 'Yeah. I was shocked to hear what happened yesterday, when I got home, like. June told me all about it. June's the wife. I couldn't believe it. I just couldn't believe it.'

Frank smiled wearily. Warrender was the third neighbour he'd had to track down at work today, and all of them were saying the same thing. What was not to believe?

'Did you know Billy well?' Frank went straight into it. The sooner he'd finished with everyone on his list, the sooner he could clock off and head for a pub. The bitch from Thrupp wouldn't know how long it had taken him, and if he managed to get through by three, he could even get a few bets down on the gee-gees.

'No, not really. He wasn't a friendly sort, and he wasn't at home much anyway, to tell the truth. Always off on that bike of his. Had a friend somewhere, he used to practically live there. I knew him to say hello to and that, but that's all. We've only lived in Aston Lea two years.'

Frank nodded. 'You see him yesterday at all? You'd have left for work, when? Eight?'

'Half past. We don't open till nine, and it's an easy commute. And no, I didn't see Billy. He's usually been picked up by the school bus by then.'

'He didn't go to school yesterday,' Frank said flatly. 'Do you come home for lunch?'

'No, the wife packs me sandwiches, like. Cheaper than eating in a cafe.'

'So you didn't go home at all during the day?'

'No. Like I said, first I heard of it was when June told me when I got home. About six. We close at half five, see. Gives people time to drop off stuff from work, if they don't have time in the morning or in their lunch hour.'

'And have you ever heard Billy Davies arguing with anybody? Seen him get into any fights, or heard anybody threaten him?'

'No, not him. More likely the other way round,' Marty Warrender said, then looked appalled. 'I mean, I don't want to speak ill of the dead or anything,' he added hastily. 'It must be horrible for the Davies family and all that,' he trailed off lamely.

'I understand. We're getting reports from lots of sources that Billy was something of a lad. Fancied himself a bit. Bit of a bully, was he?' Frank asked, smiling and putting on the all-lads-together attitude. As he'd expected, it worked, and Marty Warrender relaxed a little bit and ran a hand through his hair.

'Well, yeah, he was a bit of a bother,' he gave a rueful laugh. 'But he never bothered me, mind,' he added quickly, opened his mouth to say something else, then quickly shut it again. No, he thought silently, best not. Least said, soonest mended. It was one of his mother's favourite sayings, and Marty could truly appreciate it at that moment. Besides, he didn't know anything, not really, not for sure, and he didn't want to get mixed up in police business. They'd be bound to find out anyway from someone else. Best just to keep his head down.

Frank Ross smiled some more and made a strong note in his book. The bugger was hiding something. Or knew something he didn't want to cough up. Well, he'd pass his thoughts along to the girl wonder and she could do the secondary interview. See if she could wangle it out of him.

'Well, thanks for your time, Mr Warrender. If you think of anything else, give me a call, yeah?' He handed over one of his cards, then stepped back outside. June Warrender, he knew, worked in a cake shop in the centre of town. After her he just had two more to go.

A flotilla of ducks, passing by on the Oxford canal a few yards opposite, quacked a noisy demand for bread. A child, strolling alongside his mother, laughed with delight and duly obliged.

Frank ignored it all and climbed back into his car, checking the paper on the front seat which was folded back at the sports section. In the 3:30 at Chepstow there was a nag running called 'Billy Blunder.' Now that had to be worth a tenner of anybody's money, right? Especially at 12–1.

* * *

Hillary knocked on the Davies' side door and waited. The bungalow, even in bright sunlight, seemed to ooze a dull unhappiness, as if the very building had somehow

82

absorbed the misery of the family living within it. Even a colourful cluster of ladies' bonnets and aromatic wallflowers just under the kitchen window failed to relieve the atmosphere.

After a moment the door was opened by George Davies. He hadn't shaved, and obviously hadn't slept. He blinked at her for a moment, then absently reached down to button up the shirt that was currently undone, exposing his flabby white belly. 'Oh, sorry,' he said vaguely. 'Come on in. I'll put the kettle on.'

Hillary accepted, and wondered for how much longer she'd be a welcome visitor in this house. Not long, perhaps, after talking to Celia.

'Milk and sugar? Marilyn's in the living room, pretending to sleep on the sofa. Doc left her some pills, but I don't reckon she's taken them. We've got to talk about arrangements, she said. You know. For burying and suchlike.'

Hillary nodded, noting that George Davies hadn't been able to say his son's name yet. 'The coroner will let you know when Billy's body can be released, Mr Davies,' she said gently. 'So there's no rush.' Although there was a school of thought that said having to cope with funeral arrangements was a good way of making the mind accept the finality of death.

'Oh. Right. Didn't think of that. He'll have been . . . cut about, I suppose?'

Hillary shrugged helplessly. 'The coroner's office treats every body with the utmost respect, Mr Davies,' she assured him gently.

George Davies said nothing.

'So, how's Celia doing?' Hillary asked brightly. Perhaps now was as good a time as any to remind this grieving man that he still had one child living. And his favourite, too, by all accounts.

'Oh she's much better,' George said, his face brightening up for a moment. 'She slept the night through

— me and Marilyn kept checking on her. The pills the doc gave her I suppose. And she was up this morning, and had some breakfast. She's in her room now, colouring.'

'I'll just pop my head in then, shall I? Perhaps you'd best come too?' She knew she couldn't interview the child alone — her guts would be had for garters if she tried it — and as far as she could tell, George wasn't any more likely to fly off the handle than the little girl's mother when the questioning got tough.

'OK, but I wish you didn't have to.'

'I'm afraid we need to get the sequence of events very clear, Mr Davies. But with luck, this will be the last time I have to talk to her.'

This prospect seemed to cheer Davies up further, for he nodded and led the way happily enough.

Celia Davies looked up from the floor the moment the door opened. She was indeed using felt-tip pens to colour in a picture of Cinderella being transformed for the ball. She was dressed in a rather obviously homemade white cotton sundress, which had been clumsily stitched. Already her little arms and legs were turning nut-brown.

'Hello, Celia, remember me?' Hillary said, coming into the room and reducing her height by immediately sitting on the bed and leaning down to look at the child's work. 'Oh, that's pretty. I like the way you've given Cinders brown hair. Everybody I know gives her yellow hair.'

'I think that's silly,' the mousey-haired Celia said firmly. And her bottom lip pouted out just a little, to reinforce this serious statement. Hillary could see no signs of the shock of yesterday. Children, it was true, could be much more resilient than adults.

'So do I. I've always been glad my hair isn't yellow,' Hillary said, just as seriously. She glanced up at George Davies, who was hovering anxiously in the doorway.

'Celia, I need to talk to you about yesterday again. Just for a bit, it won't take long. Do you think you can do that?'

Celia Davies reached out for a green pen and started to colour in Cinderella's shoes. 'Course I can.'

Hillary nodded. 'That's a good girl. Now, I know your mum sent you to see if you could find Billy at the allotments. And I know you went to the shed. Now, the door to the shed's really narrow isn't it?'

Celia nodded her head emphatically. 'Billy had to turn sideways to get in, he was so thick,' she said, then giggled.

George opened his mouth to remonstrate, then closed it again.

'But I bet you didn't have to turn sideways when you went in,' Hillary said softly, and the little girl instantly shook her head.

'No, I could just walk in.'

'And that's what you did yesterday. Just walked in?'

'Uh-huh,' the little girl said, giving that over-emphatic nod that children were prone to.

'And you saw Billy. He was sitting on the sack of potatoes wasn't he?'

'Uh-huh.' Again the giant-sized nod.

'And you went up to him?'

'He wouldn't answer me when I called him. He did that sometimes, pretended not to hear me.'

'Bet that made you mad,' Hillary said with a grin, and noticed George Davies begin to shift uneasily in the doorway. 'Did you go up to him and shake him, Celia?'

'How did you know?' The little girl raised her head for the first time and stared at her, round-eyed.

'Oh well, I'm a policewoman,' Hillary said solemnly. 'We know things. So, what did you do then? Billy still didn't answer, did he?' she added gently.

'No. And I could see his shirt was all red,' Celia said. And scowled. 'I didn't see that before. I don't know why.'

'That's because it was light outside, and dark inside. It takes time for our eyes to adjust,' Hillary explained patiently, knowing they were coming to the crucial bit and wanting to take it steadily. 'So what did you do when you saw how red he was. Did you touch it?'

'Oh no. Ick!' The little girl screwed her face up, then looked down at her pens. 'I think I'll make her dress orange.'

Hillary nodded. 'Good choice — it goes with her nice brown hair. Celia, did you see the shears in front of Billy? The ones that were, well, sitting on his chest?'

'They weren't sitting on him, they were sticking out of him,' Celia said at once, boldly, and without the least hint of distress. And in that moment, Hillary knew that Celia had never loved her brother.

There was nothing wrong with that, of course. Young children who were at loggerheads with siblings very often didn't form strong emotional bonds with them until they matured and became more understanding. It was then that affection finally came into play. But in the case of Billy and his younger sister, that could now never happen.

Celia's apparent callousness certainly didn't indicate anything sinister. In fact, it made it easier for Hillary, because now she could proceed without feeling as if she was walking on eggshells.

'Yes, of course they were,' Hillary said carefully. 'Celia, did you touch them at all? The shears, I mean.'

Celia frowned and ducked her head down, and began scribbling orange all over Cinderella's ballgown.

'No,' she said petulantly. Hillary saw that the colouring pen kept slipping outside the black outlines of the dress. The previous pieces she'd coloured in, however, were all neatly done, and flush to the edges. Obviously her question had hit a nerve.

And Hillary thought she might know why. Celia had sensed she'd done something wrong, or might have, and was retreating into denial. Quickly, Hillary slipped from the bed and on to her knees. Over by the doorway George Davies took a step inside, and Hillary prayed he wasn't going to interrupt now.

'Celia, it's all right if you did,' Hillary said softly. 'Nobody's going to tell you off. I just need to know, that's all.'

'What's going on?' The voice was high-pitched and very nearly hysterical. Hillary felt Celia wince, and she slowly sat back on her heels with a resigned sigh, and looked up at Marilyn Davies, who'd just pushed her way into her daughter's bedroom.

'Hello, Mrs Davies,' Hillary said calmly. 'I was just having a chat with Celia here. She's very good at colouring in, isn't she,' she said, allowing her voice to harden just a shade, warning the other woman that she wasn't going to take any flak.

'I can hear what you're doing,' Marilyn Davies said angrily. 'Just what do you mean, asking her if she touched . . . if she touched those . . . things . . . What the hell are you trying to say?'

'Now, come on, love,' George Davies said uneasily. But it was obvious he was relieved to see her and Hillary had no doubts about who was going to be the primary force in this scene. Before it could get out of hand, she stood up and faced the mother hen who was intent on guarding her remaining chick.

'Mrs Davies, your daughter's fingerprints were found on the shears that had been used to stab Billy. Now, I just need to find out exactly how and when that happened.'

'You think our Celia did it?' Marilyn Davies shrieked, her face going from red to white with alarming speed. 'How could you be so bloody stupid? You can see she's just a little girl.'

And in that moment, Hillary realised why Marilyn Davies was so terrified. She thought that her daughter might have killed her own brother. Which was why she'd been so quick to transfer her own darkest suspicions on to the police officer investigating the case.

Suddenly, Hillary understood that the sibling rivalry between those two must have been vicious. Far worse than mere big brother/little sister jealousies. Had they come to blows before? Had Billy been violent? Or had Celia devised ways to torment her brother, and did Marilyn Davies fear that she'd gone too far?

'I tried to pull them out.' The words, quiet and defiant, slipped into the sudden fraught silence, and Hillary turned and looked down at the little girl.

Celia had put the top back on her pen and had closed her book. She was looking at Hillary, not her mother, and she was holding one shoe underneath her and rocking slightly on the floor. 'I went in and saw him, and thought the shears must be hurting him, so I tried to pull them out. I got hold of them real hard and tugged but nothing happened. Then I thought I'd better get Mum. She's stronger, and she could pull them out.' Celia shrugged. 'So I came home, and Dad went instead.'

Hillary nodded. 'Thank you, Celia. That's all I needed to know.'

She turned round and saw a look of relief pass between the Davies. Relief because they believed their daughter, or relief because Hillary had seemed to? It was impossible to say.

'I'll let myself out, shall I?' she murmured.

Outside, she stood in the small garden, taking long, slow breaths. What a nightmare it was. For all of them. Did Celia know, or sense, that her parents had thought she was a killer? Had the mother and father, in fact, even openly admitted their own private fears or had they kept it all bottled up inside? Just what had been going on in that family that could lead to such a possibility even existing in their minds?

Hillary walked to her car and again went through the ritual of opening all the doors and windows to release the accumulated heat. Suddenly sick of the hot day, she decided to head back to the office and spend the afternoon reading the preliminary interview reports and forensics.

She needed a breathing space from the mess of all these human emotions.

As she drove back to HQ she wondered if she believed Celia Davies's story of what had happened when she found her brother.

And, on the whole, thought that she probably did.

CHAPTER SEVEN

Janine glanced at her watch, scowling to see that it was nearly five past six. Still, with a bit of luck she could be home by half past seven and tucking into a takeaway. Nowadays that and *The X Factor* were the highlights of her social life. She was simply going to have to find another man — otherwise Mel might start thinking that he was irreplaceable.

The bastard.

She got out of the Mini and looked over the middling-sized bungalow in front of her, feeling distinctly disgruntled to even be here. Strictly speaking this was Frank's call, since he'd been given the task of following up on the interviews of all the Davies' neighbours, but neither of the Cleavers had been available at work and, of course, Frank had clocked off on the dot of five. Worse, she'd been the only one in Hillary Greene's line of sight when she'd noticed the oversight. She could have foisted it off on Tommy in her turn, she supposed, seeing as she had seniority, but what with his transfer in the offing, and his marriage coming up next month and all the hundred and one details that generated, she'd reluctantly decided to give him a break.

So here she was, back in the thriving metropolis that was Aston Lea. As she sighed and walked up the small, weed-free path, she couldn't help but compare this place with its neighbour, the Davies residence. Although the Cleavers' bungalow was the same basic design, there all similarities ended. 'Sunnyside' was obviously privately owned, and had recently had money lavished on it. Attractive diamond-paned windows had been installed and the external walls had been freshly painted a deep cream. Hanging baskets festooned with red, white, blue and purple flowers hung from every available wall. A trellis supporting huge, pale pink clematis clung to the walls and, through the windows, rich silk mulberry-coloured drapes tied back with velvet ribbons could be seen. The gardens were immaculate as well, and sported a little fountain tinkling away in a small pond, where goldfish darted.

Janine rung the bell and rummaged in her bag for her ID. The man who answered was unexpectedly good-looking, with dark hair and a well-sculpted body; somebody who obviously worked out and bought Armani. It was like being confronted by Pierce Brosnan or George Clooney when you were expecting Chris Evans, and Janine blinked a bit before introducing herself. And firmly reminded herself that the man was married.

Presumably, happily.

'Mr Cleaver? DS Tyler. I wonder if you have a few minutes to discuss William Davies?'

'Sure, but I've already spoken to a constable.'

'Yes, sir, this is a follow-up interview. It's strictly routine.'

'Better come inside then.' He stood aside and Janine brushed past him, catching a whiff of expensive cologne as she did so.

Inside, the bungalow had been opened up, with the narrow corridor that was still in existence in the Davies' home having been ripped out in preference for a more open-plan arrangement. The walls were uniformly white, and French windows had been added at the rear, leading out to the back garden and a patio furnished with white chairs and tables, and tubs of scarlet geraniums. Two massive white leather sofas dominated the room, and a small, neat marble fireplace played host to an arrangement of gladioli.

'Nice place,' Janine mused. The Cleavers obviously had money, and plenty of it. Either that, or they were in debt up to their eyeballs.

'Please, have a seat,' Darren Cleaver offered. 'Drink? I have a fine Oloroso?'

'Better not, not when I'm driving,' Janine said and got out her notebook. 'Your wife not at home, sir?'

'No, she's still in London. She works for a PR firm with a branch in Oxford, but just lately she seems to be doing most of her work in the London office. I think there's a promotion in the offing, and she wants to get in good with the bosses. You know how it is.' Janine nodded, trying to pretend she didn't feel jealous. 'Is she due back soon?'

'She'll be home around eight, half past eight I expect. Depends on traffic.'

Janine sighed. In that case, Frank could bloody well pencil her in for tomorrow night. Let him put in some unpaid overtime for once, she thought sourly. 'I see. Have you lived here long, Mr Cleaver?'

'About seven years, I think. We bought the place privately when the whole hamlet came under the housing association way back.'

'So you know the Davies well? They're right next door on the left, yes?'

'Yes. I have to say, we were both very shocked to learn of Billy's death. It was terrible.'

'You were at work yesterday?'

'Yes, I manage a big dairy, just outside of Banbury. We're national — provide milk and milk products all over — as far afield as Glasgow.'

Janine nodded, uninterested. 'Did you see Billy Davies yesterday?'

'No.'

'And do you or your wife ever have cause to visit the allotments? You don't own one, do you?'

Darren Cleaver laughed, showing gleaming white, perfectly straight teeth. 'Good grief no. Neither Jenny nor I have green fingers, I'm afraid. Besides, when would we ever get the time?'

'Did you know Billy Davies used to frequent the allotments regularly?'

'No. No reason why we should.'

Janine nodded, but caught a sudden sharpness in his voice. He'd poured himself a sherry and was standing with his back to the fireplace and for the first time he looked a little nervous. She might have told him the gladioli were getting pollen on his expensive fawn slacks, but didn't bother.

'Did you ever see anybody threatening Billy Davies? Or hear about any bad arguments he'd had with somebody. Did you ever see him talking to strangers, perhaps getting into a car you didn't recognise? Anything of that nature?'

Darren Cleaver shook his head decisively.

'No, nothing like that. And I have to say, I don't think Billy was the sort to be so foolish. He had a very wise head on his young shoulders. He always struck me as the sort who was well able to look after himself.'

'Well, evidently he wasn't, sir, was he?' Janine said softly, and watched the other man flush.

'Well, no. No. As I said, we were both very upset by what happened.'

Janine nodded and rose slowly to her feet. 'And you have nothing you want to add to your original statement? You haven't thought of anything which you think we might like to know since talking to the constable?

Sometimes memories can take a while to come to the surface.'

'I wish I could help,' Cleaver said, spreading his fingers in a helpless gesture. Janine noticed they were impeccably manicured. He might manage a dairy, but she doubted this man ever saw a cow, let alone handled one.

'Well, thank you, Mr Cleaver. A colleague will be getting in touch with your wife at some point.'

'That's fine,' Darren Cleaver said, and smiled as he showed her out.

Janine got in her Mini and headed for Oxford. At this time of night, at least the rush hour was over. She tuned the radio to Fox FM and hummed along to an old Carpenters' song.

She was in the mood for chicken tikka. Or maybe Chinese.

* * *

Hillary too was headed for home, although in her case this meant a barely three-minute drive from HQ to the tiny village of Thrupp. She was waiting on the main Oxford–Banbury road to make the right-hand turn into the lane, making time for an approaching lorry to pass her; the moment it was gone, she started to move out, but behind him, almost unseen, came a cyclist, and she had to quickly jam on the brakes. As the cyclist nodded a thanks as he sped by, Hillary finally made her turn, then, almost at once, jammed on the brakes again. Puff the Tragic Wagon came to an obliging halt underneath a flowering laburnum tree.

Hillary hit her hand lightly on the steering wheel. That's what it was! The cyclist had triggered what had been niggling away at her all day. Suddenly she was back at the Davies' bungalow, stepping outside the door and looking into the shed, and seeing Billy's mountain bike. At the time it had struck her as a sad and poignant sight. What should have struck her was the cost of it.

Most definitely, she'd been off her form that night, otherwise her first thought would have been to wonder how a fifteen-year-old boy from a poor working-class family had been able to afford a new, multi-geared, state-of-the-art mountain bike.

Although she herself had been eleven or twelve the last time she'd owned a bike, she was pretty sure that nowadays, such a sleek vehicle could cost as much to buy as some second-hand cars. She could distinctly remember seeing a mountain bike in a shop not so long ago, and gasping at the price tag.

Thoughtfully, she put the car back into gear and drove the few hundred yards needed to pull into the large car park of The Boat pub, where she habitually stabled her trusty Volkswagen. The landlord didn't mind since, more often than not, Hillary ate her Sunday lunch in there. Now, as she closed and locked the door, she glanced at her watch. Nearly seven. Time for a quick drink and maybe she'd treat herself to a pie. She couldn't be bothered with cooking tonight.

She walked to the pub door, making a mental note to ask Tommy tomorrow to check out the bike and make sure it really was as new and expensive as she remembered it, then question the Davies as to how Billy had come by it.

The pub was still largely deserted so early in the evening, so when Hillary walked in, she spotted him right away. Sat on a window-seat in the snug, he looked up at her and smiled the moment she walked in the door. A lean man, only a few inches taller than herself, with thinning dark hair, and a narrow, intelligent face. She had no doubt at all that he'd been sat by the window in order to see her arrive.

She smiled back, trying to pretend that her heart rate hadn't just gone up a notch, and walked to the bar. There she ordered a white wine spritzer and the salmon salad, paid for both, then took her drink to his table. 'Hello, Mike,' she said to DI Mike Regis. 'Glorious evening.'

Outside, on the canal, a mother duck and a dozen little ducklings were slowly cruising past, ignoring the swallows and house martins who were hawking for flies or skimming the surface for water to help build their mud nests.

'Sure is. Got a new case, I hear?'

Hillary nodded. It was easy to talk about work, so she filled him in, keeping to the basics of the case and her lack of progress so far. The usual copper's lament.

'You'll crack it,' he said, with flattering certainty. 'And congratulations on the medal. I wanted to be at the ceremony, but you know how it is.' He nodded at her drink. 'Get you another?'

'No, thanks, I'll make this do. And as for the medal, well, you were there that night. It was no big deal.'

Mike Regis, as a Vice squad member, had been there the night she and her team, Superintendent Jerome Raleigh and Mel had raided Luke Fletcher's farmhouse. Fletcher, a well-known drug dealer, suspected murderer and all-round villainous piece of scum, had died that night, and Hillary too had been shot.

'I wouldn't say that. You saved Mel's life, no question. The medal was well deserved, so be proud of it.' Regis took a sip of his own pint, then pinned her beneath an emerald gaze. 'I was surprised to hear that Raleigh up and quit. He left pretty damn quick didn't he, considering he'd only been at Thames Valley a few months?'

Hillary smiled grimly. She knew Regis was fishing, and wasn't about to bite. 'I daresay he had his reasons,' she said flatly. Namely, if he hadn't, he'd probably have been arrested.

But she wasn't going to go there.

'So, how's things with you? Colin all right?'

Colin Tanner was his sergeant, and the two had worked together for years. Some said they were telepathically linked.

'He's fine, and I'm fine.' Regis paused, then added quietly, 'And free. I wondered if you might fancy going out for a bite to eat some time?'

Hillary sucked in a long, slow breath. So here it was, at last. Regis, divorced and available.

When they'd first met, she'd had to acknowledge the mutual attraction that had flared up between them. They had worked well together, saw things the same, and obviously connected. Then she'd learned that he was also married, and had quickly given him the bum's rush. A while later he'd told her that he and his wife were getting divorced, and again, she'd more or less told him to come back when the divorce was real. An attitude so lacking in trust that it hadn't exactly endeared her to him, it had to be said. For a while there she'd been afraid that she'd seen the last of him. But now here he was, back again and having metaphorically picked himself up and dusted himself down, ready for round three.

But this time, there were no more excuses. If she said yes, there was no point kidding herself that she was doing anything other than taking her first step towards getting herself a man. And yet taking the plunge into another relationship wasn't something that she could do lightly. After her fiasco of a marriage with Ronnie Greene she'd thought she'd never want to get mixed up with another man for as long as she lived. But it had been three years now. And that was a long time to be celibate. And perhaps she'd healed.

Time, anyway, to find out.

She took a deep breath. 'Sure, I'd love to,' she said, but a momentary sense of panic had her adding quickly, 'but I'm up to my eyeballs at the moment with Billy Davies. Call me next week, yeah?'

Mike Regis smiled and his green eyes crinkled attractively at the corners. 'I'll do that.'

Hillary took a hefty gulp of her wine.

* * *

Janine pushed open the door of the three-bed semi she shared with two other working women, and dumped her plastic bag of Chinese takeaway on the kitchen table. It was her turn for kitchen duty, the three of them having a roster, but for the moment she ignored the pile of dirty dishes in the sink, ladled her meal on to a plate, and headed for the living room.

Nobody else was home. Of course, they all had lives. She hunted around for the remote and turned on the telly. The end credits for *Emmerdale* filled the empty house with noise, and she sighed as she tucked into spicy beef.

During the adverts for *Coronation Street*, she tackled the washing up and when she came back, noticed the answer phone blinking. They were probably all messages for her housemates, and she quickly skimmed over the familiar voices of Joyce's mum and Miranda's latest fella. Then froze as she heard Mel's voice.

'Hi, Janine. Just thought I'd give you a call. Now we're not seeing so much of each other at work, I just wanted to make sure you were doing OK.' There was a moment's pause, as if he was unsure of what to say next, then, 'I wondered if you might like to get together for lunch one day, when you're not busy. I know you've got a murder case on at the moment. Why don't you give me a call sometime, when you're free, and we'll get together. Just as friends, naturally. OK? Call me.'

He sounded anxious to ring off. No doubt he'd been having second thoughts already.

Janine turned off the machine and stared down at it. Just friends? Who was he kidding?

And what was really behind this let's-get-together offer. Feeling his lonely bed at night, was he? Well, he had nobody but himself to blame for that. And did he really think all he had to do was snap his fingers and she'd come running back?

Hah!

Janine stomped into the kitchen and switched on the kettle, reached for her mug and the teabags, then abruptly changed her mind, grabbed her bag, and slammed out of the house, heading for her local. Damnit, she wasn't going to sit at home watching telly and pining for an old flame.

She just wasn't.

* * *

The next morning, Tommy was only too pleased to spend the morning with Hillary. When he'd got in and she'd explained about the bike, he'd hit the internet, printing off pictures of various bikes and price lists. Now, as they pulled up outside the Davies bungalow once more, he reached behind him for the papers he'd tossed on to the back seat.

'So, the wedding's in — what — six weeks' time now?' Hillary asked, opening the passenger-side door and stepping out. 'Where are you going on honeymoon?'

'St Lucia. Jean has relatives out there. They've offered us the use of their beach bungalow free for a couple of weeks. I don't suppose it's anything fancy, but with a Caribbean beach on your doorstep, who cares?'

Hillary grinned. She'd bought the couple a sofa-bed for their wedding present, since she was feeling so flush after selling her house, figuring it would always come in handy for a couple buying their first home. She'd chosen a neutral oatmeal colour scheme, and only hoped they liked it.

'Let's not bother the family just yet,' she said now. 'If the bike's still in the shed, we won't need them anyway. It looked to me as if they kept it unlocked,' she added as they walked up the narrow, cracked concrete pavement towards the outbuildings.

The shed door was indeed open, and inside the blue bike gleamed as new-looking and impressive as she remembered it. Tommy checked it over and whistled silently through his teeth, then quickly checked the printout. 'Yeah, I reckon it's this model,' he said, pointing to a photograph of a man on an identical bike, pedalling up what looked like K2 but was probably in Scotland somewhere. 'Twelve gears, superannuated . . .' Tommy began to list the bike's merits with the usual male appreciation of all things mechanical, but Hillary had already tuned him out, and only paid attention again when he mentioned the price tag. '£650 new.'

Hillary sighed. 'I thought so. Where did he get the money for that?' Blackmail once more seemed to be firmly in the picture. Either that or drugs.

'Didn't you say he had an expensive camera as well, guv?' Tommy asked.

'Yeah, but his dad said he and his mum saved all year for it and it was his only Christmas present from them that year. How long has this bike been in circulation?'

Tommy went back inside to check the serial number on the crossbar, then consulted his paperwork again. 'Only came out three months ago, guv,' he confirmed. 'So it couldn't have been the year before last's Christmas present.'

So, once more she had to disturb the Davies family. But when she knocked on the door there was no answer. She walked around and looked in windows, but nobody was home.

* * *

Tommy pulled into the petrol station/garage and craned his head to look into the small shop window. 'I reckon that's Mrs Davies serving. Seems a bit soon to be back at work. Reckon the bosses are slave drivers?'

Hillary shrugged. 'Possible I suppose. But according to Frank's report, the Wilberforces seemed to be on friendly terms with them. It's more likely Celia wanted to go back to school, and George and Marilyn decided that going in to work was better than sitting in an empty house.'

When they got out of the car, a man appeared in the open square of the garage entrance, took one look at them and then went quickly back inside again. A moment later, George Davies appeared and walked reluctantly towards them, wiping his dirty hands on an even dirtier rag.

'Hello,' he said dully. 'Now what?'

He didn't seem angry, or upset, but merely bone tired, and Hillary wondered if he'd managed to get any sleep since she'd last seen him. 'I'm sorry to keep bothering you, Mr Davies. I was wondering what you could tell me about Billy's bike.'

George Davies stared at her for a moment, as if she'd started speaking in a foreign language, then a slow, dull red flush crept up his neck and on to his face.

'What about it?' he asked hopelessly.

'Did you buy it for him?'

'No. He got it for himself. Second-hand, off a boy at school, he said.'

'The model's brand new, Mr Davies,' Hillary said quietly.

'Aye, I thought it looked like it. But our Billy said this boy's mum didn't like him having it, said it was too dangerous, and made him sell it cheap, like.'

Even as he spoke, Hillary could tell that Davies hadn't believed it. She didn't either. 'Did he mention this boy's name?' she asked gently.

'No, he didn't.' Davies didn't even bother trying to meet her eyes. It was as if, bit by bit, he was beginning to accept the futility of trying to guard his son's reputation.

'Do you know how he paid for it, Mr Davies? It would have been £650 new. This boy couldn't have parted with it for less than £500.' She was willing, for now, to go along with this fictitious boy. Of course, she'd have to check it out, just to make sure. That could be a job for Frank. He'd love questioning schoolboys, trying to find one who'd sold a second-hand bike.

'Billy did odd jobs like. Worked on Saturdays with that best pal of his, Lester. I dunno what it was. Paper round maybe.'

Davies said it forlornly, but with a lingering sense of defiance, as if daring her to contradict him.

Hillary nodded. 'I see. Well, thank you, Mr Davies. I'll let you get back to work.'

In the car Tommy said flatly, 'He doesn't have any idea where his boy got the money, does he?'

Hillary sighed. 'No. And I don't think he wants to know now, either.'

* * *

Back at HQ, Hillary noticed a yellow Post-it sticker on her phone and quickly peeled it off. It smelt of fish and chips and had a grease stain on it, and Hillary didn't even have to check the name at the bottom to know that the untidy scrawl belonged to Frank Ross.

'Marty Warrender knows something he's not spitting out. Thought you might like to have a crack at the nut. F.R.'

Hillary sighed and crumpled it up and chucked it in the bin. 'Tommy, remind me to talk to the Warrenders sometime soon, when there's a half hour to spare. Janine, do a rundown on them for me, will you? See if there's anything iffy there.'

'Boss,' Janine said flatly.

Tommy quickly pencilled the reminder in his diary as Hillary scribbled something on her own yellow Post-it and slapped it on Frank's desk. It explained about the bike, and asked Frank to find the mysterious vendor. She smiled happily as she returned back to her desk. That should make his day.

Janine began to report back on her findings, but had nothing of any use to add. Some more forensics reports had trickled in, but again, nothing that took them a step further. So far, all the fingerprints found in the shed belonged to members of the Davies family, so no surprises there.

'If we don't get a clear lead soon, we're going to struggle,' Hillary said gloomily. 'Any luck with the Cleavers?'

'I only spoke to him, boss, the wife was still at work. He's a bit of a looker. Seemed a bit tense, but that's probably just because he wasn't used to having the plod in his living room.'

Hillary sighed and rubbed a tired hand over her forehead. She was getting a headache. Already they were into their second day, and they didn't have even so much as a sniff of a possible suspect. Still, at this point, she supposed there was some comfort in the thought that things couldn't possibly get any worse.

Just then, the door to Danvers's cubbyhole opened and his handsome blonde head appeared. 'Ah, Hillary. I was hoping to catch you. Any chance of a progress report on the Davies case?'

Hillary briefly closed her eyes, then stood up, gathering the files. 'Of course, sir,' she said, with a nice bright smile.

CHAPTER EIGHT

Janine checked her notebook and glanced at the tiny terraced cottage in front of her. She was parked in a narrow side street at the back end of Bicester and, according to her notes, Marty and June Warrender had bought this place nearly two months ago. It was hard to see why.

The street was lined on both sides with two-up, two-down Victorian terraced houses, with a handkerchief-sized lawn, three steep steps leading up to a front door set flush to the neighbour's wall, and tall, now surely obsolete, chimney stacks. The whole road looked cramped and mean-spirited.

Janine shrugged and climbed out of the Mini. The front door of number 32 stood open, and she could hear the sound of hammering and sawing as she approached. She walked straight through the door and into the building's main room, and coughed as the combined dust motes of sawdust, plaster and old insulation tickled her nostrils.

'Hello?' She could hear the inane chatter of DJs coming from the back somewhere, where the wall dividing kitchen from tiny parlour was being demolished. The makings of a breakfast bar were going up in one corner. Crouching down by a newly installed sink was the almost obligatory butt crack belonging to a plumber. His jeans were riding so low, Janine wasn't sure they'd stand up with him when he did. 'Hello,' she called again, and the man, still squatting, turned around. He had a red, sweating face, the very short cropped hair of somebody going bald and trying to hide the fact, and red-rimmed eyes. He stood up slowly, revealing an open shirt and beer belly. Luckily, he didn't part company with his trousers.

'Yeah?'

'I'm looking for the owner, Marty Warrender,' Janine lied. She knew Marty was at his day job in Banbury, but she also knew, after a quick trawl through the trusty internet, that he and his wife were the proud owners of this place. Funny that neither one had mentioned it to Frank. Nor had they fallen over themselves to tell them they were leaving Aston Lea. When Hillary had given her the job of checking the Warrenders out, she'd thought it was scraping the bottom of the barrel time. Now though, she was beginning to wonder. If their vic *had* been into blackmail, the Warrenders were proving to have surprising financial resources.

'Not here, luv. He's a fly-by-night.'

Janine blinked. 'Translation?'

The plumber grinned. 'One of those geezers who buys cheap, knackered properties, gets a gang in for two weeks to blitz the place, buys some tubs of pansies to stick in the garden, gets going with a lick of paint at night, and sells on, quick as lightning. Then on to the next one. Been working for this particular bloke for the last three years or so. But I reckon the balloon's about to burst though. First-time buyers are getting wise, and doing it for themselves — buy gaffs like this cheapish and then upgrade. Mind you, the price of houses nowadays, even these old clunkers are selling for a mint.' He looked around the bare walls and flaking plaster and shook his head. 'Wouldn't believe it, would you?'

Janine, who knew all too well the price of houses in Oxfordshire, would. 'Good boss is he?' she probed. 'Pays on time, no worries?'

'No. And what business is it of yours anyway, luv?' he asked, better late than never. Janine shrugged. She didn't show her warrant card, because she didn't want news of their interest getting back to Warrender. At least, not yet.

'Just being nosy. I might be in the market to buy,' she added. 'Only the one bedroom upstairs I suppose?' And when the plumber, still looking suspicious, nodded, she sighed. 'Too small then. Thanks, love,' she added, and turned and strolled out.

Back in the Mini, she started up the car and turned the air conditioning on to full before writing up her notes. The heatwave could continue all summer long as far as she was concerned, but she didn't like baking.

For a man who ran a dry-cleaner's, and a wife who worked in a shop, the Warrenders were doing all right. And if they'd been in property developing for some years, as the plumber said, then they must have a bit put by. Had Billy-Boy Davies found a way to help himself to some of that loot? She was blowed if she could see how. She checked her watch and put the car into gear. Time to head back to HQ and trawl the databases. If she could follow the Warrenders' trail through the Land and Property Registry, then with the help of a calculator and a little imagination, she might just be able to come up with a good estimate as to their net worth. Something that she was sure Hillary Greene would want to know.

* * *

Frank stared at the school, a sneer on his rounded face. It made him look like Winnie-the-Pooh after he'd just eaten a bad load of honey. Beside him Tommy Lynch also glanced at the mass of windows and straight, box-like structures, and was instantly transported back to his own school days. He'd gone to a comprehensive very much like this one, back in Cowley. Tommy had been only an average student, he supposed, but a fine athlete, and had reasonably fond memories of those days.

'We're wasting our time,' Frank said. 'And I'm blowed if I'm buggering about, questioning snotty-nosed little kids. I'm off to the office, see if I can persuade the headmaster's secretary to put out an announcement on the loudspeaker asking the boy who sold Billy Davies his bike to report in.'

Tommy said nothing.

'And if that ever happens, I'm a bloody flying squirrel. It's a waste of time. That boy was up to no good. Gotta be drugs.'

Tommy sighed. 'I imagine that's why the guv's asked me to poke around and see if I can't nail down some proof.'

Frank snorted. 'Best of British, mate. If my job's a no-hoper, yours is a dead duck. Get a schoolkid to admit to buying drugs off a dead classmate? You might as well save your breath and come down the boozer with me.'

Tommy watched Frank march off into the nearest building, glad to get shot of him at last. In his hand he had a list of classes and break times, and decided to hang around until lunch break. Frank was right about one thing — there'd be no point going from class to class and asking for information from a group of twenty kids. Nobody was going to speak up in front of their peers. But if he could get a feel for the users and likely lads, he might be able to get one or two on their own during a break and persuade some information out of them.

Yeah. Right.

* * *

The secretary didn't like Frank Ross, and didn't like his suggestion of a public announcement, but the head, anxious to be seen co-operating with the police, gave his permission. And so, at just gone 12:15 p.m., the secretary's voice was piped into every classroom, and echoed hollowly in every corridor, asking for the boy who'd sold William Davies his mountain bike to report to his or her teacher. After a muffled silence, in which another male voice could clearly be heard whispering, the head's PA then added that if anybody had any information at all about William Davies's bike, they were to report to the head's office.

Apart from a lot of speculative looks between themselves, and a few frowns of surprise from the teachers, the announcement might as well have been made on the moon, for all the difference it made.

Frank waited until all of 12:30, then left. Unlike Hillary Greene, he had been inside The Fox pub before. There weren't many pubs in Oxfordshire that he didn't know. And it wasn't until he'd ordered his first pint that he realised he should have talked to Heather Soames, Billy's girlfriend. If anyone had known where the bike had come from, she would. She might be only fifteen, same age as the vic, but in Frank's opinion, women of any age quickly learned about finances. And especially all about their boyfriend's finances.

Cursing, he used his mobile to phone the head's office again, but the secretary quickly confirmed that Heather Soames was not at school that day.

Her sister had brought in a sick note for her.

Frank shrugged. He'd try her again tomorrow. Couldn't go chasing after the poor girl if she was sick, could he? Might get had up for harassment or failing to show proper political correctness.

Instead, he went to the bar and ordered another pint. He always made it a point to know where traffic were patrolling with their little breathalyzer kits, and none of them were due around here today.

* * *

Tommy heard the bell ring for lunchtime, and smiled as the doors began to open and children poured out. Some headed for the dining room, and the horror that was school dinners, while others headed for the playing fields to eat packed lunches. Several headed off to the surrounding suburbs to eat lunch at home.

And one boy got on a very new, very fancy-looking mountain bike and pedalled away. Tommy watched him, his ginger head glowing in the fierce sunshine, and reached for his mobile.

Back at HQ, Hillary was still at her desk. She'd been debating accepting Paul Danvers's offer of joining him in the canteen after he'd listened, po-faced, to her report on the Davies case. Now, with the jangling of the phone, she rather hoped that she might be getting an excuse to beg off his offer of treating her to the special. Which today, being a Thursday, would be the vegetable lasagne.

'DI Greene.'

'Guv, Tommy. Can you tell me if Lester Miller is a carrot top?'

'Yep, complete with freckles and the creepiest pale eyes you've ever seen. Why? Have any of the kids fingered him as a dealer?' she asked quickly.

'No, guv, nothing like that. But I've just seen him pedal off on a bike that's almost a twin to the one Billy Davies has. Had.'

Hillary slowly leaned back in her chair. 'That's interesting. But not necessarily incriminating. Kids who are joined at the hip often imitate each other.' She paused, thinking it over. 'Tommy, forget about the school for a minute, and get on the blower to Miller's father and find out if he bought his son a bike recently. You say you saw him pedalling away from the school?'

'Yes, guv. Lunch break, I reckon.'

Hillary nodded. Middleton Stoney was only a three-mile journey on mostly flat roads from Bicester Comprehensive. Perhaps he was going home for lunch.

But more likely, like his friend Billy, Lester liked to play hooky every now and then.

'OK, Tommy, I'm going to drive to Middleton Stoney, see if I can shake loose some information from him. When you've finished chatting with the father, I want you to check in with Melanie Parker over at Juvie. When I mentioned Billy Davies's name to her, it didn't ring a bell, but perhaps Lester Miller's will. She's got her pulse on the kiddies' drugs scene around here and offered to liaise with us if we needed it. She's even got a snout at the school, so now's a good time to take her up on the offer to make use of him. Until we can rule drugs in or out of this case once and for all, we're just spinning our wheels.'

'Guv,' Tommy said, and hung up.

* * *

Janine parked her Mini beneath a resplendent copper beech tree, not far from St Mary's Church in downtown Oxford, and checked the address.

The offices of the Elite Public Relations Company were housed in one of those splendid Gothic monstrosities that looked so cute on tourist-board brochures. As Janine climbed out of the car, a gaggle of camera-festooned Japanese tourists, led by a guide, washed around her, chattering like escapees from Babel. 'Next, we're going to go up The Broad, and see if Trinity College has its doors open. Trinity is situated almost next door to Blackwell's, the famous book shop, so if anybody wants to do some reading . . .' the chatter of the guide drifted off into a sleepy early-afternoon waft of heat as the troop moved away.

Janine walked across a short expanse of gravel and checked out the bell pushes on the door. 'Elite' shared the Gothic hall with a couple of private interior-design companies, a very upscale dentist, and several varieties of accountants (but not turf).

Janine pressed the buzzer for Elite and was exhorted by an invisible Sloane Ranger to, 'Come on up to the second floor. We're behind the turquoise door.'

Janine stepped into a cool, black-and-red tiled hall with stark white walls. She could smell some kind of furniture wax and a floral air freshener. Several of the windows lining the massive main staircase had pieces of stained-glass in them, which gave the building the air of a part-time church. Elite must certainly do well for itself if even the more obscure Oxford branch could afford digs in this place.

As she climbed the stairs, and easily spotted the turquoise door, Janine decided to treat herself to a pub lunch after the interview, for a change. It was hot, and she could do with a glass of something cold.

'Hello, can I help you?' The Sloane Ranger turned out to be someone who'd obviously modelled herself on a 1970s Joanna Lumley, despite having neither the looks nor the figure for it. Stick-thin, and with obviously dyed short blonde hair tortured into a Purdey cut, she was wearing enough mascara to choke a duck. And she had to be sixty if she was a day. Janine smiled at the receptionist and flashed her warrant card. The old girl looked at it and her jaw dropped open.

Janine got the impression she'd never seen one before.

'Oh my,' she said helplessly.

Janine smiled. 'I have an appointment to see Jenny Cleaver,' she said flatly. She'd already phoned to make sure Cleaver wouldn't be in the London office and had spoken to her secretary, who'd confirmed that she'd be available that lunchtime.

'Oh, yes, of course. That poor boy. I read about it in the papers, and I remembered that Jenny lived in Aston Lea. Please, go right on through. Second door on the left.' She pointed to one of three doors, housing, it was supposed, the executive offices.

Janine imagined that there was very little that escaped the receptionist's attention. She had the air of one of those women who made it a point to know everything. Janine tapped on the door indicated, and without waiting for a summons, opened it and walked in.

* * *

If Lester Miller was surprised to see Hillary Greene show up on his home territory so soon after seeing her at the school, he didn't show it.

He simply stood back, a sandwich in one hand, and waved her in. 'Come on in,' he said, and took a bite out of what looked suspiciously like a tomato ketchup special. Some of the red gloop splurged out over his hand, and he licked it off as Hillary stepped past him.

'I said I'd have to speak to you again, Lester,' Hillary said, glancing around. The Millers lived in a big, detached house with mock-Tudor pretensions, situated on the very outskirts of the village. Middleton Stoney was cut in half by a main road, but there was no sound of it here. Through a pair of open French doors, Hillary could make out a large area of grounds, consisting of manicured lawns, flowering shrubs and weed-free flowerbeds, all proof of a professional gardener's services. The three-piece suite in the lounge was black leather, the glass tables smoky, and the paintings on the walls were originals. Not good ones, in her opinion, but originals.

'Want something to eat?' Lester asked, waving his gory sandwich in the air.

Hillary smiled. 'Thanks, but no.' She'd missed lunch, but she'd have to be desperate before taking pot luck with someone of Lester's culinary preferences.

'Sit down then. What can I do you for?' Lester threw himself on to a reclining chair, all but bouncing. His feet, encased in dirty, sweaty sneakers, left a distinct mark on the leather. Hillary wondered if it would be his mother, or a maid, who had to wipe it off.

'Tell me about Billy,' Hillary said, taking a seat opposite, and taking out her notebook.

'I already told you,' Lester said, taking another bite of his sandwich. Beside him, on a table, stood a tall glass of Coke or Pepsi, filled to the brim with ice cubes. Hillary felt her mouth water, and quickly looked away.

'I notice you came home on your bike,' Hillary said, and Lester, after a moment's startled silence, abruptly laughed.

'Funny things you coppers notice. Yeah, I came home on the bike. So what?'

'Nice bike. Expensive. Billy had one just like it.'

Lester flushed. 'I got mine first,' he said petulantly. 'But that was Billy all over. No class. He only wanted one 'cause I had one.'

'Really?' Hillary said, sensing a way under his skin. 'Funny that. From what people have been saying it was Billy who was the leader, and you were the one who followed him around, like a sheep.'

Lester laughed again, and reached for his glass of Coke. 'Bollocks,' he said, and took a long drink. His Adam's apple bobbed angrily in his scrawny neck, and Hillary noticed that his freckles marched all the way up from his chest to his ears.

'How did Billy pay for his bike, Lester?' Hillary asked quietly. 'His dad and mum work in a garage. He get one on the cheap? Only way for someone like Billy to get kit like that, wasn't it?'

Lester shrugged. 'I dunno. I never asked him.'

'Oh come on, Lester,' Hillary said, with a sceptical laugh. 'Are you seriously trying to tell me you don't know? According to his dad he had some sort of a job. You both did.'

'A job?' Lester squeaked in echo, as if she'd just mentioned a dirty word. 'That's a laugh. We don't work, Billy and me.'

Hillary nodded. Again he was speaking in the present tense. Had it really not sunk in, even yet, that his friend was dead? She knew that sometimes children, including teenage boys, could form really tight emotional bonds. But usually there was a dominant personality and a worshipper. She was beginning to think that this was the case here, with Lester firmly in the acolyte mode. But she was out of her depth, if so. She'd have to have a word with the department shrink, perhaps have him interview Lester Miller. You never know — it might give her some insights.

'And what about your bike, Lester? How did you come by it?'

'My dad bought it for me,' Lester said at once, and gave her a telling look. It was the sort of smug, you-don't-get-me-that-way look that made Hillary smile. If only he knew it, he'd just given her a big stick to beat him with.

'He buys you a lot of stuff, I bet. Only child, fruit of his loins and all that. Things just drop in your lap, don't they, Lester? But for Billy it was different. His dad was dirt poor — he had to graft and scheme for what he got. No wonder he was the one with all the brains.'

Lester flushed. 'He wasn't as smart as he thought he was, though, was he?' he snapped, leaning forward on the chair, his sneakers making squeaking noises against the leather as he moved.

'Wasn't he?' Hillary said calmly. 'What makes you think that?'

'Well, look how he ended up,' Lester pointed out, going for callous, but his voice wobbled as he spoke. And he swallowed hard. He stared at the half-eaten sandwich still in his hand then abruptly tossed it on to the glass tabletop, where it smeared the expensive glass with grease. He looked a little green around the gills, as if he suddenly felt sick.

'Lester, do you know where Billy got his spending money?' she asked quietly. 'Was it drugs?'

Lester shook his head. 'No. It wasn't drugs. And before you ask, I dunno. Why don't you—' He broke off and then smiled as he heard the front door open and close. A moment later, Hillary rose to her feet as a man pushed his way into the lounge. He was almost humming with aggression.

Gareth Miller glared at Hillary Greene from his height of six feet three or so. His son must have got his colouring from his mother, for Gareth had dark brown hair and greyish eyes. 'I thought I might find one of you lot here,' Miller said ominously. 'When I got a call from that DC Lynch asking about Lester's bike, I got the feeling I should make my way home pretty sharpish.' He shifted his eyes from Hillary to his son and then back to Hillary again. When Hillary looked at Lester Miller he was calmly eating his sandwich once more and smirking at her.

Of course, he felt untouchable now that Daddy had come home.

'You are aware that my son is only fifteen years old . . . whoever the hell you are?'

Hillary quickly held out her card. 'Detective Inspector Greene, sir. And—'

'You can't interview him without either his mother or me present. I've a good mind to complain about this.'

Hillary counted to three and smiled blandly. 'Of course you're free to do so, sir. My immediate superior officer is Superintendent Philip Mallow,' she lied. She didn't want this getting back to Danvers just yet, if Miller actually followed through on his threat. And she could trust Mel to smooth things over. 'And I apologize if I've made either yourself or your son uncomfortable,' she lied brightly. 'It didn't occur to me that Lester might not want to help me find out who killed his best friend. And as a parent yourself, I felt sure that you would identify with the tragedy the Davies family are going through and be only too eager to help. But,' Hillary reached for her bag and hefted it on to her shoulder, 'I can assure you that the next time I want to speak to Lester, I'll inform you first.'

Gareth Miller, who'd had the good grace to look a little guilty during her speech, just as she'd intended, suddenly stiffened his backbone and nodded curtly. 'See that you do.'

Hillary nodded back just as curtly, turned and smiled sweetly at Lester, then walked slowly and stiffly out of the house.

That was the second time Lester Miller had got under her skin.

She was still fuming as she got back into her car and her fingertips hurt as she all but poked them through the pads on her mobile phone as she dialled Tommy's number. 'Tommy,' she gritted, the moment he answered. 'You at Juvie yet?'

'Just pulling into the car park, guv.'

'Let me know right away if Melanie has anything on Miller, yeah?'

'Right, guv,' Tommy said, sounding surprised. As well he might. It wasn't her usual style to breathe down her officers' necks like this. Hillary took a slow count of three and took several deep breaths, then sighed and told herself not to be such a prat. 'OK, Tommy. See you later.'

She hung up and wiped a hand across her forehead, unsurprised to find it coming away wet and sticky. 'This damned heat,' she muttered, and started up her car, wound down her window and headed back to Kidlington.

* * *

Janine didn't like Jenny Cleaver. This was almost certainly because she was even more beautiful than herself. Although Janine didn't actively trade on her looks to get what she wanted, she was very much aware of how much they could help, or hinder. So whenever she met a woman

116

even better endowed in the looks department than herself, it always raised both her hackles and alarm bells. Seriously beautiful women, especially if they were also bright, could be trouble.

Jenny Cleaver was taller than herself, leaner, and had a mass of auburn hair that looked natural, a triangular-shaped face, and clear white skin with wide, sea-green/grey eyes. It wasn't hard to see how she'd managed to land a catch like her husband. They certainly made a striking couple. Although Janine wondered which one of them had first dibs on the bathroom in the morning. Or did they have matching his-and-hers full-length mirrors, in which they could primp and preen?

'Detective Sergeant Tyler,' Janine said, showing her badge briefly. 'Thank you for giving up your lunch break to see me. We've kept missing you the last few days.'

'Sorry. I was in London yesterday. This is about Billy, yes? Darren said you'd spoken to him last night. I honestly don't know how I can help.' Jenny Cleaver, who'd risen to her feet when Janine had come in, now indicated a swivel chair in front of her desk, and dropped back gracefully into her own chair. She watched Janine cross her long legs and smiled.

Something, Janine wasn't sure what, feathered a warning across the back of her neck, and then was gone. 'You might think, because Aston Lea is such a small place, that we all know our neighbours' business,' Jenny Cleaver carried on, 'but I'm afraid that's not the case. I know George and Marilyn, of course, as I often call in at the garage for petrol and such, but I can't remember the last time I even spoke to Billy.'

Janine nodded. Jenny Cleaver was wearing an iron-grey raw-silk trouser suit that she would kill to own, and the jade and silver pendant hung around her neck was nice too.

'So you have no idea who might have wanted to kill him?'

Jenny Cleaver shook her head. 'It's horrific, isn't it? I don't feel safe in my own home anymore. Darren and I have seriously discussed moving, I can tell you.'

'I see,' Janine said. Self-absorbed or what? She didn't seem to care at all that a boy was dead. But Janine, who was nothing if not honest with herself, knew that she was probably just feeling bitchy because Jenny Cleaver had it all. The good-looking husband, the ideal home and garden, the gorgeous wardrobe and glamorous job. 'Well, if you remember anything you think I should know . . .' Janine was fiddling in her bag for her card. Finally she found a rather dog-eared one and handed it over. 'Give me a call. I don't suppose you saw Billy on Tuesday, the day he died?'

'No, I have a six thirty a.m. start when I'm working in town.'

Poor you, Janine thought savagely, smiled and left. In the outer office once more, she was just in time to see the Joanna-wannabe slip her bum back into her seat. What was the betting that she'd been standing with her shell-like ear glued to the boss's door?

Janine smiled blandly. 'Busy lady,' she said pleasantly.

'And might be even more so, if Holy Orders gives her the promotion.'

'Huh?' Janine said, wondering if her ears were full of wax. 'Holy Orders?'

The receptionist giggled. 'Sorry, Mrs Orbison. We call her Holy Orders around here 'cause she's a strict Jehovah's Witness. She's our boss. Well, our boss here. And if Jenny wants to get the jackpot she's hankering after, she'll need Mrs Orbison's recommendation.'

'Oh, yes, her husband mentioned she was in line for promotion. Be working out of London permanently then, I guess.'

'Phwar, London be blowed,' the Sloane Ranger drawled. 'New York more like. Elite are international you know.'

Janine managed another smile and left the office feeling slightly sick. Why did some women seem to have it all?

Then she thought about the shell-shocked face of Marilyn Davies and abruptly stopped feeling sorry for herself. She made a mental note crossing the Cleavers off her list and headed back for the car.

Maybe she'd pop in and see Mel after getting back to HQ. Just to say hello, like. Maybe take him up on that offer of lunch. It didn't hurt to stay friendly with the boss, right?

CHAPTER NINE

Hillary turned off the engine of her car and sat for a few minutes, simply letting her head clear. It was nearly seven, and the sun, although not yet setting, was giving out a softer, more golden glow. She was back in Aston Lea, parked on the side of the road and feeling just a shade depressed.

Her case seemed stuck in a go-nowhere groove.

Through the open window of her car, she could hear a blackbird singing sweetly. Then a group of swifts came streaming low over the hedge like black arrows fired from a crossbow, screaming their way over a field of barley, and she felt the gloom begin to lift. The first early dog roses were beginning to bloom amidst a blackthorn hedge, and somewhere in the hamlet in front of her a dog barked. Although she had worked out of Oxford in her youth, Hillary couldn't understand people who preferred city life.

Sighing wearily, she climbed out of the car and walked slowly to the allotment gate. A waft of something cooking, maybe barbecued meat, swept past her on the evening breeze and her stomach rumbled. If she'd had any sense, she'd be home on the boat now, cooking dinner for herself. She knew the uniforms had interviewed all the allotment holders, and had come up empty.

She'd also read all the other interview notes, and knew that Lester Miller was safely accounted for in a class when Billy had died, and that his girlfriend, Heather Soames, had been hanging around with friends on the tennis court, during a 'free' period. At some point she was going to have to reinterview Heather Soames herself, and Mel would probably have said that she had higher priority, but something was drawing Hillary back to this place.

The scene of the crime.

What had Billy Davies seen in his final moments? Who had he been talking to? Had he arranged to meet someone here, or had he been surprised by someone? Had he known his killer? Had he been afraid, or surprised, in those final moments, when he felt the cold blade slip between his ribs?

A victim's final moments weren't something she often dwelt on. It only hurt her, and it served no good purpose. But tonight, on such a lovely spring evening, it was hard to ignore the ghost of the dead boy, here, where he'd died.

Suddenly she had the sensation that she was being watched. It was not something that frightened her. A country girl born and bred, she knew the eyes probably weren't even human. Anything could be watching her, finding her presence intrusive and wishing she'd leave. A young rabbit, out in the wide world on his own for the first time. A hunting stoat, with his eye on the rabbit. Maybe even a cat from one of the bungalows. Once, when she'd been about thirteen or fourteen, she'd been sitting under a tree, totally alone and deep in the countryside, eating an apple, and quite happy until she'd felt the hairs on the back of her neck stand up; but no matter where she looked, she couldn't see the cause of her alarm. She'd been by a river, but there were no river birds or voles, and there were no grazing sheep or cattle in the fields surrounding her. She was beginning to get seriously alarmed until she thought of looking up — the one place she hadn't tried — and discovered a pair of barn owls staring down at her.

Now, Hillary slowly straightened up from her leaning position on the top of the five-barred gate and looked around. This time, however, her audience was definitely human — an old man, to be specific, standing in the midst of a patch of what looked like sweet williams and pumpkins. He was leaning on a hoe and, in deference to the heat, was wearing a pair of wide shorts that highlighted comically thin white legs, pockmarked with the odd red, angry-looking bite. That was the trouble with heat. It brought flies with it.

Hillary opened the gate and walked in. The old man watched her as she walked up the grass path bisecting the plots towards him, then nodded as she smiled a greeting at him.

'Nice evening. Won't last though,' he said obligingly.

Hillary shrugged. 'I can do without the heat myself,' she said. 'Especially if it turns sticky.' There were very few disadvantages to living on a narrowboat, but excessive heat in the summer months was one of them. Sometimes the inside of the *Mollern* could feel like a sauna.

'Arr, it'll end in a thunderstorm no doubt. You the woman in charge of finding out who killed young Billy then?' he added, deciding they'd had enough pleasantries.

Hillary nodded. It didn't surprise her that he knew who she was. But she was in no hurry to get down to the nitty-gritty. Sometimes witnesses opened up more if they liked you. 'This your patch?' she asked unnecessarily, surveying the neat rows of mounded-up potatoes, the tangle of peas curling their way up sticks, and a patch of rhubarb that was ready for pulling.

'Yes, 'tis,' the old man acknowledged. He was going thin on top, and his dome shone red where the sun had caught it. 'Want some onions? Spring onions, I mean. I need to thin them out.'

Hillary grinned and shook her head. She knew how hot they'd be. Her father, before his death, had kept two chains of allotments, and she remembered the kick his scallions had had. 'I was hoping you could help me,' she said instead. 'I'm finding it hard getting to grips with what Billy was doing here on the day he died. I've heard he hung around here sometimes, but nobody seems to know why, exactly. His mother said something about him taking photographs?'

The old man looked at her for a moment, then scratched his no-doubt itching head and shrugged. 'He always had a camera slung around his neck, I'll grant him that,' he said at last. 'And now and then he'd take some snaps, like. If the weather was funny. We had a snowstorm last winter. Right queer it was. Only lasted five minutes and we had a bit of a rainbow with it too. It was eerie, for a minute or two, I can tell you. A bit scary even. I was out here checking on the Brussels, making sure I'd have some for Christmas, and I nipped in my shed quick. Saw Billy then, snapping away. His dad reckons he won some sort of prize for one of 'em, in one of them geographical or nature magazines. The ones that bang on about the glory of nature, and all that.'

Hillary nodded. Well, here at least was independent confirmation of Marilyn's evidence. Her son might have been fond of the place. And yet, there was something hesitant about the old man's attitude that made her linger over it.

'Still, the day he was killed, it was just another hot spring day,' she pointed out. 'I wouldn't have thought there was anything to interest him here. Especially if he wasn't well.'

The old man grunted. 'I wouldn't take much notice of that,' he advised, then added as she raised an eyebrow in question, 'Him being ill, I mean. Little bugger had a very convenient constitution, you ask me. Any time he wanted to skive off school he'd come down with something.'

Hillary smiled. 'Yes, I got that impression. So you see, I'm still puzzled as to what he was doing here. Did you ever see him meet anyone here?' she asked flatly.

'Not that I can recall,' the old man said after some thought. 'If I saw him here at all, he usually headed straight for his dad's shed. You checked it out I suppose? No dirty magazines in there?' His face creased into wrinkles as he smiled slyly. 'Young lad that age . . . well, you gotta wonder.'

Hillary smiled and shook her head. 'First thing we thought of,' she said, not altogether untruthfully. She imagined SOCO had gone over the shed with hiding places in mind. 'Nothing like that.'

'Ahh. Well. You know, I often saw him slip through the back, like. But I can't see no harm in that.'

'Out the back? Back of where?' Hillary asked sharply, glancing over at the Davies allotment, and the still taped-off shed.

'That bit of derelict land behind the shed,' the old man pointed. His fingers, she noticed, were yellowed with nicotine stains. 'Used to belong to old man Humphries, kept the forge. Used to let his old horse roam around there. Kept a pig, too, in a stone-built pigsty. Course, it's all thistles and dock now. Too small to rent out to a farmer for sheep, too inconvenient to get to for anybody to build on. It's just a mess of elder and stuff now. Can't think what mischief the lad could have got up to in there. Reckon he was just curious, like. Either that or he was photographing stuff. Spiders, or whatnot. Bird's nests. Plenty of them in there, bound to be.'

Hillary recalled admiring one photograph hanging on Billy's bedroom wall — a spiderweb, with morning dew on it. It seemed to be hanging from two blackened thistle stems. Could have been taken back there. It made sense. But she was sure there'd been no mention of a camera being found in the vicinity in the SOCO reports she'd read. And his digital camera had been in his bedroom that first night they'd interviewed his parents. So unless Billy had a second camera, and one that his assailant had stolen from him, it didn't seem likely Billy had been here pursuing his hobby. And if he didn't have a stash of porn, or something even more unhealthy in the shed, why had he been here at all, if not to meet his killer?

'Well, thanks,' Hillary said. 'Can you point me in the direction of your fellow allotment owners?'

'Sure. Phil and Glenys live in the second bungalow on the left, and Pete the one next door. And the Coopers live on the first one over on the right. They took over the Warrenders' old plot.'

Hillary, who'd just lifted one foot, intending to swivel around and walk away, put it slowly back down again. 'The Warrenders? I didn't know they had a plot.'

The old man guffawed. 'They don't, not now. But they asked for one as soon as they moved in. I reckon they had some daft idea of growing their own veggies and living the good life. Soon found out it was more hard work than they bargained for. Plot went to weeds within a week. Next year, the allotment committee agreed to give it to the Coopers.' Hillary nodded. Was that so? So the Warrenders would be familiar with the allotments. And Billy Davies wouldn't be particularly alarmed or surprised if one or the other of them had approached him.

'Well, thank you, Mr . . . ?'

'Ferris. Nigel Ferris. Anytime. Want some rhubarb?'

Hillary, who rather liked rhubarb, let him pull some for her and deposited it on to the back seat of her car before walking on into the hamlet to interview the others.

* * *

It was getting dark by the time she pulled in to Thrupp. As she'd thought, none of the other allotment keepers had been able to help, but two of them did confirm Nigel Ferris's statement that they'd seen Billy either going into, or coming out of, the derelict land behind the shed.

Now, as Hillary pulled into the pub car park, she supposed at some point she was going to have to check out the land herself. Make sure she was wearing her oldest clothes and trousers that tucked into some sturdy boots. Stinging nettles and six-legged things that bit would no doubt be the order of the day, and she was damned if she was going to pick up ticks, even in the line of duty.

She parked and locked up, and hefted her bag over her shoulder. From *Willowsands* she heard the sound of music; a familiar tune that, as she drew closer, she identified as Simon and Garfunkel's 'Mrs Robinson' from the film *The Graduate*. It made her chuckle. Only Nancy had a sense of humour that wicked.

She walked on by and hopped lightly on to the back of her own boat, already reaching into her bag for the padlock key. When she'd first moved on to the boat, she'd just left Ronnie after finding him out in yet another extra-marital affair. It had been the final straw. Her uncle had bought the boat in a fit of over-exuberance on his retirement, only to find out, after a few trips, that his wife wasn't that keen on living 'out of a pencil box.'

It was a sentiment that Hillary had at first shared, but since Ronnie had been careful to put the house in his own name, and wasn't about to be generous in any upcoming divorce, it had been the boat or nothing. Then he'd died in a car crash, and some crazy animal liberators had tried to commandeer his assets, including the house, and what with one thing and another, she'd found herself still living on the boat when she'd been shot a few months ago.

It had been during her recuperation that she'd finally admitted that life on the canal suited her, and she'd bit the bullet and bought the boat outright from her uncle. The housework it needed was minimal, it was convenient for work, and the rhythms of the water and the reliability of the seasons had worked some sort of magic on her. Now she couldn't imagine living in a brick-and-mortar house that didn't bob about occasionally, and couldn't be moved whenever the fancy took her.

She stepped inside, automatically ducking her head so that she didn't bang it on the metal frame, and turned on the light. She went straight through the narrow corridor to the prow of the boat, where the galley was. A glass of wine and some salad, and an early night. Not very exciting perhaps, but . . .

She tensed as she heard a thud and felt the boat move, ever so slightly, beneath her. She knew what that meant. She turned, alert but not yet alarmed. A kitchen knife lay in the rack on the sink.

'Hello on board? Mind if I come down?'

Hillary bit back a groan and hurried forward. 'Not at all, sir. Please, mind your head.'

'Call me Paul,' DCI Danvers said, bending in half as he came down the stairs. He was wearing a pair of silver-grey trousers and a pale blue sports shirt. His arms were tanned, as was the V-shape under his neck. His blonde hair was fast turning silver as the heatwave continued, and he grinned a white smile at her as he reached the bottom.

'You've redecorated since I was last here,' he said. He'd been on the *Mollern* only once before, when Hillary had still been but a lodger. Since buying the boat, however, she had lightened the paint scheme, added a few shelves, and some watercolour sketches an old friend from her college days had painted for her. She'd also bought some mint-green covers for the armchair and her bed, and matching curtains.

'Only a bit,' she agreed. 'Drink? I've only got tea or coffee in,' she lied. She didn't want to do anything that would encourage him to linger. Or get ideas.

'Fine,' Danvers said. He moved forward, following Hillary as she retreated back to the galley. Apart from her bedroom and the tiny shower room, the *Mollern* had an open plan, and the galley also housed a bookcase and a single armchair, a fold-down table and a small portable telly. Danvers glanced out of one of the windows, where a waxing moon shone ripples of light on the dark canal water.

'I can understand why you like it here, Hillary. It's hard to believe Kidlington is just a half mile up the road. It's like a different world out there.'

Hillary smiled and pointed to the armchair. 'Please, have a seat.' She reached for a folding deckchair beside the sink and opened it out for herself. As the kettle began humming, she talked about the Davies case, and he listened closely.

'Any progress on the drugs angle?' he asked, when she'd finished.

'I'm waiting for Tommy to get back to me. Melanie Parker won't hang about. If there's something there, we'll know it soon.'

'And the family's in the clear?'

'As much as they can be,' Hillary said neutrally, 'given that husband and wife and eleven-year-old daughter all alibi each other.'

'Get any vibes there?'

Hillary blew out her lips. 'I don't think either of them were under any illusions about their son,' she said at last. 'I got the impression they were doing an ostrich act. But they're not completely off my radar yet.'

Danvers nodded, then watched her make the coffee. He accepted his with a brief smile. 'Mel seems to be settling down in his new job OK.'

Hillary nodded and took a sip of her own brew. It was too hot and tasted surprisingly bitter. She felt hot and sticky after another scorching day, and wanted a cold shower. The boat felt close too, and she got up and opened the window behind her. The *Mollern* was deliberately moored under a long line of willow trees, which provided nearly day-long shade, but even so, she could feel the sweat begin to gather between her breasts.

She wished Danvers would go. His knee was so close to hers they were almost touching.

* * *

Janine watched the waiter pour a Chilean Chardonnay into her glass, then looked across at Mel. 'The linguine all right?' he asked, and Janine nodded, spearing a forkful and chewing quickly.

She was hungry.

'Nice place,' she said, looking around the Italian restaurant. She hadn't been here before, and wondered how long it would last. Restaurants seemed to have a short shelf-life nowadays.

'Glad you like it,' Mel said. 'The tiramisu here is really something.'

'What's going on, Mel?' Janine said flatly. 'Why the invitation to dinner?'

Mel shrugged. 'I could ask you the same thing. You didn't have to accept.'

Janine grunted. 'Free food. What's a girl gonna do?'

Mel smiled and reached for the shaker of parmesan cheese. 'Fancy dancing later?' He knew Janine loved to dance — anything from line dancing to ballroom to retro disco.

Janine smiled wryly. 'Sure, why not?' This was better than staying at home and watching the telly any day. Mel wanted to get back into her bed, she knew it. She could feel it. And she . . . well, she wasn't sure whether or not she'd let him, or just amuse herself watching him squirm trying.

* * *

'Well, I'd better be off,' Paul Danvers said, putting his empty coffee mug in the sink. Hillary, sitting in the low deckchair, found herself struggling just a little to get to her feet. When Danvers reached down to grab her hand and pull her up she felt her breath catch. She was careful not to take a step towards him.

'Thank you, sir. It's been a long day.'

'Paul.'

Hillary smiled. 'Paul.'

She walked him to the back of the boat and watched him walk away down the towpath. She was going to have to face it. The man was after her. And what the hell was she supposed to do about that? If she mentioned it to Mel, he'd think it was sour grapes because he'd got the job and she hadn't. And there was no way she was going to make an official complaint to Donleavy. It would be the kiss of death to her own career, and besides, to be fair, the man hadn't even so much as made a pass. Perhaps she was reading too much into it. Didn't Danvers have a girlfriend, anyway? Some sort of svelte legal eagle, if she remembered. Well, there was no point worrying about it now. She'd cross that bridge when and if she came to it.

She was about to go back down the steps when a long, slow wolf whistle pierced the night air. 'Way to go, Hill,' Nancy Walker said. She was lying on the top of her boat, and looked, at first glance, to be naked. Then Hillary saw that she was, in fact, wearing a skin-coloured bikini.

'What the hell are you doing?' Hillary said.

'Too damned muggy to sleep indoors,' Nancy said. 'I've got a mattress out here. You should try it.'

Hillary shook her head. 'You're bloody mad, you know that? What if some mad rapist came along?'

Nancy grinned. 'I'd shout for you, of course. Who's the Adonis?' she asked, nodding in the direction Danvers had taken. 'Finally stopped living like a nun then? About time.'

'It was work,' Hillary said shortly. 'He's my new boss, Detective Chief Inspector Danvers,' Hillary added firmly.

'He fancies you something rotten,' Nancy said, matter-of-factly, lying back down and smiling as a bat swooped low across the water, its call, in spite of the folklore that would have it otherwise, being perfectly audible to the human ear. 'Trust me, I can tell. And you ain't immune girl, either, no matter what you've been telling yourself.'

'What, you can tell all that, even in the dark, at a distance of twenty feet?'

'Better believe it.'

Hillary had the uncomfortable feeling she was right. 'He's younger than me,' she said flatly.

'So?' Nancy gurgled and Hillary sighed. Probably not the best argument to use on the toy-boy queen of north Oxford.

'He's my boss.'

'So?'

'He's the one who investigated me that time when they thought I might be bent!'

'Ooooh, seriously sexy!' Nancy said. 'He can investigate me for corruption any time he wants to. I won't let him down.'

'Oh, shut up,' Hillary grinned, ducking back down the steps.

As she shut the door firmly behind her, she heard Nancy call, 'If you really don't want him, can I have him?' Hillary was still laughing when she fell into bed a little while later.

* * *

She was back at work at 8:30 the next morning. It was Friday, three days after the discovery of Billy's body, and already the temperature was high enough to have her nicking someone's electric fan.

She attacked her in-tray as if she hated it (which she usually did) and fell on Tommy's neck the moment he walked through the door. The news wasn't good though. Melanie had nothing on Lester Miller and, worse, her snout was almost positive neither Billy Davies nor Miller had been dealing.

'Although the snout did say that everybody at the school thought Davies had some sort of scam going. He always had money, and nobody knew where it came from,' Tommy finished his report, just as Janine came in through the door.

Hillary watched her take her seat, wondering why she was smiling like the cat that had been dining on canary pie.

'Drugs a washout then?' she asked, having caught the tail end of Tommy's report.

'Looks like it,' Hillary agreed. 'Any reports of an increase in thefts in the local area?' she asked sharply, but Tommy was already shaking his head.

'Thought of that, guv, but nothing unusual. If Billy was thieving, he wasn't doing it on his own back doorstep.'

'Blackmail's got to be back on the hotlist then,' she mused, then added, 'Did either of you know the Warrenders used to have an allotment?'

Before either of them could respond, Frank Ross stuck his head around the door, but made no move to cross the big open-plan office to his desk. Instead he gestured at her like a belligerent gnome.

Hillary sighed and got up. She didn't want to leave the cooling reach of the electric fan, but she knew it was only a matter of time before its furious owner claimed it back. 'What is it, Frank?' she asked flatly, when she reached the door.

'Bird downstairs asking to see you,' he said back, just as flatly. 'About the Davies case. I was passing the desk when she started in and I offered to help, but only you will do, apparently.'

Hillary nodded. 'Right. You'd better sit in obbo,' she said, referring to the room where another officer could watch and listen in on an interview.

'Gee, thanks,' Frank drawled.

The witness had been taken to interview room five, she was informed, and when she walked in, the teenager turned immediately to look at her. She wasn't very tall, and she had too much puppy fat. Her skirt was too tight, and the shirt she had tied at the waist revealed a bulging belly button. She had a line of silver stud earrings in one lobe only, and her make-up was already beginning to run in the heat.

Hillary took a seat opposite her and smiled. 'Hello, I'm Detective Inspector Hillary Greene. I'm heading up the William Davies murder inquiry. You wanted to see me?'

The girl nodded. She had long, damp brown hair and hazel eyes a little too close together.

Hillary got out her notebook. 'Your full name please?'

'Deborah Eloise Soames.'

Hillary glanced up at her. 'Any relation to Heather Soames?'

Debbie Soames nodded sullenly. 'My sister, yeah.'

Heather Soames, if Hillary's memory was accurate, was the same age as her boyfriend had been — namely fifteen. But this girl looked older. Maybe seventeen or so. What's more, Heather Soames was known to be something of a looker — one of the school's popular people. It must be a bit tough on a girl like this to have a little sister who was such a looker.

'I've yet to speak to your sister, Miss Soames,' Hillary said mildly. 'My officer tells me she wasn't at school yesterday. She was ill?'

Debbie Soames snorted. 'Ill my arse. She's up the duff, isn't she.' She reached into the pocket of her skirt and pulled out a stick of Juicy Fruit and opened it up.

Once in her mouth, she began to chew it vigorously.

Hillary slowly leaned back in her chair.

'I see. I take it Billy is the father?'

Debbie shrugged. 'Probably. Not sure. Heather's not all that fussy, know what I mean?'

Hillary thought she did. Debbie Soames bitterly resented being the dumpy, unattractive one, and was enjoying this rare chance to drop her sister in it. So she'd have to take Heather's supposed nymphomania with a big pinch of salt.

'What makes you think your sister's pregnant?' Hillary asked curiously.

'Spewing up in the morning. Not being on the rag. Clothes getting too tight. You don't need to be a rocket scientist, do yah?' Debbie Soames snorted. 'Besides, I found a pregnancy testing kit in her room.'

Hillary smiled. 'That was very observant of you, Miss Soames. Did Billy know she was pregnant?'

Debbie shrugged. 'Mighta done. Not sure. I know Heather didn't go spreading it around. Scared Dad'll find out. He'll kill her when he does,' she added smugly.

'You haven't already told him?' Hillary asked, surprised. A girl with this much repressed sibling jealousy, she would have thought, would have blurted it out to Dad straight away.

Debbie Soames looked uneasy and shrugged.

'I ain't no grass,' she finally said.

Hillary nodded. There was something there, obviously. Some reason why she hadn't informed her father. Well, there was no time to waste now. She'd have to speak to Heather Soames right away.

She questioned Debbie Soames about the day of Billy's murder, but she'd been at school and knew nothing. Now that she'd spewed her venom she seemed in a hurry to get away, and Hillary was only too pleased to let her go.

Outside, Frank Ross smiled happily. 'About time we got a break,' he said.

Hillary glanced at him sourly. 'Ask Janine to meet me outside,' she said, and before he could open his mouth said flatly, 'Forget it, Frank. I'm not letting you interview a pretty pregnant teenager.'

Ross shot a two-fingered salute to her back when she turned and walked away.

'Same to you,' Hillary said, without turning around.

CHAPTER TEN

Heather Soames answered the door herself. She was the same height as Hillary, but far more slender, with shoulder-length ash-blonde hair and big green eyes. If she was pregnant it wasn't yet obvious, although she was dressed in a long, loose, flower-bedecked robe, so perhaps she was beginning to show and was anxious to cover up. Her face was pinched and pale, and free of make-up. She looked ill, and Hillary was glad she hadn't brought Frank.

Beside her, Janine held out her ID. 'DS Tyler, and this is Detective Inspector Greene. Heather Soames?'

'Yes? Dad isn't here.' Heather Soames stepped away from the door, indicating them to come inside. Hillary, mindful of her tongue-lashing from Lester Miller's father recently, found herself hesitating.

'Heather, since you're only fifteen, there should be an adult present. Would you like to call your father?'

'Hell no,' the teenager said at once. 'Come inside. I'll make you a drink.'

Hillary nodded to Janine to go first, but once inside, tried again. 'How about a neighbour? Do you have a favourite aunt or uncle you'd like to call?'

'No, I'm fine. It's fine. I want to talk about Billy.'

Hillary nodded, but once the teenager had turned her back to lead them through to the kitchen, she snapped her fingers in Janine's direction and pointed to her phone, and mouthed the word 'father.' Janine nodded and moved off to one side and began to dial.

Hillary went after Heather and found her in a small but cheerful white and yellow kitchen, with a tiny round dining table, and all the worktops gleaming with old-fashioned Formica. The house had once been a council house, but now looked as if it was privately owned. Out back was a big and colourful, if rather overgrown, garden. The Soames lived on a big but fairly well-respected housing estate in west Bicester. Somewhere a church clock, probably St Edburg's, chimed the hour of ten.

'You've not been well,' Hillary began, watching the girl as she filled the kettle and reached into a cupboard for mugs. 'You've not been back to school much since Billy died?'

'No, probably a tummy bug. Tea or coffee?'

'Coffee for both of us, thanks. One without sugar, one with. Do you want me to do it?'

'No, I'm not helpless. Please, sit down. Move the cat if he's on the chair.'

But there was no cat and, outside, she could hear Janine talking quietly on the phone. Soon, Francis Soames would be here and, although she was not supposed to technically question the witness, Hillary saw no harm in just chatting. All girls together, and that sort of thing.

'Heather, are you expecting a baby?' she asked casually, and the girl almost dropped the sugar packet she was holding. She turned and stared at her for a moment, then sighed.

'Who told you? Mary-Beth? Or Colleen? They swore they wouldn't tell. Should have known I couldn't trust them.' She sounded merely tired though, rather than seriously put out.

Hillary smiled. 'Your best friends? Yes, well, our information didn't come from either of those, so it looks as if you chose your friends well.'

Heather Soames nodded listlessly and went to the fridge for milk. Janine wandered in, nodded casually at Hillary and took a seat as well.

'So, are you many weeks along?' Hillary asked.

'Not so many. Eight or nine, I think.'

'You've been to see a doctor?' Hillary asked abruptly, suddenly alarmed, but already the girl was shaking her head.

'Not yet.'

'But you will?' she pressed, her mind mentally going through a register of people she could call on for help in these matters.

'Not sure,' Heather said carefully, and poured boiling water into the mugs, brought them to the table then sat down. She tucked a strand of hair behind her ear and stared at a half-empty marmalade pot on the table. 'Billy wanted me to get rid of it,' she admitted frankly. 'He said he'd pay. He even found some places I could go. On the train, like. Couldn't get it done around here. Bloody gossipy town, you ask me.'

Hillary nodded. 'Does your dad know?'

'No!' Heather almost shouted. 'And you mustn't tell him! He'll be sick as a parrot. Please! He's got really paranoid since Mum . . .' Her bottom lip began to quiver. 'Since Mum died.'

Janine glanced up from her notebook, not liking the way the girl's voice had begun to oscillate. Although she could, and had, dealt with many weeping and hysterical witnesses, it wasn't her favourite pastime.

Hillary got up, walked around, and put an arm around the girl. 'Your mum die recently, love?'

'Two months ago,' Heather choked out and began to sob. Janine jumped up and looked around, spotted some kitchen roll on the windowsill and yanked off a few squares. Hillary took them from her and handed them silently over, hugging the girl as she wept into the tissue. The crying storm lasted a few minutes, but when it was over, the teenager looked calmer. And even more exhausted. Hillary went back to her seat.

'It was cancer,' Heather said quietly, holding the sodden and crumpled mass of paper in her hands. She began absently to shred it. 'We knew for months beforehand that she was going to go, but Dad wouldn't have it. He kept talking about us all going on holiday next year, as if by pretending it wasn't happening, it wouldn't happen.'

Hillary nodded. 'I understand.'

'But she went. And ever since then, Dad's been mad around me and Debbie. Won't let us stay out after ten. Can't go on the back of Debbie's boyfriend's motorbike, even with a helmet on. Stuff like that. If he knew I'd got pregnant, he'd . . . well, he'd do his nut. Please don't tell him. You don't have to tell him, do you?' she asked pathetically.

Hillary opened her mouth, then closed it again, as she heard a car pull into the drive outside. 'That's your father,' she warned, then put a hand on Heather's shoulder as she made to get up. 'Don't worry, we had to call him, but we don't need to talk about the baby. It was Billy's, yes?'

'Of course it was. He's the only one I've been with. You know, my first and everything.'

Hillary nodded. 'Did you feel angry when he asked you to have an abortion?' she asked quickly, aware that their time was fast running out. Outside, a car door opened and slammed.

'Well, not really,' Heather said, looking from her to the door and back again. 'I was a bit scared. I don't want a kid, not really. I thought Billy would come with me though. Hold my hand. Now I don't know what I'm going to do.'

'There's people you can talk to,' Hillary said quickly, and leaned back away from her as she heard the front door open. 'Go to the family planning clinic, or even the Citizen's Advice Bureau. They can give you names and addresses,' she whispered.

When Francis Soames walked into the kitchen a moment later, Hillary and Janine were sitting sipping coffee, and Heather was fiddling with the marmalade pot. Hillary rose at once. 'Mr Soames? Hello, I'm Detective Inspector Greene.' She held out a hand. 'This is my colleague, DS Tyler. She phoned you?'

'Yes. What is it. What's wrong?'

'Nothing's wrong, Mr Soames, but we need to speak to Heather, concerning the William Davies investigation, and since she's underage, we need an adult present. We thought you'd like to be here before we start questioning her. As you can see, she's made us feel right at home while we were waiting for you,' Hillary added, holding up her mug.

Francis Soames nodded. 'Good girl,' he said absently, but he looked wary. He was one of those lean, sparse men, who had quick, birdlike movements and lots of energy. His hair was as blonde as his daughter's, but looked set to go grey any second, and his nose was on the hooked side. He looked like a man who knew how to handle himself and life, but you could tell he'd had a bad knock recently. There was something in the hollows under the eyes, the stiff way he walked, that gave it away.

'Any tea in the pot, lovey?' he asked, sitting down and shoving a black briefcase out of the way under the table.

Heather got up wordlessly and made her father some tea.

'So, perhaps we can begin?' Hillary said guilelessly, pretending not to notice the look of gratitude the teenager sent her. 'You were at school the afternoon that Billy died, I believe?' she carried on smoothly.

'Yes,' Heather said. 'We had a free period, just after double French. Mary-Beth and Colleen and me hung around the tennis courts. Colleen always watches Wimbledon, fancies her chances as a pro and all that, and she was practising her forearm smash. Or pretending to. Mostly we just drank Cokes and chatted.'

Hillary nodded. 'I know you've already gone over all this with a constable, but sometimes it takes a few days for the shock to wear off, and then witnesses can remember things they didn't think of before.' She said this more for Francis Soames's benefit than anything else, and it was to him that she turned.

He nodded, but didn't speak. He was watching his daughter carefully though, Hillary noticed.

'Were you expecting Billy to be at school that day?' She turned back to Heather.

'Course. It was the day after the bank holiday. Everyone was back at school.'

'But you're not in the same form as Billy?'

'No. First time I knew he wasn't there was at the morning break. We usually spent it together. We'd meet up in the locker room where I had my locker.'

Hillary nodded. 'And had Billy seemed odd in any way, before the bank holiday? Did he seem worried, or upset, or anything like that?'

Heather shook her head. 'No, he was the same as ever. Asked me what I wanted for my birthday. It's next month. Said he was going to buy me a diamond necklace, but I told him not to be daft. He said he was though, said he'd seen this tiny diamond drop pendant in a jeweller's in Banbury. He was always like that; he loved buying me stuff. He was just a big kid, really.'

Hillary tried not to smile. At fifteen, that's exactly what Billy-Boy Davies had been. A big kid. But there was no point in trying to explain this to Heather. Girls grew up faster than boys, and a girl like Heather, who'd already been through so much, would almost certainly regard herself as a fully-fledged adult.

Francis Soames shifted uneasily on his chair and his daughter shot him a quick look. 'I know you always thought he was showing off, but he really meant the stuff he said, Dad.'

Francis Soames opened his mouth to contend with this, then considered his daughter's wan face, and shut it again. In the end, he merely shrugged.

'Dad didn't really like Billy,' Heather explained to Hillary, rather unnecessarily. 'And Billy was dead scared of Dad. But they'd have got on all right though, in time. I know they would have.' She paused, then took a deep breath. 'Do you know who killed him?' she asked, staring at her with big moist green eyes.

Hillary smiled gently. 'I'm afraid I can't discuss an ongoing investigation, Miss Soames. Can you tell me what the deal was between him and Lester Miller?' she asked, abruptly changing the subject.

Heather's lips instantly twisted. 'Oh, him. Ginger nut. He was all right, but he was a bit of a hanger-on. You know, like pop stars have roadies, Billy had Lester. Billy was the one with all the ideas and all the brains, and Lester, well, his dad is loaded, or so Lester always said, and Billy let him tag along with us sometimes. Billy always said that as soon as he left school, Lester would be history though.'

Hillary nodded. The picture was becoming clearer. Billy had tolerated Lester because of the computer, the liberal pocket money, the nice house where he could freeload and get away from the bungalow. She doubted that he'd ever really thought of the boy as a true friend.

'Heather, do you have any idea who might have killed him?' Hillary asked softly.

'No,' Heather said at once. 'I'd have told you if I had,' she added simply.

'Did Billy ever talk about his family? Did he get on with them?'

'He never really said much. I think his dad got on his case from time to time, and he said his little sister was a real pain in the . . . I mean, a big pain,' she shot her father a quick look, hoping he hadn't caught the near-slip. 'Said he couldn't wait to leave home, but I think he got on with his mum all right. Just the usual stuff, you know?'

Hillary did. 'All right, Heather. Well, that's all for now. I hope you feel better soon,' she added, getting slowly to her feet. 'Mr Soames, if you'd like to see us out?' she murmured discreetly.

Francis Soames got instantly to his feet, his mug of tea still untouched in front of him. Outside, they walked in single file to Hillary's car.

'I understand you lost your wife recently. I'm very sorry,' she said quietly. 'But your daughters must be a comfort.'

'Yes they are. I don't know what I'd do without them. Debbie's taken on the housework and cooking and everything. She's my rock, I always tell her. Heather's a bit more delicate. Well, you saw. She's not been well. This thing with Billy has really knocked her sideways. And after losing her mum so recently too. I'm worried about her. Good job Debbie's so strong.'

Hillary nodded, suddenly seeing it all. Heather, the pampered favourite. The dumpy Debbie, relied upon and largely ignored. She was beginning to think she'd done the elder daughter a disservice. The reason why she hadn't told their father about Heather's pregnancy was now obvious — she didn't want to heap yet more misery on his plate. Yet being taken so much for granted must chafe, after a while.

Perhaps it was a cry for help, rather than malice, that had brought Debbie Soames to the station that morning? She'd like to think so.

'You were at work when Billy Davies was killed, Mr Soames?'

Francis Soames smiled. 'Not very subtle, Inspector,' he chided wryly. 'And yes, I was. I run a carpet cleaning service out of Glory Farm.'

Hillary nodded. 'Well, we'll let you get back to it,' Hillary said, holding out her hand once more. Francis Soames shook it, but didn't return to his own car and went back inside the house instead. Hillary tossed her car keys to Janine and slipped into the passenger seat.

'When you've got a minute, I want you to visit the carpet cleaners,' Hillary said, the moment Janine was buckled into her seat. 'Find out if Soames really is alibied or not. It's one thing to say, "Oh, I was at work," but what does that actually mean? If he helps out with the actual house calls, he could have been anywhere. He could have cleaned a lounge carpet in half an hour, logged it as an hour, and been in Aston Lea for the other half hour, killing the kid who'd been messing about with his underage daughter. Both Debbie and Heather could be wrong about Daddy not knowing about the pregnancy.'

'Could be,' Janine mused. 'Losing the wife could have sent him a bit funny. And if he knew or suspected that Billy wanted Heather to get rid of his grandson or granddaughter, it might have been enough to tip him over the edge. He's obviously still a man in mourning.'

Hillary agreed. She'd seen ample examples of how an otherwise sane and emotionally well-balanced person could do extraordinary things when in the grip of grief. 'Mind you, he didn't strike me as the type who liked to get hands-on. Notice the briefcase? I think he sees himself as strictly managerial. So if he was in the office, make sure you question the secretary well. Does his office have another exit? Could he have slipped out? How often did she see him? If he was on the phone, who with and for how long? I want Francis Soames's whereabouts for the whole afternoon of Billy's death tied up with pink ribbons.'

'Boss,' Janine said, and turned the ignition key.

Back at HQ, the desk sergeant nobbled her the moment she walked through the door.

'Hey, Hill. DI Parker wants you over her neck of the woods ASAP.'

Hillary shook her head at Janine silently telling her not to bother accompanying her, and turned and headed off towards Juvie. It wasn't yet eleven, and she was curious to hear what Melanie wanted.

The unit dealing with juvenile crime was a large one, and — a typical sign of the times — growing larger all the time. The criminals caught TWOCing, ram-raiding, drug-dealing, stealing and mugging would soon all be under the age of sixteen — or so Hillary sometimes felt. She didn't envy Melanie her posting, or have any desire to join her.

Melanie Parker wasn't at her desk, and a fresh-faced DC (who looked about ten, and was probably used to infiltrate raves on a nightly basis) quickly pointed her in the direction of the interview rooms. There she was met by a DS Vernon, who knocked on a door and ushered her in, before leaving them to it.

Melanie was sat at a table smoking in blatant violation of anti-smoking laws. Opposite her a teenager with so much metal clipped, clamped, threaded and pierced on to his face that he must set off metal alarms at a distance of twelve feet, puffed as enthusiastically away. Hillary felt the back of her throat tickle and bit back the urge to cough.

'Ah, DI Greene. Kevin, this is the officer I was telling you about. Kevin is a pusher at Bicester Comp. Why don't you tell DI Greene what you were just telling me?'

'First off, I ain't no pusher, right?' Kevin said, stubbing out his cigarette in an ashtray, displaying the spiderweb tattoo on the back of his hand to perfect advantage. 'That's just a little joke the inspector here likes to play. I never done time for dealing, yeah?'

Melanie Parker smiled beatifically. 'Just give us time, Kev,' she said softly. 'We're only waiting until you turn eighteen when we get to send you down to the big boys' prison.' Kevin snickered, but his eyes flicked nervously between the two women. Hillary pulled out a seat and made herself comfortable. 'Just so's we're clear. I'm just here doing my bit. Being a good citizen, like.'

'You're here because we pulled you, Kevin,' Melanie corrected flatly. 'And don't think that, even now, officers aren't pulling the plumbing apart to find out exactly what it was you flushed down the loo.'

'Can't prove it was nothing to do with me,' Kevin said at once. And accurately. Hillary knew that Melanie's people wouldn't really be inspecting the loos. It would be a waste of time and effort. And with what genuine plumbers cost nowadays, the budget would never stretch to it.

'Just get on with it,' Melanie said, almost affectionately, as she lit up another cigarette. Hillary felt her eyes smarting, and blinked furiously. She hoped they'd get down to it soon, or else she was going to start breaking out in a rash. She was mildly allergic to cigarette smoke.

'Right. But I ain't no grass or nothing,' Kevin reiterated. He had dyed blue hair with a zigzag cut straight across the top of his dome, and matching zigzagging blue eyes. Hillary wondered what he was on. No doubt Melanie could tell her if she asked.

'That's understood,' Melanie said impatiently. 'Stop mucking around like a junkie at an Oasis concert and get on with it.'

'Who's Oasis?' he asked, genuinely puzzled, making both women feel about a hundred-and-six years old.

'You want to spend a couple of days in Branston House?' Melanie snapped, naming a notorious young offenders' institute near the lunatic asylum in Broadmoor.

'Hey, OK,' Kevin held up his hands defensively. 'You was asking me about the kid that got his throat cut, yeah?'

'It was a stabbing to the chest, but close enough,' Melanie said. 'Now get on with it.'

'Right, well, he wasn't dealing. Not that I'd know from experience, like, but some of my friends ain't as clever as me, and they sometimes buy the odd naughty tablet or two, know what I mean. And that kid that got offed never did no offering.'

'We already know that,' Melanie said, letting her impatience show. 'I wouldn't drag DI Greene over here just to listen to you snivelling. Tell her what you told me, and cut the acting performance. This isn't the BAFTAs.'

'Yeah. OK. No comeback on me, we agreed.'

Melanie sighed elaborately and nodded.

'Yeah, well, this kid I know, he thought Billy-Boy might be interested in making a few quid, right, so he asked him if he wanted in. But Billy-Boy got really sniffy, and said it was a mug's game. The bigger boys got all the profit, and kids like my mate got thrown into Juvie if they got caught. Said he didn't need no dimwit two-bit dealer to help him get his hands on readies. He was doing all right as it was.' Kevin ran the back of his tattooed hand under his leaking nose and sniffed. 'This really pissed my friend off, right. I mean, who did he think he was? Thing is, Billy-Boy had just come to school on this mean bike, and everyone knew he was boffing the choicest babe in school, giving her gold bracelets and stuff. So he was coining it somehow, right enough.'

Hillary leaned forward on the table. 'Did your friend know how?'

'Nope. He only knew he wasn't doing it by dealing. Didn't reckon he was thieving either, since his brother has the patch around here. But Billy was cocky, you know? The kind of cocky you only get when you're doing all right for yourself. Know what I mean?'

Hillary did. She also wondered why Heather Soames hadn't mentioned any gold bracelets, then supposed that they hadn't really had much time to chat before her father had appeared on the scene. Besides, to be fair, she had mentioned that Billy liked buying her expensive gifts.

146

Perhaps a diamond pendant hadn't been just wishful thinking after all.

'Didn't your friend lean on Billy a bit?' Hillary cajoled craftily. 'After all, if he had a source of income, surely your friend wanted a slice of the action? No crook likes independent operators on his patch.'

'Naw,' Kevin said. 'He'd been told by his main man to keep things nice and easy, right. Don't frighten the chickens. Don't do nothing to attract the law. He couldn't have had Billy-Boy kneecapped without drawing attention to himself like. And certain people wouldn't have stood for that.'

Hillary saw Melanie twist her lips in a grim smile and shook her head.

'No,' Hillary agreed flatly. 'You got any idea what Billy was into?'

'Me?' Kev squeaked in surprise. 'Nope. Not unless it was selling porn. He had a way with the camera, I'll tell you that. And his girlfriends were always lookers.'

Hillary nodded. It was possible, she supposed. Nowadays, porn didn't pay all that well — there was too much of it about and cheap at the price. But to a boy of fifteen, selling pictures of nude girls for twenty quid a pop could make him feel as if he'd hit the jackpot. And it would all mount up.

'OK, Kevin,' Hillary said. 'If you hear anything let me know, yeah?'

Kevin snorted, 'Yeah right,' and Melanie Parker cleared her throat loudly, and his cheesy grin quickly faded.

'Go on then, sod off,' Melanie Parker said, stubbing out her cigarette in a tin ashtray. And when the boy had got to the door added cheerfully, 'Catch you next time, Kevin.'

* * *

Hillary returned to her desk thoughtfully. Melanie had assured her that the intelligence, in spite of the unprepossessing source, was probably good. She'd also promised to keep an ear out for any gossip concerning the dead boy and pass it on.

Hillary sat down at her desk and quickly explained to her team about the possible porn angle, finishing briskly, 'Frank, this is right up your alley. Find out if Billy-Boy had any contacts he might have been selling to regularly.'

'Right, guv,' Frank grinned. 'Mind you, he could have been selling directly to *Playboy* and whatnot. That "Readers' Wives" racket would stretch to nubile teenage girlfriends, I reckon. I'll have to buy a range of mags and get in touch direct. Any chance of raiding the slush fund?'

Hillary was still laughing over that when her phone rang. 'Yes? What? Here now? OK, no, send him up.' She hung up then frowned. 'George Davies is downstairs. He probably wants an update on his son's case.'

Janine gave her a double take. According to protocol, they should have talked to him downstairs in an interview room but, after a moment, she thought she understood why the boss had asked to have him brought up here. The room was big and full of busy men and women, working flat out. If you'd had a child murdered, the sight of computers being used and phones ringing would reinforce the impression that something was being done.

Hillary stood up when a uniformed WPC ushered in George Davies. The garage mechanic looked around, but his eyes were dull. To her surprise, he didn't speak, not even in answer to her greeting, but dug his right hand into his back pocket and came out with a small, dark blue book. Hillary recognised it straight away as the kind that building societies handed out to savers.

'I found this hidden at our place,' George Davies said flatly. 'It's Billy's. I know all his hiding places. He thought I didn't, but I found it this morning. Thought I'd better bring it in. I haven't told his mother,' he added, the short staccato sentences betraying how agitated he really was. 'I gotta get back to work,' he finished, backing away, then turned and walked quickly to the door.

Tommy looked at her quickly, wanting to know if she wanted him to stop him, but Hillary shook her head.

She reached for the book instead and opened it. The building society was a high-street name, and the book belonged to their Bicester branch. Hillary opened it and ran a quick eye down the columns. In the ten months since he'd opened it, Billy had amassed just over £1,550. There were a few withdrawals, but by far the most interesting item was a regular payment of £150. It had been paid in at the beginning of every month for the last six months. There were also lesser, but still regular payments of between £30 and £60.

She tossed it to Janine who scanned it, whistled, then passed it to Tommy, who had it snatched out of his hand by Frank.

Frank snorted. 'Nice work if you can get it.'

'It's got to be blackmail,' Hillary said flatly. Porno by itself wouldn't pay so regularly.

'Janine, I want you to bring in Marty Warrender. We'll start with him, really sweat him, then go on to the rest of the neighbours. If one of them doesn't know something about this, then I'm Peter Pan.'

CHAPTER ELEVEN

Marty Warrender looked around the interview room nervously. His gaze skidded off the uniformed PC stood at the door and dropped back down to his cup of tea. He'd never been in a police station before, and he wasn't quite sure how he was supposed to behave.

Even when the shop he'd been working in a few years ago had been broken into, it had been the then manager, Clifford Waythorpe, who'd had to deal with it all.

It was so quiet he had to fight the urge to cough, just to hear a reassuring human sound. He began to feel just a little bit sick, and pushed the cup of tea away from him, across the scarred and somewhat battered table.

When the pretty blonde sergeant had called into the dry cleaners to ask him if he could come down to the police station in Kidlington to answer a few questions, he'd thought at first that she was joking, but it had taken only a few moments to realise that she wasn't. He'd had to ask Sylvia Dodd, the woman who worked with him, to take over for an hour or so, very much aware that she'd been watching the whole procedure with her mouth hanging open, and barely able to contain her excitement.

Sylvia had worked at the dry cleaners since the year dot, and although hard-working and very knowledgeable about what shifted gravy from linen, she was an inveterate gossip. He cringed, wondering what she was telling the customers, even now. Unless, of course, she was on the phone chatting to her endless list of equally gossiping friends. It would probably be all around Banbury by now that he'd been asked to 'help the police with their inquiries.'

Thinking of what that ominous phrase usually meant — at least to most people's minds — Marty felt the nausea roll around in his stomach and hoped he wasn't going to make a spectacle of himself. He took a deep breath and tried to calm down, but he could feel his hands shaking, and slipped them out of sight on to his lap and underneath the table.

Surely they weren't going to actually arrest him? He'd done nothing wrong! And they hadn't read him his rights or anything. Perhaps he should just get up and go? If he had more gumption, he'd do just that, he thought miserably. How long had he been in here, anyway? He checked his watch, and saw that it was nearly half past twelve. The drive from Banbury had taken over half an hour and it would be the same back, no doubt. And it wasn't as if he didn't have work to do.

'All right, let's get on with it,' Hillary Greene said at last. She was standing in the observation room, and, from the suspect's body language, she gauged that he was wound up good and tight. Beside her, Janine nodded.

Marty looked up, almost in relief, when two women finally walked in through the door. The blonde he recognised at once, and the older, attractive brunette with the curvy figure he instinctively pegged as someone with clout. He found himself straightening up in the chair.

'Mr Warrender? I'm Detective Inspector Hillary Greene. I'm the senior investigating officer on the William Davies inquiry. Thank you for taking the time to come in and see us. Something has come up, and we need your help. It shouldn't take long.'

Marty Warrender let out a long, tense breath. He saw the older woman notice, and shrugged sheepishly. 'I was thinking it was something serious. You know, getting a bit worked up.'

Hillary smiled briefly and nodded. 'Well, it is serious, Mr Warrender. The murder of a fifteen-year-old boy is bound to be. And I'm sure you'll help us in any way you can.'

'Oh, of course,' Marty said, reaching for his cup again but merely fiddling with it, turning it around and around on the saucer. Funny, he'd expected them to give him a mug, not a cup and saucer.

'We've been building up a picture of young Billy during the last few days,' Hillary began, opening the folder she'd brought in with her and turning a page or two as she spoke. 'And the picture that's coming through isn't altogether a kind one. Billy seems to have been a bit of a lad. Oh, not outright criminal. That is, nothing that we've been able to pinpoint yet.' She suddenly looked up and caught him nodding. 'None of this surprises you, I can see, Mr Warrender.'

'No. Well, not really. I mean, we all knew Billy was a bit of a handful. But George and Marilyn are so nice, and young Celia's a poppet. You don't, you know, like to say anything unkind, for the family's sake, do you?'

Hillary nodded understandingly. 'I suppose not. But when it comes down to it, the police have the responsibility of solving Billy's murder. And we can't always afford to speak well of the dead, especially if we have reason to believe that flaws in the victim's character are what led to the fatality in the first place. You see what I'm getting at?'

Marty Warrender felt his stomach roll again, and swallowed hard. He could feel bile biting at the back of his throat, and forced himself to take a sip of the tea. The attractive brunette was harder, and sharper, than he'd first thought. He'd allowed her soothing voice and reasonable manner to fool him.

'Yes,' Hillary carried on, giving him the uncanny feeling that she'd just read his mind. 'Now, in Billy's case, we know he was up to no good, but there's nothing obvious to help us. For instance, he wasn't dealing drugs, or stealing, or even, as far as we can tell, hanging about with a bad crowd.'

She cocked an eye at him, and again Marty Warrender nodded. 'But, you see . . .' Hillary pulled out a piece of paper and turned it around on the table to face Marty Warrender. 'Here's our problem.' She tapped one finger on the photocopied sheet of paper, which showed Billy Davies's bank balance. 'Somebody was paying Billy regular and quite sizeable sums of money.'

Marty didn't want to look down, but felt himself compelled to. The amount of savings indicated wasn't huge by today's standards, but when he realised that it belonged to a fifteen-year-old boy — moreover, one from a working-class family that was struggling to make ends meet — then it became shocking.

'And Billy Davies had no paying job that we've been able to discover,' Hillary carried on smoothly. 'So we have to wonder where it all came from. Don't we?'

He knew he must have gone pale, and took another long, shuddering breath. When he looked up both women were staring at him and he felt his stomach heave. Again he hastily swallowed. 'Don't look at me,' he said at once. 'It's nothing to do with me.'

'Of course, to us, this bank account screams blackmail,' Hillary said, almost conversationally, and turned the sheet of paper back towards her. 'Now, Billy didn't have much of a social life,' Hillary smiled. 'He spent the vast majority of his time either at school, at a friend's place or at home in Aston Lea. And since I can't see that schoolchildren could come up with such sums of money, the only place William Davies could have got his hooks into someone was in Aston Lea. You follow our logic?'

Marty Warrender slowly leaned back in his chair and frowned. Janine wondered where he'd suddenly got his spine from, and frowned herself when he began to shake his head from side to side. 'Not me,' he said flatly, a look of triumph flashing across his face. 'I refused to pay the little bugger so much as a penny.' Now that it was all out in the open, he felt, oddly enough, far happier and much more able to cope.

Hillary, who'd met this phenomenon before, merely nodded. 'So he did try to blackmail you,' she said matter-of-factly. 'Over what exactly?'

'None of your business,' Marty Warrender snapped right back. 'And I didn't kill him, so that's that. I'm not saying anything more. I want a solicitor.'

Hillary smiled gently. 'You're not under arrest, Mr Warrender,' she pointed out gently. 'But you do realise, I hope, that we can get a court order to check your bank records. And if you have any withdrawals which match the deposits in this book,' she tapped again the photocopy with her finger, 'then that situation may well change.'

'Go ahead,' Marty Warrender said, again with that surprising flash of triumph. 'You won't find any payments that match. Me and June work hard, what with our full-time jobs and the property developing we do. We plan to retire when we're both fifty-five, and find a place by the sea. Enjoy ourselves while we're still young. And I wouldn't let that sly little hooligan get his hands on a penny. Lazy little bugger, let him work for it, the same as the rest of us have to. That's what I told him.'

Hillary nodded and closed the folder with a snap. Then she stood up and smiled. 'Janine, would you like to run Mr Warrender back to his place of business?' She glanced at Janine, indicating she wanted a quick word. 'Mr Warrender, if you'd like to wait outside a moment?'

Marty Warrender got quickly to his feet. His knees felt distinctly weak, but he moved quickly across the floor and out the door that the uniformed policeman held open for him. He looked both vastly relieved and pleased with himself.

'Take him back to Banbury, then have a word with his staff,' Hillary instructed quietly. 'Billy had something on him all right, and I'm betting he had some sort of photographic evidence to back it up. Him and that camera of his seemed to be joined at the hip, and I can't see a wannabe paparazzo not making the most of photographs to put the bite on someone. I want to know what it was he had on Warrender. Then get that court order for his bank records. I don't think he actually did pay out any money: he seemed too pleased with himself about that not to have been telling the truth. But we need to check anyway. Besides, the fact that we can tell everyone that we've been able to gain access to *his* accounts might help loosen a few stiff upper lips when it comes time to talk to the other neighbours.'

Janine nodded, scribbling furiously in her notebook. 'Right, boss.'

* * *

Hillary more or less followed behind Janine's car for ten miles or so back towards Banbury, but then veered off at the Adderbury traffic lights, to head towards the Davenridge Dairy. Situated on a small, rural industrial park not far from the village of Aynho, it was a large square building with fake-orange brickwork and a lot of smoky glass. Beyond it lay huge storage facilities, and rows of white milk tankers.

Darren Cleaver looked surprised to see the police again, especially at his place of work. His secretary though, a smart, tiny woman, showed her efficiently into his office and came back almost at once with a pot of excellent coffee and some shortbread biscuits.

'Please, sit down, er, Inspector.' Darren Cleaver pointed to the comfortable, ergonomically designed swivel leather chair that was situated in front of his desk. His office was large and airy and — almost inevitably — was painted pristine white. Large, smoked-glass windows gave a darkened view out on to the surrounding countryside. 'I believe I saw a colleague of yours a few nights ago? A blonde woman?'

'DS Tyler, yes, sir,' Hillary said. 'I'm the officer in charge of the investigation, however, and some new details have come to light. So I'm doing follow-up interviews on all of Billy's neighbours.'

'Oh, I see,' he said, and sat down. He was wearing a navy blue suit and white shirt with a mother-of-pearl coloured silk tie. Hillary could understand why Janine had called him a prime hunk; although men who were prettier than herself had never appealed to her. Into her mind flashed the somewhat battered face of Mike Regis, with his cat-green eyes and attractive crow's feet. Instantly, she shook the image away.

'It seems Billy may have been something of an amateur blackmailer, Mr Cleaver. We've reason to suspect that he had approached at least one of his neighbours in Aston Lea and attempted to extort money. I was wondering if he had approached you?'

'Good grief, no!'

'Or your wife?'

'I hardly think so,' Darren Cleaver blinked hard and fast. 'Are you sure? Poor George and Marilyn! Mind you that probably explains—' He broke off abruptly, and reached for the coffee pot. 'Biscuit, Inspector?'

'Explains what, Mr Cleaver?' Hillary pressed, accepting both a cup of coffee and a finger of shortbread.

'Hmmm? Oh, nothing. Just thinking aloud.'

'Mr Cleaver, I don't have to remind you that this is a murder inquiry, do I?' Hillary asked, still using her flat, calm voice, but this time injecting just a hint of steel into it. Darren Cleaver heard it, glanced at her uncertainly, then looked down at the coffee cup in his hand.

Eventually he sighed. 'I suppose not. It's just that, well, I don't want to get the poor man into any trouble. Not after all that's happened, he doesn't need any more hassle. And with the new laws they have nowadays and everything I suppose it was, strictly speaking, illegal. But really, after what you've told me, I can understand why he did it.'

Hillary smiled patiently. 'Do you think you could make yourself just a little bit clearer, sir? And start at the beginning?'

Darren Cleaver sighed. 'It was earlier this year. Sometime in March, I think. I was driving past the Davies's place. The council had the road up just outside, and I was having to be careful getting around the bollards, otherwise I don't suppose I would have seen. I'd just bought this new Saab, you see, and I was a bit paranoid about scratching it. Anyway, I had to glance across towards the Davies' bungalow, to see how close my paintwork was to the hedge on that side, and I just happened to see into the window. It would be the . . . kitchen, I think. Or maybe their lounge. I'm not sure.'

Hillary nodded. 'Go on.'

'Look, like I said, it's going to sound worse than it actually was. Only I saw George giving his boy a bit of a walloping. Oh, not with his fists or anything!' Darren Cleaver added hastily. 'I'm not talking about child abuse. I would have reported that right away. No, I mean a good old-fashioned bum-smacking. Had the lad over his knee and was paddling his arse. I thought at the time, he should be careful about that. I mean, Billy could have sued him or something, and he was just the type to . . . well, never mind. As I said, I just saw it in passing, and only the once. Next day I saw Billy and he was right as rain and cocky as ever so I know his dad didn't really hurt him. Not bruise him or anything, you know? And now, after what you told me he'd been up to . . . well, you can't really blame George can you? Trying to knock some sense into the lad. I mean, I know it's the law and all that, but I have to say I think it's gone too far when a father can't discipline his kids without being scared of being jailed for violating their human rights or what have you.'

Darren scowled and poured some more cream into his coffee cup. Hillary wondered, briefly, if it was cream from the dairy, or if his secretary bought it cheap from Asda.

'I see,' Hillary said at last. There was nothing to be gained by pointing out to him that he should have reported what he'd seen to social services. 'Well, I think that's all for now, sir,' she said, getting up and letting him walk her to the door.

Once outside, she walked slowly back to her car, deep in thought. It hadn't gone unnoticed that, as soon as she'd started to mention blackmail, Mr Darren Cleaver had been very quick to change the subject and give her another bone to chew over. On the other hand, his story had that unmistakable tang of truthfulness.

She sighed and slipped behind the wheel of her car. Another trip to the Davies bungalow seemed to be in order. But first, she reached for her phone.

Jenny Cleaver was, for once, in her Oxford office and her PA put her straight through to her private line. She sounded a little wary to be hearing from the police again, but agreed to see somebody later that day. Once she'd hung up, Hillary phoned HQ and asked Tommy to pay her a visit. She wanted someone to be face to face with her when questioned about the possibility of being approached by Billy with blackmail in mind. That done, she turned the key in the ignition, and headed back south.

* * *

It was little Celia who answered the door to her knocking, twenty minutes later. 'Oh hello. You're the big police lady.'

Hillary smiled, hoping the child meant that she was 'big' as in the 'big chief,' as opposed to being just 'fat.'

But she wasn't sure.

'Hello, Celia. Is your mummy or daddy in?'

'They both are. It's lunchtime.'

Hillary glanced at her watch, surprised to see that it was only ten minutes to two. 'Mummy and Daddy come home from the garage for lunch, do they?' she asked, as the little girl opened the door wider for her.

'Course,' she snorted, as if Hillary was being particularly dense, then nearly made her jump out of her skin by suddenly yelling, at a pitch and volume that would have made a jet engine envious, 'Mum! Daddeeeee! The big police lady's here again.'

Hillary glanced up as the door to the kitchen opened and Marilyn Davies looked out at her dully. 'Come on in, the kettle's on. Want a slice of Madeira? Millie Verne baked it and brought it over yesterday, so it's still fresh. Everyone's being so kind.'

Hillary accepted the invitation to come into the kitchen, but turned down the cake. Instead, she tried to convince herself that a pot of low-fat yoghurt and an apple, waiting for her back at her desk at HQ, was what she really wanted.

George Davies was at the sink washing out his mug, and he turned to look at her as she pulled out a chair. 'Found who did it yet?' he asked flatly, and just a shade belligerently. Hillary recognised the tone immediately. It had been four days now, and the worst of the shock was wearing off. Disbelief was being replaced by anger, and the police were the obvious targets for that anger. She didn't take it personally.

'We're getting closer, Mr Davies,' she said, and meant it. She was sure, now, that the blackmail angle was the course to follow. And it could only be a matter of time before she found whoever it was who'd rather kill than pay up.

Perhaps something of her confidence sounded in her voice, because the anger was gone when he next said, 'So what brings you back here?'

Hillary sighed. 'In the course of a murder investigation, Mr Davies, the police uncover all sorts of things. Things not necessarily related to the crime, but things that come to light anyway. Family secrets, things best left undisturbed. But things that we have to follow through with, just to make sure that they're not relevant after all. Do you understand what I mean?'

'Not sure I do,' George said, and Hillary saw his wife also frown and shake her head.

Hillary sighed and decided simply to take the bull by the horns. 'We've had reports that you sometimes used to discipline your son, Mr Davies. Physically, I mean. Is that true?'

Shockingly, Celia Davies, who'd been standing unnoticed in the doorway, giggled loudly. When Hillary looked at her, she clamped a hand over her mouth, but her eyes danced wickedly. 'Daddy used to smack his bum,' she said, then clamped her hand back over her mouth again.

'Oh, that weren't nothing,' Marilyn Davies said at once. 'George never hit him around the head, or nothing dangerous. He never would, would you, George?'

'No, nor never took my belt off,' George agreed, sitting down heavily opposite her. 'My dad used to take his belt off to me, regular like, when I was a nipper. Suppose it never did me no harm, but I never forget it. It hurt like blazes, and I swore that when I grew up I'd never hit my kid like that. And I never did,' he added, staring at Hillary defiantly. 'You gonna do me for it then?'

Hillary shook her head. 'No, Mr Davies,' she said softly. 'I can't see that the Crown Prosecution Services would think that charging you would serve any useful purpose. You're hardly a danger to the public are you?'

George shrugged, but his big shoulders slowly relaxed.

'I do, however, want to know why you smacked him. Surely he was getting a bit too old and big for that?'

George sighed wearily. 'Oh, I don't know. I caught him once pinching a tenner from his mum's purse.'

'Then he threw a stone at Mr Cooper's cat,' Celia chanted and hung her head as her mother shot her a furious look. It made Hillary wonder, uneasily, how often Celia had snitched on her brother and earned him a smacking. And how Billy Davies would have retaliated in kind. Once again, Hillary found herself wondering if Celia Davies could have swung those garden shears after all. Perhaps in a fit of childish rage and managing a very lucky — or unlucky — strike that had slipped between her brother's ribs without too much force being necessary.

Quickly she shook the image away. It was useless to speculate like that. She had to stick to facts. And the fact that Billy was blackmailing someone was looking more and more likely.

'Mr Davies, Mrs Davies, did Billy ever say anything about photographing his neighbours?' she asked casually. 'You know, for the photo competitions, or simply for fun? Maybe he thought he might be able to sell them on, if they were really good? Some people like candid photographs of themselves, after all.' It was weak, but there was no point in asking outright if they knew that their son was a blackmailer. They'd only deny it, even if they knew.

Marilyn looked a little puzzled, but clearly thought about it for a moment or two, then shook her head. 'No, I don't think so? George?'

George Davies also shook his head. Hillary turned and looked at Celia, but the little girl was staring vacantly out of the window, looking bored.

* * *

Back at HQ, Hillary deposited her bag on her desk, sat down wearily and reached into her drawer for her lunch. The apple was a little wrinkled Cox's Orange Pippin, the yoghurt was blueberry. She was just scraping the very last dregs from the bottom of the carton when Janine came back. She went straight to Hillary's desk and threw herself into the chair opposite.

'You were right about Warrender's staff. Or his one co-worker, to be exact. Sylvia Dodd was only too happy to chat. Warrender sent her out on her lunch break as soon as he got back, and I hung around and treated her to a currant bun at the cafe by the canal. That reminds me — I need to clock it off to expenses.' She fiddled in her notebook and Hillary sighed, waiting patiently for her to get on with it.

'Anyway, she's worked there forever, since long before Marty Warrender first showed up,' Janine carried on, 'and after saying what an OK boss he was, and all the usual, she dived right in. She'd met the wife a couple of times and thought she was a bit of a mean-fisted dowdy old so and so, and wasn't at all surprised to see her boss one Friday night holding hands with a woman who definitely wasn't Mrs W. At some pub or other in Cropredy, it was. I thought I'd drive over there and see if the barmaid knew who the girlfriend was. She might do, if they made a regular habit of meeting up there. Or if the other woman lives in Cropredy itself.'

Hillary nodded. 'You think Billy might have taken a picture of Marty and his bit of skirt on the side and tried it on?'

'Might have,' Janine agreed. 'The Warrenders are in on this property developing deal together — the payments and signatures are equally divided between the two of them. Marty might be in the soup financially if the wife learns he's playing away, so he wouldn't want to risk getting taken to the cleaners in a divorce.'

162

Hillary sighed. 'But Marty denied paying up. Perhaps Billy approached the wife. Frank did the initial interview with June Warrender didn't he?' she asked glumly.

'Yup. And you know what that means,' Janine said, rolling her eyes and then spotting the empty yoghurt pot. 'Got another one of those?'

'No, and believe me, you're not missing anything,' Hillary said shortly. 'OK, go out to Cropredy, but check on Mrs Warrender first. Test the waters, see if you think she knows about hubby and his lady friend. And if you get anything interesting, ask her outright if Billy tried anything on with her, vis-a-vis touching her up for a bit of blackmail money.'

'Right, boss. Where are you going?' she asked casually. She always wanted to know what her boss was up to. Not only did DI Greene have an envious clear-up rate for her cases, and Janine learned lots by studying her methods, she also liked to make sure that Tommy didn't get better assignments than she did.

Hillary, not fooled for a moment, smiled grimly. 'I'm off to explore some derelict wasteground full of thistles and ticks. Wanna come with me instead?'

But Janine was already on her feet and heading for the door.

* * *

The allotments were deserted when she parked there at a quarter to three that blazingly hot Friday afternoon. The police tape still hung limply from the Davies' shed, and Hillary glanced at it in passing. Behind the shed the mock orange blossom was now blooming, and the heady, wonderful fragrance enveloped her as she pushed her way through it. It was surprisingly easy to do, confirming the reports she'd had that Billy Davies used to come this way regularly. She certainly didn't have too much difficulty pushing through the shrubbery and emerging on to the other side.

The overgrown paddock was small, and surrounded on all four sides by hedgerow. Nesting birds flew in all directions at the first sign of the human interloper, and Hillary gazed around her curiously. Elder grew thickly all around, but there was a distinct and obvious pathway through it, where the grass and dock had been flattened.

She followed this trail cautiously, careful to keep her ankles well away from the worst of the nettles whilst admiring the beautiful colours of the thistle flowers, and the even more beautiful colours of the butterflies that were feeding off them. Orange-tips, yellow brimstones and early commas, along with all kinds of bees and flies, found the flowers irresistible.

A chaffinch sang from the hedgerow, and was echoed by a yellow hammer, and Hillary was so busy nature-watching, she almost missed the dark, oblong outline of a building. It was low to the ground, covered in moss, lichen and bindweed, and for a moment she couldn't think what it could be. And then she remembered the old-timer from the allotments telling her about the pigsty.

She moved forward and crouched down, finding the warped wooden door with ease, for here the low-growing elder branches had been hacked back. By Billy Davies?

She reached for the door, intending to go inside and hoping that any resident rats or spiders were out foraging, and was brought up short. For there, gleaming and relatively new-looking, was a big brass padlock.

So Billy Davies had managed to find a hiding place that not even his dad had rumbled, Hillary mused. She picked the padlock up in her hand and gave it an experimental tug, but it held fast. She sighed, and reached into her bag for her mobile.

'Tommy? You back from talking to Mrs Cleaver? No, you can fill me in later. I'm in the paddock behind the Davies' shed. I need you to get yourself over here as quick as you can with someone from SOCO and a good pair of bolt-cutters. We may have hit the jackpot.'

CHAPTER TWELVE

Hillary watched as Tommy bent down in front of the padlock and positioned it in his palm. Although he had a pair of bolt-cutters with him, he reached into his shirt pocket for a small leather case with a zip around three of its edges. It reminded Hillary of one of those portable little sewing kits that Victorian ladies used to carry with them when embarking on the Grand Tour.

But what Tommy extracted was a pair of long, thin, stainless steel instruments with hooks on the end. He inserted one all the way inside, and with the other, began to probe delicately. Hillary let out a long, slow, impressed whistle. 'You've been taking lessons from Mick the Pick,' she accused. Michael Pritchard, a now retired sergeant from burglary, was still something of a legend at Thames Valley. He was, she knew, very fussy about those he chose to be his 'apprentices.'

Tommy, from his crouching position in a patch of dock, grinned. 'He offered, and how could I say no? I bet he'd have this done by now though . . . ahh, got it.'

The padlock fell sweetly open into his hand, and he stood up and slipped it into a plastic evidence bag he kept in his other pocket. Throughout the procedure he'd been wearing ultra-thin latex gloves to protect fingerprint evidence.

'Well done, Tommy,' Hillary said, slapping him on the back. 'Headington don't know what an asset they're getting. But now you've got it open, we don't even know that our vic was ever here. For all I know, this pigsty could belong to a neighbouring farmer.'

Tommy paled slightly. 'We have got a warrant, haven't we, guv?' he gulped.

Hillary grinned. 'Never fear. I phoned Danvers after I phoned you. It should be being signed even as we speak.'

Tommy paled even further. 'What if the judge turned it down? Aren't we being a bit previous, guv?'

Hillary laughed. 'Worried about being nabbed for illegal entry, Detective Constable?' Then she shrugged. 'Yes, we'll have to be careful,' she agreed more soberly. 'No one sets foot inside until we get the go-ahead,' she added, mostly for the benefit of the two forensics experts Tommy had brought with him. She recognised one as a fingerprints man, the other she didn't know. Both of them, at her words, started looking around for a place to sit and make themselves comfortable. Eventually they flattened an area of grass underneath a flowering elder and stretched out. Gnats immediately began to gather around them, making them flap their hands above their heads as they began to talk about football. Neither were yet wearing their white boiler-suit outfits, so presumably they weren't worried about tracking any 'trace' into the pigsty.

Hillary, not wanting to get down on to the ground, leaned against the smooth bark of an ash tree instead and wondered how much longer the heatwave was going to continue. If it was like this in May, what was July going to be like? Perhaps she'd go to Greenland for her holidays this year. Or to that place in Canada where you were supposed to be able to feed polar bears or whatever.

It was twenty minutes before Paul Danvers called back to say that the warrant had been signed. Hillary nodded over to the two SOCO officers, and watched them suit up and go in. They had to leave the door open to let in light, and from their muttered comments, Hillary knew they'd found something. Which came as something of a relief. Her biggest fear had been that the place was empty and that she'd wasted everybody's time.

It was nearly an hour before she and Tommy were able to root about inside themselves. The pigsty was, of course, tiny, being barely six feet square, and was lined, incongruously, with old wooden filing cabinets. Grimacing at the ubiquitous black powder the fingerprint man had left everywhere, Hillary chose a cabinet and pulled out the first file. It was a cheap beige paper folder (probably pinched from the school stationery cupboard), and had the name 'Gordon the Wanker' written on it in big black felt-tip pen.

Hillary's eyebrows shot up as she opened it, and was presented with large colour prints of a man urinating against a wall. He was stood with one hand out in front of him and braced against a brick wall, and his other hand was holding his flaccid member, which was clearly visible. It looked as if it had been taken in a town — Bicester, Banbury, maybe Witney, somewhere like that — for the man was obviously in an alley, and in the top right-hand corner there looked to be some kind of lettering. The sign from a pub or club? Probably some boozed-up customer had left after one too many and instead of going back inside to relieve himself in the Gents, had simply chosen to do so in the alley. It was dark, but there were streetlights either end of the alley, and from the building he was leaning against, light shone from an open window.

The photograph had obviously been taken by someone who knew what they were doing for the focus was sharp, and the lighting superb. The man was heavy-set, grey-haired, and was wearing what looked to be a good quality suit. She moved the photograph a little closer to her face, and squinted. Yes, she was sure she could make out a gold watch on the wrist of the hand that was leaning against the wall. A man of some prosperity then. The face was in profile, but she had no doubt that he would be perfectly recognisable to anyone who knew him.

She turned the top photograph over and found several more of the same man, one with him almost full-on to the camera and in the process of stuffing himself back into his trousers. That photograph, more than any of the others, could have been misconstrued if taken out of context. She could almost see Billy Davies approaching him with a copy of it. Maybe at his place of work, or even at his home, piling on the pressure. Had he threatened to say that the man had propositioned him, flashed him, threatened him if he didn't have sex with him? And would a no doubt perfectly respectable man, probably married and maybe with a business reputation to protect, then pay up to keep the boy quiet and happy?

Of course he would. In today's climate, where paedophiles were hated and rightfully prosecuted as often as possible, no man would want to run the risk of being classified as such.

Hillary sighed, and passed the folder on to Tommy. 'We're going to have to find out who this is. Get Larry to get a head shot from that, and pass it around the troops. Someone might know him. If we don't get any joy, we might have to ask the local papers to run it with the usual "Do you know this man?" angle.'

'Right, guv,' Tommy said.

Hillary went to the next folder in the drawer and withdrew another set of photographs.

These were snaps that had been taken in broad daylight. A naked woman, lying on a towel in what was evidently her own back garden. In the background Hillary could see one of those round, revolving clotheslines, with a few children's clothes hanging limply from it. The house looked small — a one-time council house maybe — and now probably privately owned. It could have been in any suburban cul-de-sac in any town. The woman was blonde, but not a natural, as some of the more revealing pictures only too clearly showed. Attractive in a plump kind of way. Stretchmarks clearly showed in one or two close-up shots. The little sod must have used a zoom lens to get such detail.

Would the woman have paid up, if only to prevent strangers and neighbours from seeing her physical defects? On the other hand, if she was extrovert enough to sunbathe naked in her back garden, maybe she'd told the little sod to sling his hook. Hillary rather hoped she had.

'Tommy, another one we need to track down.' She looked around at the filing cabinets, wondering how many more victims were in here. 'This is going to take some time.' She looked at the front of the folder she was holding and grimaced as she read 'Big Tits Linda' in the same bold black lettering. Well at least they had first names to go on. 'With a bit of luck we'll find a notebook or diary or something with their proper names and contact details in,' she muttered.

'Guv, I think you should see this,' Tommy said, handing over another file he'd taken from the bottom drawer.

These photographs were different from all the rest, in that they were indoor shots, and carefully posed. Whereas all the others had been clandestine shots taken of people unaware of the lens, these were taken with the full consent of the model.

The girl was very young, beautiful and ash-blonde. Heather Soames's face stared at her, full of health and youth, obviously taken before pregnancy and loss had put dark shadows under her eyes. She was lying on a black leather sofa, the contrast with her smooth white skin and fair hair almost painful. She was totally naked.

Sighing, Hillary flipped through them. There was nothing ugly about them. Nothing deliberately provocative or crude. She wondered if the girl thought of them as art;

if her boyfriend had promised they were for his eyes only. And maybe they had been. And maybe not.

'See if you can find any more like these, but of different girls,' Hillary said. 'If so, he might have been trying to sell them to the dirty mag trade. Heather is obviously underage, so some might have been willing to shell out a few readies.'

Tommy nodded and began to pull out drawers.

Hillary reached for the phone and reluctantly called in Frank Ross to come and help out. Then she took a few of the Heather Soames pictures and slipped them into a plastic evidence bag. 'Tommy, I'm going to have a word with Francis Soames. See if he knew about these,' she waved her hand in the air. For a protective papa, they had motive written all over them. 'Better get a catalogue going of all these folders. Pull in some uniforms to help — every piece needs to be properly noted and logged into evidence. It's going to be a long night.'

Tommy nodded and watched her go. Before leaving the station, he'd signed the last of the forms accepting his promotion to sergeant, and agreeing to the move to Headington. Next Wednesday was going to be his last day. He wondered where they'd take him for a drink and how he'd feel knowing that his life was about to change irrevocably. Now that the time had come, he felt almost sick.

He shuddered, then went back to trawling a pigsty for evidence of blackmail.

* * *

In the car, Hillary speed-dialled Janine's phone.

'DS Tyler.'

'Janine, it's me. You checked out Francis Soames's alibi right?'

'Yeah, boss. You wanted to know if he was out on a call cleaning carpets. He wasn't. He was in the office all that day. Secretary confirms it. The office has only one door in and out, but it's on the ground floor. He could have slipped out the window. I checked — it has windows that open, it's not sealed or anything. Looks out over the car park, so if he picked his moment right he might have been able to nip out without being seen, but he'd have to be lucky. I couldn't pin the secretary down, though, on just how long he might have been in the office on his own. She thinks she was in and out with letters to sign, cups of coffee, queries, etc. all day long. She reckoned he couldn't have been on his own for more than twenty minutes at a time, if that. It seemed unlikely to me that he'd have been able to get out, kill Billy, and get back again without her knowing.'

Hillary sighed heavily. 'Pick up any vibes from her?' she asked hopefully. If she and the boss were sleeping together, she might have been prepared to give him a false alibi.

'Not one.'

'OK, thanks. Ring Tommy, we've had developments this end,' she added abruptly and rung off.

* * *

Francis Soames didn't look particularly surprised to see her again so soon. When she came in, he was already on his feet, and he nodded to his secretary, a fifty-something with good bones and large waves of striking grey hair. 'Yvonne, some coffee perhaps?'

Hillary watched the woman leave, then took a seat in front of his desk. She waited until Soames had sat back down before reluctantly pulling out the photographs, still encased in their plastic covering, from her briefcase. 'Mr Soames, you're probably going to find these upsetting, but I need to know if you knew about them.' She pushed the photographs across the desk towards him and saw his jaw drop.

He stared at them for a moment, and then slowly reached out and drew them closer. He swallowed hard once or twice, then croaked deliberately, 'It's Heather.'

He looked back up at Hillary, then down at the pictures of his naked daughter and abruptly flushed bright red and pushed them away from him. Hillary hastily scooped them up and put them back in her case. Unless the man was a better actor than Hoffman, he'd never seen them before in his life.

'Her mother would have been horrified,' Francis Soames said at last, and still unable to meet her eyes. He himself looked mortified. 'I suppose that boy took them,' he added bitterly.

'We think so, yes,' Hillary said, very calmly and matter-of-fact, trying to lower the embarrassment factor a bit. 'I take it Heather never said anything about posing for art shots?'

'Art?' Francis opened his mouth to rail bitterly, then changed his mind, and closed it again. After a few deep breaths he shook his head and said instead, 'I never thought Heather would do something like that.' He sat with his elbows on the table, his hands covering his face, then he took them away and stared at her. 'Who else has seen them?' he demanded, his voice rising in pitch. 'Were they in his locker at school? Did he show them around to his friends? To that freakish-looking Miller boy? Have they been laughing at her behind her back? Tell me!' His voice had risen to an almost hysterical shout by now, and suddenly the door opened.

His secretary came in with a tray of coffee, pretending not to have heard him. Francis watched her put the tray down on his desk and made a visible effort to get himself under control. His face was now bright red, with white blotches. He swallowed hard and mumbled, 'Thank you, Yvonne. Would you hold all my calls for now. Oh, and cancel my meeting with the reps at four?'

'Of course, Mr Soames.'

Hillary waited until the door closed behind her before continuing. 'I have no reason to suppose that anyone other than Billy and Heather herself have seen the pictures, Mr Soames,' she said quietly. 'The photographs weren't found at his school, or even at his residence, but in a well-concealed and secure hiding place. Is Heather still at home?' Hillary asked. 'We'll need to talk to her about these at some point.'

'What? Oh, no, she said she'd go back to school this afternoon.' Francis Soames slowly leaned back in his chair, visibly growing calmer now. 'She wants to get back to normal, catch up on the schoolwork she's missed and be with her friends. You know how teenage girls are. She's sleeping over at her friend's house tonight. Mary-Beth's. Perhaps it's just as well. I need some time alone to come to grips with this.'

Hillary nodded. 'Probably the best thing for you both. Well, we'll leave it 'til tomorrow then,' she said, getting to her feet. Francis Soames nodded, but didn't rise himself, and she doubted he even heard the door closing behind her. The secretary glanced up at her curiously as she walked by her desk, but didn't speak.

Hillary stood in the parking lot for a moment, thinking. Francis Soames was an emotional man, clearly still upset at losing his wife and maybe on the verge of a breakdown himself. It wasn't hard to imagine him, in a moment of unthinking crisis, reaching out for the nearest weapon and striking the boy who'd stolen his daughter's innocence. The trouble was, Hillary didn't think he knew anything about it. And why would Billy agree to meet Francis Soames at the allotment shed? As far as she'd been able to make out, Billy had been afraid of his girlfriend's father.

No, she just didn't see it, somehow.

Hillary glanced at her watch. Nearly ten minutes past four. She could go back to Tommy and the others, but there was little point now. She supposed she should head back to headquarters and update her new boss on the latest developments.

Or she could tackle Lester Miller again.

* * *

This time she called Mr Miller senior first, and he was waiting for her as she pulled up outside his mock-Tudor residence, leaning against a silver/blue Daimler Sovereign with his arms folded across his chest, and one foot tapping impatiently away on the tarmac. The epitome of a busy man with better things to do than talk to the likes of herself.

Hillary smiled at him widely as she got out of her car. Her cream-coloured jacket was creased and probably smelly from the heat, her matching slacks green-smeared and covered with grass seeds from her trip through the paddock. She hoped her shoes were dirty enough to leave marks on his carpet.

'Mr Miller, hello again. I take it Lester's home from school?'

'He is. And I do hope this is the last time you'll need to see him, Detective Inspector Greene.'

Hillary grinned. 'So do I, Mr Miller. So do I. Shall we go in?'

Lester was sitting in the same leather chair as before, but this time his feet were bare and he was drinking from a can of lager. His father noticed, but said nothing, and Hillary wondered if he'd get a bollocking after she left, or if Gareth Miller was the sort of man who'd approve of his teenage son showing what he was made of in front of the hoi polloi.

'Hello again, Lester,' Hillary said brightly, taking a seat on the sofa opposite without waiting to be asked. She pulled out her notebook, smiled at the ginger-haired boy, waited until he'd taken a significant swig of Foster's, then said brightly, 'So why didn't you tell me about your mate Billy's blackmail scams?'

Lester didn't spout the lager from his nostrils, or choke, or do anything so entertaining, but he did swallow hard and have to clear his throat. From a lounging position against the unlit fireplace, Gareth Miller suddenly shot upright. 'What?'

'Please, Mr Miller, don't interrupt,' Hillary said flatly. 'If you insist on making things difficult, we can always carry on this conversation at the station. With solicitors and all that that entails.' The look she shot him made him slowly lean back against the mantelpiece, but his eyes narrowed on his son.

Lester Miller shrugged, then laughed. It wasn't a very convincing laugh. 'Nothing to tell.'

'That won't do,' Hillary said, slowly shaking her head from side to side. 'We found his hidden stash, Lester. Don't tell me that you weren't in on it. A bright lad like yourself.'

'Don't say a word, Lester,' Gareth Miller growled, and to Hillary snapped, 'Look, I'm not having this. Are you accusing my boy of something? Because if so, I want to know what.'

Hillary sighed. 'Mr Miller, let me make things clear. I'm not interested in making trouble for you or your boy. But I need to know the facts. Why don't we just let Lester speak, hmm?'

'It's OK, Dad, I think I know what she's talking about, and it's no big deal, yeah? Billy took photos see, of people. There was this woman who used to sunbathe in the nude, right, and it drove her husband spare. He was always telling her off about it. Well, Billy took pictures, see, and said he was going to see if she'd pay him off, otherwise he would show them to her husband. I don't suppose he went through with it though. Billy just did it as a joke.'

Yeah, right, Hillary thought sourly.

'It doesn't sound funny to me,' Gareth Miller growled.

'Me either,' Hillary put in tartly. 'Tell me, Lester, how did Billy know about this woman sunbathing nude?' she asked curiously.

'Huh? Oh, somebody at school told him. This kid in the third form was bragging about it. She lives just down from him, apparently, and he was telling everyone how, when he goes home from school, he gets his old man's bird-watching binoculars and does some real bird-watching. Get it? Anyway, when Billy heard him he decided to follow the kid home and see if it was all just bullshit, or on the up-and-up. And when it turned out to be true, he goes over there on the next sunny day and — wham. Pictures.'

Hillary sighed heavily. 'I'll need this boy's name. The woman's neighbour, I mean,' she clarified, and wrote it down when Lester told her. At least that was one victim they'd be able to trace with ease. 'And what about the other pictures, Lester?'

Lester Miller shrugged one bony shoulder and took a sip of lager. 'Don't know about them,' he lied.

'You don't, huh?' Hillary said sceptically and saw the boy's father frown. 'But isn't that where Billy got all his money from, Lester? You know, to buy the mountain bike, and the fancy zoom lenses for his camera. The gold jewellery for his girlfriend?'

Lester shrugged, but his eyes refused to meet hers. He looked less cocky now and more angry. And suddenly, Hillary twigged.

'He was holding out on you, wasn't he, Lester?' Hillary said softly and with mock sympathy. 'What was it? At first he kept you in touch with what he was doing. The nude sunbather, the man waving his willy about.' Out of the corner of her eyes, she saw Gareth Miller jerk against the wall, and carried on quickly before he could break her momentum. 'And it was fun, wasn't it? Watching Billy con or bully or threaten all these men and women, these so-called adults and grown-ups, out of their hard-earned cash.

But things changed, right? He began to keep secrets. Not tell you stuff. Maybe even deliberately kept you out of the loop. Is that how it was?'

Lester Miller stared down at his lager can. 'He thought he was so clever. He used to take me along, when he confronted them, like, letting them know that he wasn't the only one who knew. And in case they got stroppy, like, I was to call the cops straight away. But the last few months or so . . . I could tell he'd got on to something good. Really good. But he wouldn't tell me what. He kept denying it, but I knew.'

Hillary leaned forward on the chair, unable to mask her sudden tension. 'You think he arranged to meet someone that afternoon, don't you? The day he was killed. You think one of his victims turned ugly, don't you, Lester? And you know what? So do I. So if you have any idea, any idea at all who it was, you have to tell me.'

'Lester, tell her,' Gareth Miller urged. 'Have some sense for once in your life.'

'But I don't know, do I?' Lester Miller suddenly shouted, leaping to his feet and throwing the can of lager to the floor in a fit of childish temper. His eyes, though, were full of genuine tears. 'You think I don't know that if I'd been there, like before, I could have stopped it happening? If only he'd told me, I'd have gone with him and he'd be alive today. If I knew who killed him, I'd tell you. But I don't. I don't.'

By now the lad was sobbing, and his father, nonplussed, went across and patted him awkwardly on the back. But the boy pushed him away and angrily wiped the tears from his face with the back of his hand. Mucus from his running nose hung in strings from his hand and he wiped it vaguely on the side of his jeans.

Hillary got up slowly. 'All right, Lester,' she said softly. 'All right.' She nodded across his carrot-coloured head to his father, and let herself silently out of the house.

She felt tired all of a sudden. Perhaps she'd head back to HQ after all, have a drink in the canteen, catch up on some of her other cases while she waited to hear from Tommy. Do something normal, something that didn't have human misery and sin stamped all over it.

* * *

It was nearly six when Tommy came back from the pigsty. Frank had driven off on the dot of five, of course, leaving him and two uniforms to bag up the proceeds.

Janine had also been and gone, citing a hot date for not hanging around. Something about the way she'd said it had caused alarm bells to go off in Hillary's head, but she'd been too tired to pursue it. Besides, Janine put in so much unpaid overtime, there was no way she was going to comment about her getting away on time for once.

Tommy wasn't surprised to find only Hillary at her desk, but as he went by the DCI's cubbyhole, the door opened and Danvers came out.

'Guv,' Tommy said in passing, but didn't stop, since he had an arm full of evidence that looked ready to totter over and spill across the floor. He made it to Hillary's desk just in time and dumped the lot in the middle of the table, catching some of it before it spilled over. It was only then that he was aware that Danvers had followed him across the room.

'This the lot?' Danvers asked. 'Hillary's informed me of your find out at Aston Lea. Good going.'

'Yeah. Er, right, thanks, guv. No, it's not the lot. I've logged most of it into Evidence downstairs. But I thought the guv should see these. They're a bit odd. We can't figure out, me and the lads, what they're doing in with all the rest,' Tommy said. 'We found more naked women shots, by the way; some of older women too — who the hell knows why they posed for him. And some other shots of a couple making out in the back of a Volvo, plus two men in a Gents out at Woodstock park. We reckon Billy took them through an open window. One face is clear, the other,' Tommy coughed, 'isn't.'

Hillary nodded. More blackmail victims.

'But like I said, guv, these don't seem to fit the pattern.'

Intrigued, both Hillary and Paul Danvers took a beige folder each and opened them out.

In Hillary's pile, the now-familiar style of Billy Davies's camera lens showed photograph after photograph of the same man and woman. The man was of medium height and build, rather effeminate-looking, with carefully styled brown hair and a perfect complexion. Sometimes he was wearing a suit, sometimes something casual. In one or two he had on sunglasses. In all of them he had the look of a man who had regular face massages at a club where they also manicured his nails and clipped his nose and ear hair. Hillary guessed he'd have cabinets full of those products for men that ranged from fancy shower gels to moisturizing shaving lotion. The woman with him had a similar pampered look. She was about his height, with long dark hair and big eyes bristling with mascara. Like her partner, she was always expensively dressed, be it a plain white tennis dress that must have cost more than a month's worth of Hillary's salary, or plain, extremely tailored trouser suits designed to look like a man's outfit from Brooks Brothers.

They were pictured getting in and out of cars, always together, always going to, or coming from, different, respectable-looking and well-maintained houses. There was nothing in them that could possibly be material for a blackmailer.

She frowned up at Paul Danvers, who was looking equally puzzled at his own folder, and, catching his eye, wordlessly swapped with him.

His couple were a little older, a little plumper, but the photographs were the same. In fact, all five folders were filled with men and women going to and coming from houses. Nothing more, or less.

'What the hell?' Danvers said.

'Exactly, guv,' Tommy said. 'We can't figure it out. The nude sunbather, or the bloke peeing up a wall, OK. I can see how it could be embarrassing for them, and why they might pay out the odd fifty quid just to save them the hassle of explaining them away. And maybe the gays in the bog might want to avoid the hassle of being outed. But these? What's the big deal?'

Hillary sighed. 'I don't know, but we're going to have to track them all down. No sign of any names I suppose?'

'No, guv. No little black book, nothing.'

'Well, we need to find them and interview them. Tommy, you and Frank get on to it first thing tomorrow morning.'

'Guv,' Tommy said. 'Do you mind if I get off now? Only Jean's picking up the bridesmaids' dresses and she needs a ride out to Marsh Gibbon.'

Hillary nodded and Danvers watched him go, smiling. 'The wedding's next month, right?' he confirmed.

Hillary nodded.

'You're going to miss him. He's a good officer. Fancy coming for a drink?'

Hillary sighed, but nodded. It was easier than thinking of an excuse not to go.

She only hoped he didn't choose a pub where anybody knew them. The last thing she wanted was for the gossip mill in this place to start linking them together.

CHAPTER THIRTEEN

Janine reached up and accepted the glass of red wine being offered to her. She smiled, and curled her legs up further under her on the big white sofa. Whoever would have thought she'd be back sitting in her favourite place in all the world?

In front of her, the empty grate was filled with a dry flower arrangement that was becoming a little dusty now, but it was still considered by the woman who came in to clean for Mel twice a week to be the last word in interior design. Oddly enough, Janine found that even the desiccated purple petals and dyed-orange grass stems looked good to her now — like long-lost friends that you meet after a time, and find have improved with age.

'So, how's the case going?' Mel asked smoothly.

'Nowhere,' Janine shrugged and took a sip of the Bordeaux. 'Or maybe we'll have it solved tomorrow.' As she drank, she filled him in on the latest developments. Although, as a superintendent now, Mel had a wider field of responsibility and wasn't, in any case, in overall charge of the Davies murder inquiry, he listened closely and nodded when she'd finished.

'Hillary thinks the murderer is a blackmail victim, and it's only a matter of time before pinning him or her down?'

'It makes sense,' Janine agreed. 'It would explain why he was at the shed — because he'd arranged to meet someone there to put the bite on them — and why someone would want to kill a fifteen-year-old boy that doesn't involve a sex-gone-wrong scenario. And we know there'd been nothing of that sort from the autopsy report.'

Mel sighed. 'Let's not talk about it now. We get enough of the squalid side of life at work. Try some of the brie.' He pointed to the platter resting on the little coffee table in front of them, which contained crackers, biscuits, an assortment of cheese and a bunch of grapes. Janine looked at it and laughed.

'The old seduction kit, huh? Have you forgotten that you offered me the same thing the very first night you brought me back here?' Here being Mel's place in 'The Moors' area of Kidlington, which comprised most of the old village, before Kidlington morphed into an anonymous town. It was one of the most elite areas going, and Mel had been awarded the big detached house during his divorce from his second (and stinking rich) wife. In return, wife number two had left for London with Mel's son. But father and son, as Janine knew well, seemed to stay in touch and keep close and, as far as she could tell, Mel had never questioned the arrangement. Like most men, he seemed to believe that children belonged with their mothers.

'Of course I didn't forget,' Mel said now, rubbing the side of his face with his palm. 'I wanted to remind you. It used to be good, didn't it? Between us, I mean?' he added softly.

'I thought so,' Janine said flatly, taking a sip of the wine, 'until you dumped me to get your promotion.' Oddly enough, the words weren't angry, or even resentful, and Mel smiled grimly.

'If the promotion had been going your way, you'd have done the same thing, and you know it.' His words weren't accusatory either, simply a statement of fact. 'Let's face it, Jan, we're both as ambitious as hell. Or at least, I thought I was. Lately, I'm beginning to wonder if it's all been worth it.'

Janine slowly put her wine glass down on the table in front of her, her heartbeat picking up a notch, and casually selected a grape. 'That sounded curiously plaintive. Don't tell me the air is too thin, up there with the big boys?' she mocked.

'You're a sarky cow.'

'Job not all it's cracked up to be?'

'The job's fine. And you know damned well what I'm trying to say. I miss you. I miss us, being together, like this.'

'Forget it, Mel,' Janine said flatly. 'The brie could be imported from France for all I care, I'm not getting into bed with you again. Is that what dinner the other night was all about? And now this quaint little trip down memory lane?'

Mel sighed heavily and turned to face her on the couch. He was wearing jeans that were almost white after so many washes, and clung to his thighs in a way he knew Janine really liked. He was also wearing one of his Ralph Lauren silk white shirts. His hair was freshly cut and he'd shaved before going out to meet her, and had splashed on the cologne she'd given him for his birthday, just weeks before they split.

Slowly he reached out with one finger and pulled a strand of her long blonde hair from the side of her face. Janine watched him, smiling slightly, her eyes the eyes of a cat wondering whether to play with the mouse or simply kill it. It made his stomach clench in that old, familiar way.

'It was always good between us,' Mel said blandly.

'Granted,' Janine shot back tartly. 'But not good enough for you to give the brass the two-fingered salute and keep me with you.'

'Come on, how would you like it if some chancer waltzed in and snaffled your promotion right out from under you? Don't tell me you wouldn't have done the same.'

'What's the matter,' Janine jeered. 'Did the man from the Met put your nose out of joint? So this is all Detective Superintendent Jerome Raleigh's fault is it? And now he's not around anymore, you want things back the way they were? Only with you getting to keep the big new job, and still have the little woman back in your bed giving you your jollies. Well, I don't think so.' Janine swivelled her legs around and put them on the floor, preparatory to getting up and leaving. 'You don't get to do that to me again, Mel. How stupid do you think I am?'

Mel didn't move from his position on the sofa. In fact, he didn't react to her angry words at all. It was almost as if he hadn't heard them. 'No, I don't want things to go back to how they were; the same problems would still exist. Donleavy and all that crowd will start looking down their noses at us again, and all the old rumours will start up, and the sniggering. I don't fancy that any more than you do.'

Curious now, Janine slowly leaned back against the sofa again. 'So what are you saying?'

'You like this place, don't you, Jan?' Mel asked, waving a hand around the living room. It was a large, high-ceilinged room, with original pelmets and mouldings, and a large set of French doors that opened out on to a beautiful garden complete with pond and weeping willows.

Janine, thinking of the cramped semi she shared with her two housemates, laughed grimly. 'What's not to like? What's your point, Mel?'

'You were always angling to move in here permanently. You gave out enough hints that you wanted to do the whole settle down, maybe start a family thing. Did I misread the signs?'

Janine laughed again, but her heart had once more picked up a quicker beat. 'And much good it did me. You made sure I never quite got my second foot through the door, didn't you?'

'The time wasn't right,' Mel said, shaking his head. 'But now I think it is. Or could be, if you wanted.'

Janine licked her lips and slowly reached for her wine glass again, giving herself time to think. She watched him narrowly for a moment, then tossed back the contents in a single gulp. 'Let's get this straight. You're asking me to move in with you?' Janine demanded, twiddling the empty wine glass and then swearing graphically as Mel began to shake his head.

'No, that'll just put us back where we were before,' he pointed out. Then he reached out and took one of her hands in his, and began to rub the tops of her fingers with his thumb. 'I want you to marry me, Jan.'

* * *

Hillary Greene woke up when a sound like nothing else on earth shattered the early morning silence. It sounded a bit like a car exhaust backfiring after a baked spud had been rammed up it, or like some kind of machinery that had been choked with a century's worth of grime giving its last death-call. When it sounded again, Hillary groaned and turned over in her bed and yelled out the porthole window, 'Shut up for Pete's sake.'

The heron that had landed in the field opposite, no doubt to digest its early morning breakfast of stickleback and to proclaim to one and all that this was his territory whilst he was at it, took off in alarm and flapped noisily away. Although the name of her boat, the *Mollern*, was the Old English country word for heron (in the same way that a badger was a brock, or a fox was a Reynard), Hillary didn't particularly appreciate her boat's namesake waking her up at 4:30 in the morning.

Her uncle had once told her that herons were often referred to as 'Old Croak' in Old English literature, and it hadn't taken her long to realise why. They had a call that could raise the hackles on a dead dog.

She heard the same ghastly sound again, this time coming from only a hundred or so yards down the canal where the heron had re-landed, and gave up. Sitting up, she threw back the covers on the bed and put her feet to the floor, yawning widely.

It was Saturday morning, but it was not one of her days off. She took a quick shower and made herself some porridge for breakfast. Most mornings, she didn't have time for more than a snatched cup of coffee and a crust of toast, but since she was up at such a freakish hour, she supposed she might as well make the effort.

The sky had just lost the last of its pink-tinged sunrise as she pulled into the parking lot at HQ, and she'd finally managed to stop yawning by the time she pushed open the swing door and walked through the foyer.

'Bloody hell, don't tell me the Martians have invaded and all leave's been cancelled,' the desk sergeant said as she walked by, doing a slapstick double-take of the clock, which showed it to be ten minutes past five in the morning.

'If I'd had any damned sense, I'd have gone back to bed,' Hillary snarled back by way of cheery greeting, and headed for the stairs without breaking stride. She had to suffer similar comments from the night shift as she crossed the big, open-plan main office, but by the time they'd begun to filter out, and the day shift had come in, Hillary had cleared her in-tray (which was miraculous in and of itself) and had reread every scrap of paper generated by the Davies case.

Tommy was first in, and after checking her notebook for the 'to do' reminders, she gave him the name of the schoolboy who'd been so keen to watch the naked lady sunbathing. 'Find out her name from him and then interview her. Find out if she had an alibi for the afternoon of the murder. Oh, and since the hubby is apparently less than pleased with his wife's tan-lines being so seamless, find out where he was too. If Billy Davies had approached him, he might not have been in the mood to take it lying down. You never know just what the outraged jealous types can do in a fit of temper.'

'Right, guv. I'll make a start on identifying the odd couples in the pictures as well, yeah?'

Hillary nodded. 'Yeah, that's top priority. And get that lazy git Frank to . . . hold on.' She picked up her ringing phone, listened for a moment, frowned in puzzlement, and said, 'OK, Mel, I'll be right up.'

Tommy gave her a questioning look and she shrugged. It was unusual for a DI to be called to a super's desk, because it implied he was by-passing the chain of command. In this case, Danvers.

She felt her mouth go dry as she got up, wondering if someone had seen her and Danvers in the pub last night, and told Mel about it. But surely word wouldn't have travelled that quick? Besides, The Duck and Drake in a small village out near Weston-on-the-Green hadn't exactly been a hotbed of CID activity. Unless one of the two octogenarian darts players had been undercover narks, or the busy barmaid somebody's snout.

'The moment you find out the identity of one of our couples let me know,' Hillary said to Tommy. 'I want to be interviewing at least one of them by the end of the working day.'

'Guv.'

Hillary walked up the stairs to Mel's office, and went straight through, as his civilian assistant (posh word for part-time secretary) wasn't in on a Saturday morning. At his office she tapped on the door and went in without waiting for a summons. She noted at once that he was alone, which came as something of a relief. If DCS Marcus Donleavy had been there as well, she'd wonder what kind of shit she'd landed in.

As it was, Mel was smiling that particular smile he favoured when he knew she wasn't going to like something, and she felt her stomach give a distinct dip. She began to wish she'd given the porridge a miss.

'I don't have time for messing about, Mel,' she started, without preamble. 'You've got that little-boy-caught-with-his-fingers-in-the- biscuit-tin look, so what the hell have you done, and why is it any of my business?'

'And good morning to you, what a lovely day it is and why don't you take a seat. Coffee? It's that new Brazilian blend I told you about.' She watched him pour her a mug and felt her stomach do a further nosedive into her shoes as he came up with a Nash's bakery box. Inside were two plump chocolate eclairs.

Hillary took a long, fortifying breath. 'OK, not a word until I've finished it. If it's this bad, I need the chocolate fix to fortify me.'

Mel smiled thinly but let her eat and drink, whilst doodling on the report of next month's projected crime figures. When she'd licked the last of her fingers free of cream, Mel leaned back in his chair.

'I know Tommy's leaving next week, so you'll be getting a new DC, which means this probably isn't the best time to spring this. But how would you feel about losing Janine as well?'

Hillary stared at him flatly. 'She got a promotion already? Hell, that was quick work, even for Janine. You know she's not ready for the responsibilities of being an inspector, don't you?'

Mel shook his head. 'No, it's not that. But she won't be able to stay at Kidlington after we get married.'

Hillary stared at him for another second or two, then said shakily, 'You should have made that a whole boxful of eclairs, Mel. What the hell are you using for brains? No, scrap that.' She held up a hand. 'I know what you're using instead of the old grey matter. Mel, you're not serious are you?'

Her old friend grinned at her and reached for his mug. He looked young and carefree, and Hillary wanted to stretch her foot under the table and kick him on the shins.

'Donleavy and the rest of the brass will have a fit,' she said plaintively.

'Not necessarily. Think about it, Hill. All their old objections go out the window if me and Janine get spliced. It makes her legit, it means she has to transfer out of my station, so there can't be any conflict of interest so she's not always on their radar, and, besides, now that I've got the promotion, they can go whistle.'

Hillary opened her mouth, then closed it, then opened it again, and was about to say something — she wasn't sure exactly what — when his phone rang. He picked it up impatiently, listened, then frowned and nodded. 'Right, I'll tell her. Yes, right away.'

He hung up. 'That's downstairs. A Mr Francis Soames has rung up in a right state, claiming that his daughter has gone missing and wanting to speak to you. That's your murder vic's girlfriend, isn't it?' he asked, but Hillary was already halfway to the door.

* * *

Francis Soames was pacing his living-room carpet like a demented chicken when Hillary arrived a half hour later. Debbie Soames opened the door, looking pale and wide-eyed. 'Dad's going spare,' she said, unnecessarily, as she stood back to let Hillary pass. 'You don't think anything's happened to her, do you? I mean, she's a silly cow, but she's only fifteen, and she's my sister and . . .'

'Debbie! Is that them?' Francis Soames threw open the door and stared at Hillary as if expecting her to have Heather with her. 'Where is she? Have you got people out looking for her? You don't think it's just l-like B-B-Billy, do you?'

Behind her, she heard Debbie Soames draw in her breath sharply.

'Mr Soames, calm down,' Hillary said loudly. 'Now, let's go and sit down. Debbie, perhaps you could make us some tea.' Hillary turned briefly to the young girl and nodded. 'And then you, Mr Soames, can fill me in on what's happening.'

Francis Soames let her lead him back into the living room, but instead of taking a seat, he commenced pacing again. 'I told you she was going back to school for the afternoon, then staying on at a friend's house, right? Well, apparently, she didn't. The school tells me she never registered in afternoon assembly, and now Mary-Beth's mother has confirmed that Heather didn't stay the night with her at all. In fact, she knew nothing about it. When I called her this morning to speak to Heather, she didn't even know what I was talking about.'

He was shouting by the time he'd finished, and Hillary had to spend the next ten minutes getting him to calm down, sit down, drink some tea and start listening to her.

'Right,' Hillary began grimly. 'It sounds to me as if I need to speak to this Mary-Beth Chandler right away and see if she knows what's going on. It wouldn't surprise me if your daughter didn't arrange it with her, to set up a cover story. Mr Soames, try not to worry just yet.'

'Not worry? What if that maniac who killed the Davies boy has got my daughter!' Abruptly, the man started to cry, deep, wracking sobs. 'I've just lost my wife. I can't lose a child too!'

Debbie Soames immediately came to sit next to him on the sofa and hug him. She looked at Hillary silently, misery written all over her face.

'Mr Soames, I don't think that's likely,' Hillary said gently. 'I can't go into details, but we think we know now why Billy Davies was killed, and it has nothing to do with your daughter. Now why don't you take some headache pills and try to lie down for a few hours? It's possible we'll have some positive news for you very soon.'

Hillary knew that she was breaking every rule in the book in giving such assurances, but she was pretty sure she knew what had happened, and if she could give the poor man some hope to keep him going until his daughter was back, safe and sound, then why not?

White-faced, Francis Soames nodded, but whether he believed her or not, she couldn't say.

* * *

Outside, she opened up her mobile and began punching in numbers as she got behind the wheel of her car. Her call was answered almost at once.

'DS Tyler.'

'Janine, it's me. I want you to start ringing around the abortion clinics. Heather Soames has gone missing overnight, and I think I know why. Don't try any of the Oxfordshire ones: she said something about wanting to go further away from home. But my guess is not too far. Try the surrounding counties first.'

'Right, boss. Boss, about Mel and me—'

'Not now,' Hillary said curtly, and hung up.

* * *

Mary-Beth Chandler looked scared. She was facing Hillary across a kitchen table in her family's kitchen, with her mother sitting at right angles to her, watching her like a hawk. Mrs Chandler was one of those plump women who seemed cheerful and at ease in their own skin, but right now she looked ruffled and bewildered.

'I thought you had better sense,' she was saying to her daughter now, and Hillary wondered how many mothers had said the same despairing thing to their offspring over the years.

'But I didn't know, did I?' Mary-Beth wailed the typical teenager's lament. 'Heather just asked me to say that she was staying here for the night, if her dad called.'

'And why would she ask you to do that if she wasn't up to any good? Didn't you think to ask her *that?*' Mrs Chandler demanded, doing Hillary's interview for her.

'Oh, Mum! I couldn't do that. She's my best friend. She needed me.' Mary-Beth, like her mother, had a mop of dark curls and big dark eyes, and puppy fat had given her a curiously twin-like appearance with her parent. Now she sniffed inelegantly into a tissue and flicked the silent policewoman a terrified glance. 'I'm not going to be arrested, am I?'

Hillary smiled wearily. 'Not unless you refuse to answer my questions, Miss Chandler,' she said flatly. 'Do you know where Heather Soames is?'

'No, honest, I don't.'

Hillary nodded. She believed her. She was too scared to hold anything back at this point. 'When did she ask you to cover for her exactly?'

'Yesterday morning. She rang me up at school and said she had to do something, and she needed to be gone overnight, and could I just say that she was sleeping over with me if anybody asked.'

Mrs Chandler shook her head sorrowfully.

'And how did she sound? Depressed, or maybe tense?'

'No. A bit quiet, like. Dull. Sort of resigned, like when we have double biology at school.'

Hillary nearly laughed at that one. 'I see. Now, I want to go back a bit, to the afternoon of Billy's death . . .' She stopped, in genuine surprise, as Mary-Beth Chandler gave a sudden wail and began to cry in earnest.

'I knew you were going to find out about that,' she managed to gasp out at last, between genuine sobs of fright. Her mother, not a little frightened herself now, got up and scuttled around to stand behind her, hugging her in a manner not very far removed from the way Debbie Soames had hugged her father. Over her daughter's distraught head, Mrs Chandler stared at Hillary helplessly.

Hillary couldn't help her though. She had no idea what all this was about either. 'I think it's best if you tell me all about it, don't you?' she said gently.

And Mary-Beth Chandler nodded, gulped some more, dabbed at her tears and said, 'We told the policemen who asked us that Heather was with us that afternoon. When Billy died, I mean. That we all hung out at the tennis courts during our free period. But we didn't. I mean, me and Colleen did, but Heather went home. We won't get into trouble, will we?'

Hillary felt a cold chill creep down her spine as she stared at the girl's woebegone face. 'Let me get this straight,' she said, steel in her voice now. 'On the day that Billy was killed, Heather Soames left the school at what time exactly?'

Mary-Beth sniffed, her back straightening up automatically as she reacted to the authority in the older woman's voice. 'It was after maths. A quarter to two. That's when we had the free period till three o'clock. The afternoon break is for fifteen minutes so it works out at an hour and a quarter, so—'

'And did Heather come back at three?' she interrupted ruthlessly. 'Or did she stay away the rest of the afternoon?'

'I'm not sure,' Mary-Beth said shakily. 'I had IT, and Heather had, er . . . English lit, I think. So I didn't see her before going home.' Hillary was sure that Heather's English teacher had confirmed her presence for that afternoon lesson. But that still left an hour and fifteen minutes unaccounted for. It gave her time to kill her boyfriend. But, aged fifteen, Heather had no car and couldn't just drive to Aston Lea. There was no regular bus service from Bicester either, and it was doubtful that she would have been able to bike it there and back in time.

Unless she'd hitched. Unless she'd had help from another quarter.

Debbie Soames was probably old enough to have a provisional driver's licence.

Hillary mentally shook her head. No, this was going too fast. She had to slow it down, think it through. Why would the Soames sisters want Billy dead? And why would Debbie come into the station and tell them all about Heather's pregnancy if they were in it together? Unless they were playing some kind of game that Hillary hadn't figured out yet.

'Listen, Mary-Beth, I want you and your mum to come to Kidlington so that you can make a proper statement about all this.' Hillary looked at the older woman as she spoke, who nodded grimly.

Mary-Beth started crying again.

* * *

Hillary drove back to HQ, trying to fit Heather Soames into the frame as the killer, and failing. Would a fifteen-year-old girl kill the father of her baby because he wanted her to have an abortion? How had she got to Aston Lea? Why would Debbie, or anyone else, aid and abet her? It just didn't add up.

Tommy looked up as Hillary walked across to her desk.

'The woman's name was Samantha Willis, guv.' He launched into his report before she'd even sat down, tossing the photo of the naked sunbather on to her desk. 'She admitted that Billy Davies had approached her with copies of these pictures, last summer this would be, and told her he'd give them to her husband if she didn't pay him two hundred quid. She laughed in his face, apparently — told him he'd better make sure that he found her husband before he went into the pub, otherwise he'd probably be drunk and would wallop him good and proper.' Tommy grinned. 'From what I gather, she put the wind up him and sent him off with a flea in his ear. Denies flat-out that she paid him a penny.'

'Good for her,' Hillary grunted, then looked across at Janine, who was talking on the phone.

'No one of that description at all? She'd have come in last night, possibly this morning. No, all right, thanks.' Janine hung up, and immediately began dialling again, shaking her head at Hillary as she did so.

'Any luck with the couples in our mysterious photos?' Hillary asked Tommy.

'No joy yet, guv, but Frank reckons he might have a lead. He left a half hour ago.' Tommy managed to say it with a straight face, but they both looked at the clock, and realised that the pubs would now be open.

'Right,' Hillary said heavily, and explained the bombshell Mary-Beth Chandler had just dropped. Janine, able to talk and listen at the same time, got another negative from another clinic, hung up and tried the next one on her list, as Hillary outlined her problems with Heather Soames as the killer.

Suddenly, Janine's voice sharpened, and she flicked a pencil in the air, catching Hillary's attention.

'Yes, that's right. Did she register under her own name? OK, spell it out for me, please.' Janine swivelled her chair around and began typing into her computer, then grinned. 'Yes, yes, that would be her mother's maiden name. Is she still there? Right, no, don't do that. Can you just make sure you keep her there until we arrive? No, I realise you can't do that . . . Yes, fine, OK, but could you just not tell her that we've called making inquiries about her? That won't violate any of her rights, will it? OK. What time's she due to check out? Yes, we'll make it,' she said confidently, checking her watch before hanging up.

'Guv, a clinic in Northampton. Sounds like our girl. She had a termination this morning.'

'Right. We'd better get our skates on. Tommy, stay here and find those couples. I want to speak to them as soon as possible.'

'Right, guv,' Tommy said, watching them go with an envious sigh. Then he picked up one of the photographs of the anonymous couples, and wracked his brains for a new idea.

Then he clicked his fingers. He could always take a trip to the Oxford post office, see if any of the posties there recognised the streets in the background. It was a long shot of course, but you never knew your luck.

CHAPTER FOURTEEN

'These places always give me the creeps,' Janine said, as she turned into a perfectly ordinary-looking parking lot in front of a low, orange-brick rectangular building. Occupying one floor only, it spread itself around hard landscaping and tubs of flowering pots harmlessly enough. It even had cheerful hanging baskets and a tent-like grey slate roof.

'It's your imagination,' Hillary said crisply, and opened her car door. The sun was still shining as relentlessly as ever, but weathermen were promising a break in the heatwave, heralded by a thunderstorm that was headed their way later that weekend. It couldn't come soon enough for Hillary's liking. The heat reflecting off the white paving slabs surrounding the Northbrook Clinic hit her in the face the moment she stepped on to them, and the gleam of sun on pale stone made her scrunch her eyes up in order not to be temporarily blinded.

An intercom was set beside a solidly constructed door that was very firmly locked. She buzzed it and gave her name, and a moment later, with a slight hum, the door slid open. Hillary was glad to step inside an air-conditioned reception/waiting room, and stood for a moment beside a duct that was blasting out cool air, and breathed deeply.

Posters of various sorts, providing information on all sorts of dire diseases, lined the walls, along with three big pots of fake ferns. The receptionist's office was indicated by a window set into a wall with no access from the public area. As Hillary approached, she wondered whether the architect had just designed it that way, or whether the powers that be at the clinic had insisted it be that way, in order to protect their staff.

'DI Greene, DS Tyler,' she repeated quietly as the receptionist drew back a small portion of the glass in order to hear them better. 'We have an appointment with the office administrator?' There were only two women waiting in the seats, pretending to read magazines, and Hillary saw no reason to send their blood pressure soaring by letting herself be overheard. The receptionist appreciated it, for she smiled in gratitude before whispering back.

'Oh yes, Mrs Reece is expecting you. Please, go through the door.' As she spoke, she reached down to press a button, and the door a little further down the wall made a buzzing sound. 'Mrs Reece's office is the second on the left.'

Hillary nodded, and proceeded down the corridor. Mrs Reece, a woman in her sixties, with a fine head of iron-grey hair, iron-grey eyes, and no doubt an iron will to match, studied their ID intently, listened silently to Hillary's explanation as to why they were there, then told them curtly to sit and wait, whilst she consulted Miss Peacock's doctor.

Hillary was nonplussed for a moment, until she recalled that Heather Soames had booked in under her mother's maiden name.

The office was beige, with blinds, a functional desk and very little in the way of personal touches. Janine fidgeted in her chair. It was a full ten minutes before the office administrator came back and told them that Miss

Peacock was expecting them, and that they were to follow her.

Janine muttered something under her breath that, thankfully, neither of the other two women quite caught, and fiddled with her bag as they walked down a wide, beige-coloured corridor to the rear of the building. The further into the depths of the building they went, the stronger became the scent of antiseptic and the astringent tang of cleaning fluids. Hillary felt her stomach tightening. Like a lot of other people, she didn't much like hospitals, dentists, or any other place where the human body became a free-for-all for men and women in white coats.

'Miss Peacock is due to be discharged in two hours,' a man in a white coat, waiting outside the door, said before either of them could speak. 'She's supposed to be resting, and we're checking in on her from time to time to make sure there's been no further reaction to the local anaesthetic, or the drugs she's been administered. The clinic psychologist might also want to see her. If she does, I'd appreciate it if you'd suspend your interview at once and let her speak to our patient in private.'

He was a young man, but he spoke like an old one, and Hillary nodded. She did not, in any way, try to justify or quantify why they were there or what they were doing, and after eyeballing each other in silence for a moment, the doctor nodded briefly and moved away. Mrs Reece, after a surprised moment, followed his lead.

'Phew, it was like the showdown at the High Chaparral,' Janine quipped and Hillary held up her finger as if it were the barrel of a gun and blew across it briefly. Then she tapped on the door and opened it, standing aside to let Janine get ahead of her.

The room was surprisingly small, and held little more than a single bed with a bedside cabinet that housed a bottle of lemon barley water, a teenage magazine, and, oddly, a pot of African violets. Heather was not undressed but was fully clothed, half-sitting, half-lying on top of the bed. She looked pale, but her eyes were dry and she smiled briefly at them as they came in.

'Does Dad know I'm here?' were the first words she spoke, and Hillary shook her head.

'No, DS Tyler tracked you down this morning. But your father does know you didn't go to school yesterday, and didn't spend the night at Mary-Beth's.'

'Damn! I'll have to think of something to tell him,' Heather moaned, watching them curiously as they each reached for a moulded plastic chair that were hell to sit on and seemed to be standard seating in every public place where you weren't encouraged to linger.

'Heather, Mary-Beth and Colleen have both confirmed that on the afternoon Billy died you weren't at school, like you said,' Hillary began firmly. 'You do understand that lying to the police is very serious don't you? You yourself are not only in serious trouble, but in trying to cover for you, your friends are as well,' she warned her flatly.

At that, tears instantly brightened the teenager's eyes. 'That's not fair! They didn't do anything!' She leaned up and forward on her elbows and stared at Hillary earnestly. 'I just asked them to say I was with them, that's all. And they did it because they're my friends. You're not going to arrest them or anything are you? It's not as if I did anything wrong! I didn't hurt Billy, if that's what you're thinking! Why would I?'

'All right, calm down,' Hillary said sharply. Heather's voice was steadily rising, and the last thing she wanted was a showdown with the iron maiden or the girl's doctor.

Heather slumped back against the bed again, and heaved a massive sigh. 'Oh what's the use,' she suddenly wailed. 'Everything's gone wrong. Mum's dead, Billy's dead, now my baby's dead, Dad's going to pieces and Debbie hates my guts. I might as well be dead too!'

Hillary's lips twisted wryly. 'Very dramatic. You ever considered acting as a career?'

'No. I want to be a librarian,' Heather Soames said, startled. Hillary, careful to avoid catching her sergeant's face, knowing that laughter was very definitely the last thing this situation called for, cleared her throat instead.

'I'm sure your dad must approve of your career choice,' she said blandly. 'Now, let's get a few things clear. Your dad isn't going to go to pieces, he's just going through a rough time, and so are you. People in mourning don't see the world the same way as they did, and it's going to take the both of you a very long time to adjust. But you will, and the pain of your mum's loss will become more bearable as time goes by. And your sister doesn't really hate you. Don't forget, she lost her mum too, and I'm willing to bet that she was your mum's favourite. Your dad always loved you best, am I right?'

Heather flushed and mumbled something that was probably an agreement.

'Well then, cut your sister some slack. Now, being in here is tough, I grant you,' Hillary said, glancing around and suppressing a shudder, 'and what you did can't have been easy, but you must have thought about it long and hard before coming here, and in the years to come, you'll probably come to accept that the decision you made today was the right one for you. Now, can you please put a break on all this self-pity, and tell me what you were doing when Billy was murdered?'

Heather Soames sniffed and nodded, and Janine watched her, amazed. Although Hillary's voice had been gentle and calm throughout the lecture, she'd half expected the teenager to wilt under the onslaught. Instead, she seemed to be responding to it like a wilting flower to a refreshing rain.

Janine had seen this phenomenon before, of course. Hillary was well known at the station house for her interview technique. One DCI in the fraud squad was sure she must have studied psychology in college, and wouldn't have it that her degree was in English lit. And Janine could understand why. Her boss seemed to have an uncanny ability to read suspects and witnesses alike, and unerringly take whatever approach was most effective in getting them to spew their guts.

Take this girl, for instance. Janine would have tried the mollycoddling approach, sure that a teenage girl who'd just had an abortion should be treated like a cracked egg that would burst apart at the slightest pressure. Yet here she was, shoulders straightening, tears drying up, and looking at Hillary like . . . well . . . like she was the next best thing since sliced bread.

No doubt about it, Janine was going to miss watching her work. When she'd agreed to marry Mel, he'd pointed out that she'd need to move stations, and had agreed to help her get taken on at Witney. Of course, she fully expected to be promoted to DI within a year, and had made that much clear. Still, Hillary Greene had taught her a lot, and still had much she could have shown her. For a moment, it made Janine wonder whether she was doing the right thing in agreeing to ask for a transfer away from Kidlington.

'OK, I'll tell you, but it sounds so stupid,' Heather Soames said now, jerking Janine back to the matter in hand. 'You see, this girl at school, Natalie Constantine, said that her cousin's best friend had got pregnant, and because she was Greek Orthodox or something, knew that her mother wouldn't let her have an abortion, so she got some of these herbal pills from a health shop, and made a bath with really hot water and vinegar, and, well, it worked. She lost the baby. So, that afternoon, I knew Debbie would be in school and Dad would be at work, and because the vinegar would really smell out the bathroom, I had to choose a time when I was all alone. So that afternoon was perfect. So I went home and tried it.'

She paused to take a much-needed breath, and looked at Hillary with a half-ashamed, half-defiant gaze.

Hillary shook her head helplessly. In these days of the twenty-first century, for crying out loud, how could teenagers still be so woefully ignorant about such matters? 'Just as a matter of interest, what were the pills you took? And how many?' she asked curiously.

'St John's Wort,' Heather said promptly. 'I remembered it because it was such a gross name. And I took quite a few pills, before and after. For days. It's not poisonous, is it?' she asked sharply.

Hillary shook her head. 'Well, I'm glad at least that you had the sense to come here. Heather, how did you pay for it? This is a private clinic, isn't it?'

Heather flushed. 'Billy gave me some money, two days before . . . you know, he died. I kept it hidden in my pyjama case at home. Debbie's a right nosy cow.'

Hillary smiled wearily. 'OK, Heather. Just for the record. Did you see Billy Davies at all that day?'

'No.'

'Did you go to Aston Lea? Get someone to give you a lift there perhaps?'

'No! I told you — I was in the bath for, like, nearly an hour. The water had to be hot, so I kept letting some out and refilling it. But nothing happened. Except I smelt like vinegar all that night. Yuck!'

'Did anyone see you at the house that afternoon, either when you arrived home, or when you left for your afternoon lesson afterwards? A next-door neighbour, someone getting into or out of a car?'

'Don't think so. Why, don't you believe me? The neighbours all work during the day, so it's not my fault, is it? It's really dead around our place in the day.'

Then, as if realising her unfortunate choice of words, she flushed bright red.

* * *

'What do you reckon?' Janine asked as they walked out the door back towards the car park. They'd offered

Heather a lift home, but she preferred to wait and take the train back. Hillary thought she was just putting off the evil moment when she had to confront her father.

'I think the poor kid was telling the truth,' Hillary said, dialling the Soames's number and having a brief talk with a powerfully relieved Francis Soames. When she hung up, she carried on the conversation as though she'd never left off. 'Mind you, she has no witnesses to her alibi, which is no alibi at all. Still, she's not at the top of my list. Any more than Celia Davies is.'

Janine nearly rear-ended a gold-coloured Yaris as she negotiated the exit of the car park. 'Celia! The little sister? You rated her?'

'It crossed my mind,' Hillary said darkly, as her sergeant gaped at her like a stunned mullet.

Janine did, in fact, feel seriously wrong-footed. She'd always considered herself to be tough. And certainly way tougher than her DI, whom she'd tended to think of as, well, nearly past it, and certainly as a veteran of a much easier time in the police force. To learn that Hillary had considered an eleven-year-old girl as a suspect, and with such cavalier insouciance, when she herself hadn't even thought of it, left her feeling somehow reduced.

'Let's stop off somewhere for lunch,' Hillary said, glancing at her watch. It was a bit of a drive back to Kidlington, and she fancied a long cold drink in an anonymous pub. 'My treat. Besides, we need to talk about you and Mel.'

Janine felt her chest tighten, but her jaw came out pugnaciously. 'Boss,' she said flatly.

* * *

Back at HQ, Tommy was about to take a bite out of a cheese and pickle sandwich. He was still living at home with his mother (yes, Tommy had heard all the jokes) and would be until the estate agent came across with the keys, and the bank sorted out the last details of his and Jean's joint mortgage. And, just like when he'd been a kid going off to school, his mother insisted on packing him a lunchbox.

Not that he minded when it included such delicacies as sandwiches as thick as doorstops, and wedges of homemade fruit cake.

He'd just champed down on a deliciously tangy double cheddar, when someone slapped his back so hard it almost made him choke.

'Hey up, my old cocker, you want to be careful of that,' Frank Ross said, watching with malicious pleasure as Tommy's eyes began to water as he struggled to catch his breath.

'Wanker,' Tommy muttered under his breath. He should have known it would be Ross.

'Sergeant Wanker to you, laddy,' Ross said gleefully, 'and don't forget it. Just because you're off up to the boonies doesn't mean you're out of the woods yet.'

Tommy sighed over the awfulness of the mixed metaphor, and took a second, more cautious bite of his sandwich.

'Come on, no time to stuff your face. We're off to interview one of our mysterious contestants. This pair, to be precise,' Ross said, picking up one of the photographs of the couples Billy Davies had photographed arriving at a house with a green-painted gingerbread trim.

Tommy was so surprised, he nearly choked all over again. 'What? You found one of them?'

'Course I did! What do you think I've been doing all morning?' Ross demanded. 'Come on, let's get going before the girls get back from their morning jaunt.'

Tommy blinked. 'How did you get on to them? I went down to the post office, and none of the postmen recognised that street.'

'They wouldn't, would they?' Ross said, still with that annoying cheerfulness. 'Well, not this street at least. This,' he said, tapping it with a dirty fingernail, 'is a house in

Yarnton.' Tommy swallowed his bite of sandwich and looked at Ross closely. Was the poisonous little Winnie-the-Pooh clone drunk? If he'd spent the morning in the pub, as he suspected, he might well be. Not that Frank had ever come in to the office drunk before. Well, not obviously, undeniably drunk.

Frank gazed back at him with a wide grin. He knew just what the younger man was thinking. And he was not about to admit that he'd found out the whereabouts of one of their mystery couples totally by accident. He had, in fact, been in a pub all morning, in Bladon to be exact. Near enough to be close to the office in case he got his chain yanked by Hillary Greene, but far enough away from the station not to be frequented by tattle-tales. In fact, the pub was a well-known watering place for beat-up coppers trying to keep their heads down, and off the radar, for a couple of hours.

Which was how he'd run into an old mate of his from Traffic, who'd been well into his fourth pint of Coors. Frank, who'd taken an envelope full of the photographs with him, had slapped them down at his table before getting a round in. One or two of them spilled out, and when he came back to the table, he found his old oppo looking through them idly.

And he recognised the distinctive woodwork on one of the houses, because his father-in-law lived in a house in that very street.

Which just goes to show, Frank thought now, that it pays to be in the right place at the right time. Good old-fashioned dumb luck. You couldn't beat it.

'I think we should wait for the guv,' Tommy said flatly now, and Ross snorted.

'I think we should wait for the guv,' Ross mimicked snidely. 'Grow some balls, why don't you?'

But Tommy noticed that he made no move to go off on his own, but sat down at his desk, and reached for a file. Within a few minutes, Tommy guessed, he'd be snoring. Well, sod him. One thing he wasn't going to miss when he transferred to Headington was Sergeant Frank bloody Ross.

* * *

Janine drove into the parking lot at HQ at 2:15 that afternoon, feeling a little uneasy. They'd found a pub in Brackley, and both had ordered the grilled chicken salad. After she'd told Hillary about her inconclusive interview with June Warrender, Janine had tensed herself, ready for an angry lecture, but none had been forthcoming.

Hillary had, instead, simply asked her if she was sure she knew what she was doing in accepting Mel's proposal, and then sat silently as Janine had, rather aggressively it had to be said, stated her long list of reasons for accepting. Hillary had listened with no expression at all on her face, then simply nodded, and ordered herself a large gin and tonic. Janine, who was driving, had to make do with orange juice. Although a G&T would have gone down well at that point.

Now, as she followed her boss through the big, open-plan office, she found herself, very annoyingly, beginning to have second thoughts about the whole thing. Luckily, her phone rang just then, and she dumped her bag on the table, answered it, and listened intently.

Frank Ross wasted no time telling Hillary that he'd possibly tracked down one of the streets in the photograph to a nearby village called Yarnton. Hillary could hear Janine talking on the phone, and could tell by the tone of her voice that she was excited by something.

'Well done, Frank,' Hillary said, amazed to find herself actually saying those words. 'You and Tommy go and make sure. If you confirm a visual match, start going around the neighbours, discreetly mind, and find out who lives there.' She tapped the house pictured in the photograph. 'And then run a full background check on them. But don't approach them yet.'

'Right, guv,' Tommy said, already getting up. Frank, looking more disgusted, rose reluctantly to his feet.

'That was the landlord of the pub in Cropredy, guv,' Janine said, hanging up and watching Tommy and Frank disappear. 'You know, that pub where Marty Warrender and his girlfriend have been hanging out. He wasn't there when I called by, and he'd been the one serving that night, so I asked the barmaid to get him to call me back. He was a bit cagey on the phone, but I think he knew who and what I was talking about.'

Hillary nodded. 'OK. Let's go.'

Janine looked at her, surprised. Although Hillary often accompanied her on interviews (much to the disapproval of a lot of people who thought DIs should be chained to their desks, where they couldn't cause too much trouble), she wouldn't have thought this particular interview would have been of any interest to the SIO.

Still, hers was not to reason why . . .

* * *

In the parking lot, Frank Ross yanked open the door of his rusting Fiat, swearing under his breath as he did so. Tommy took one look at him, and said he'd take his own car. The mood Frank was in, he was just as likely to wrap his car around a lamp post as not.

So what if Hillary wanted to know something about the people before interviewing them? So what if she'd asked them to do the legwork. That was their job, wasn't it? Tommy just didn't know how Hillary put up with Frank Ross. Or why the brass had lumbered her with him in the first place.

* * *

The landlord of the Goat and Honeypot was watching football on the bar telly. The interior was cool and dark, and apart from one man supping beer and reading a paper, the place was totally deserted.

'Weird name for a pub, innit?' Janine commented as they approached the bar.

'Best not to ask how they came by it,' Hillary advised. 'Someone might just tell you.'

Janine was still grinning over that when the landlord drew his gaze reluctantly from the screen.

Janine identified herself, and the landlord nodded. He wasn't a heavy-set man, and had thin shoulders and a narrow waist, but he had one of the most gigantic beer bellies Hillary had ever seen. He turned watery blue eyes on them, and slowly reached out to take the photograph of Marty Warrender that Janine offered to him. His slow movements, the near-baldness of his dome and the sagging wattle of skin at his neck all reminded Hillary of a tortoise.

'Marty,' the landlord said simply.

'You recognise him? Have you seen him in here in the company of a woman, recently?'

'Yes. He often comes in to have a drink with his sister-in-law.'

'Oh,' Janine said blankly. Damn, a dead end. But the old gossip at the dry cleaners had been sure . . .

'Very close to his sister-in-law, is he?' she heard Hillary ask dryly, and the landlord chuckled.

'Very. His wife would have his guts for garters, I reckon, if she found out. A bit of a tartar, she is.'

'But no one's going to tell her?' Hillary said, still in that same, amused, dry tone.

'No one round here, any rate,' the landlord said, and went back to his screen.

Janine bit her lip. That was twice in one day that Hillary had got the drop on her.

'Find out the sister-in-law's name, then go interview her. Make sure Billy didn't approach her for dosh. If Marty Warrender turned him down, as he said he did, he might have thought he'd have better luck with the lady,' Hillary instructed as they headed for the door. 'Find out where she was when Billy died, and if she has an alibi. Check it out thoroughly.'

Janine nodded, but as she drove back to HQ, she felt oddly depressed.

Hillary went back to her desk and phoned Francis Soames. Heather had got back safe and sound and had confessed all. He sounded shaken up, and appalled by his daughter's recent traumas, but also, oddly, a lot calmer. She hoped the Soames were going to be OK.

When she lowered the receiver and looked up, Paul Danvers was just coming out of his office. He saw her at her desk and smiled, but didn't divert over.

Hillary watched him leave, wondering if he was gone for the day, in which case she wouldn't have to worry about him and whatever private agenda he seemed to be working on. Instead, she reached for one of the files in her in-tray. No matter how fast she cleared it, some malicious elf seemed to sneak in under the cover of darkness and fill it up again. It was nearly 3:30.

She had no idea her case was about to blow wide open.

CHAPTER FIFTEEN

Janine came back first and reported. 'Boss. The sister-in-law is one Felicia Cummings. She lives in Cropredy, and works in Banbury, just down the road from her brother-in-law. Very convenient,' she grinned. 'Flick — that's what she prefers to be called — admitted to the affair with Marty Warrender, but only after she realised there was no point denying it. Apparently it's been going on sixteen years! Sixteen years! Can you imagine?'

Hillary, who'd heard of far weirder things in her time, shrugged. 'Did her sister know?'

'According to Flick, no. But I'm not so sure. I mean, how's a woman going to miss the fact that her sister and husband are at it, and have been for sixteen years? She'd have to be living in cloud cuckoo land not to have twigged.'

Hillary shook her head. 'Not necessarily. I had a case once, of bigamy. This man had been keeping three different families over a period of twenty-five years, and not one of the wives or children knew about the others. A travelling salesman. He divided his time equally. Very fair-minded chap was Mr Tarkington.'

Janine shook her head. 'Well, I dunno,' she said dubiously. 'Anyway, Flick was certain her sister was in the dark about it. But she's got a rock-solid alibi for the time Billy died. She was at work — a place that sells expensive glass and crystal figurines and whatnot. You know, the sort of place you go to come Mother's Day or Christmas if you've got a yearning to buy a miniature tree made out of amethysts or whatever.'

Hillary nodded. 'I think I know the place. How many staff are there?'

'Three, and all three were at work the day Billy died. I talked to all of them separately — and the other two are adamant Felicia never left the shop.'

'Lunch hour?'

'No good, boss — they staggered it, so there were always two in the shop. Flick did go to the cafe over the road for her lunch break, but the cafe owner confirmed it. She's a bit of a regular there. He says she left about two fifteen, and the girls in the shop confirmed she was back by two twenty.'

Hillary sighed. It seemed airtight. 'Did Billy approach her for money?'

Janine frowned and tapped her pencil against her lips. 'Not sure, boss. She says not, but she seemed a bit touchy to me. If I had to guess, I'd say that he had, but that she'd told him to sod off, and then told her boyfriend all about it. I could try and get a warrant to check her bank accounts, I suppose?'

Hillary shook her head. 'Not just yet. If all else fails, we can always go back to her.' She glanced at her watch, willing the phone to ring, but it was nearly forty minutes before Tommy checked back in.

'Guv, it's definitely them,' were his first words. 'A Mr and Mrs Clive and Dawn Waring. He owns his own company, selling and setting up garages and conservatories. She sort of "does" friends' houses. You know, fancy wallpaper, paints mixed to order for a unique colour scheme, that sort of thing. Gets paid for it, but it's probably more of a hobby than a serious business. House is mortgaged but nearly paid for, the car's a new Mondeo. Seem to be doing all right. Married for nearly fifteen years, no kids. No previous. They're both in — I'm sitting outside their place now. You coming over, guv?'

'Be there in ten minutes, Tommy,' Hillary said.

* * *

The house was instantly recognisable from the photograph, the green-painted gingerbread trim being echoed in some of the other houses in the cul-de-sac. Janine watched through the windscreen as Tommy got out of his own car and walked over and slipped into the back seat of theirs.

'Frank's still questioning the neighbours, guv,' Tommy lied. He had, in fact, skived off. 'Do we three all go in, or what, guv?' Tommy asked curiously, leaning forward into the gap between the front two seats. 'Might seem a bit heavy-handed.'

Hillary thought it over, then smiled. 'It seems to me that's just what we need,' she mused. 'Shake 'em up a bit. Let's face it, we've got nothing on them. Some innocuous pictures a murdered lad took, could mean anything or nothing. If they instantly start shouting for solicitors it won't make any difference how many of us are in there. And if they decide to keep quiet, the same applies. But my guess is that Mr and Mrs Waring consider themselves average, law-abiding citizens, and a visit from three police officers, looking and sounding serious, might just be enough to get them talking to us. Unless they don't know what those pictures are all about and what they mean either. In which case, we're buggered anyway.'

Janine nodded happily. That's how she would have played it too. Perhaps she wasn't losing her touch after all.

'OK, Tommy, play the big silent menace. Look at everything and say nothing. Janine, likewise, but make a show of taking down every little cough and sneeze in your notebook. I want them to be very much aware that this is a formal interview. I'll do all the talking, unless I indicate otherwise. I want you both to watch their body language and see what you can pick up from their behaviour. We'll compare notes later. Don't interrupt me unless you've spotted something I've missed, or thought of something I haven't, in which case just lean over and whisper in my ear. Got the picture?'

Janine grinned. She loved this sort of thing. Tommy merely said quietly, 'Yes, guv.'

Hillary nodded and got out of the car. Yarnton was a village split in half by a busy dual carriageway, but this side of the road, in a quiet and unassuming cul-de-sac, Saturday afternoon life went on as it did everywhere. Someone, in one of the back gardens, was mowing a lawn. A sprinkler system turned itself on to water a front lawn, startling a blackbird that had been looking for worms. In one garden, a child's pink bicycle lay abandoned on its side.

She made her way to the door of number five, and pressed the bell. The woman who answered was definitely the woman in the photograph, although she did not have a face that a camera captured with any ease. She looked fatter, more blurred somehow in real life than she did on celluloid.

'Mrs Waring? I'm Detective Inspector Hillary Greene. This is Sergeant Janine Tyler, and this is Detective Constable Thomas Lynch. May we come in please? We'd like to have a word with you and your husband.' Dawn Waring went rather pale, which made the blusher stand out on her cheeks, giving her the unfortunate appearance of a clown. Her bright red lipstick didn't help either. Her hand went up to tuck a brown lock behind her ear in an unconscious gesture of fear, and she smiled too brightly.

'Oh, yes, of course. My, it sounds very ominous. Clive!' she raised her voice, but not much. 'Clive, darling, we have visitors.' They were now all crowded into a small hall, where a grandfather clock ticked ponderously. 'Please, come through to the lounge. My husband's out the back, feeding the fish. He's nutty about koi. I ask you, the things men like.' She ushered them through to a room where the three-piece suite was king.

A monstrous black leather sofa and two overstuffed armchairs dominated a plain, simple, square room, that contained little else but a television and, for some reason, a poster on the wall proclaiming the delights of the Caribbean island of Mustique.

Hillary nodded to Tommy and looked pointedly towards the far wall. Instantly, Tommy went over and leaned against it, folding his arms across his chest. Wearing an inexpensive dark blue suit, he suddenly looked like a bouncer hired to sort out trouble at a notoriously violent nightclub.

Janine, without being asked, took a seat at one end of the sofa. Hillary, also without being asked, took a seat at the other. This left the two chairs free for the Warings.

Clive Waring was as portly as his wife, going bald, and looked startled to see them. His wife, hovering in the open doorway, looked from them to her husband, then to the poster, then out the window. She was still very pale.

'Please, won't you sit down,' Hillary said, her tone of voice making it an order rather than a pleasantry. She noticed that Clive Waring obeyed immediately, rather like a well-trained dog. Dawn Waring took her own seat rather more slowly and reluctantly, but it was not defiance so much as fear that held her back.

Hillary smiled briefly, opened her briefcase, and took out a set of photographs. She went through them, leaving the picture of the Warings on the top. 'These photographs have come into our possession,' she said flatly. 'Would you please look at them, and tell me what you know?' She handed them to Clive Waring first.

Puzzled, he took them, and stared down at the top one, his jaw falling open. He had, she noticed, false teeth. 'But that's us! Look, Dee.' He handed it over and his wife reached out and took it; then his gaze fell on to the next photograph in the series, and he paled conspicuously.

Wordlessly, he turned to the next, then the next. When he'd finished, his hand was visibly trembling as he handed them over to his wife.

'As you can see,' Hillary continued pleasantly, 'the photographs are all similar. All are of couples, taken outside private residences. You obviously know them,' she added flatly, giving him no chance to deny it. 'Can I have their names and their addresses please?'

Clive Waring, who'd been staring at his wife, cleared his throat. 'What makes you think we know these people?' he said to Hillary, his attempt at bluffing them rather ruined by the way his voice wavered alarmingly.

Hillary smiled grimly. 'Mr Waring, I'm heading up the William Davies murder inquiry. I don't appreciate being lied to. You can be charged with wasting police time if you refuse to co-operate. Do you understand what I'm telling you?'

'Murder!' It was Dawn who spoke. Or rather squeaked. She stared at Hillary, then at her husband, then back to Hillary again. 'We don't know anything about a murder. There's nothing wrong with us!'

The last came out as a wail, but it was a curious sentiment. On first hearing, Hillary thought that she was simply saying that they weren't murderers. Then she had immediate second thoughts. There's nothing wrong with us. Just repeating it in her head made Hillary think that the Warings believed that there was indeed something very 'wrong' with them. But what? What were they trying to hide?

'I never said there was, Mrs Waring,' Hillary said calmly. 'But I need to speak to these other people, and I have reason to believe you know who they are. So, their names and addresses please. My sergeant will take down their particulars.'

Janine straightened up and turned smartly to a fresh page of her notebook, and fixed her blue gaze on Clive Waring.

Waring flushed, looked helplessly at his wife, then shrugged. 'Well, I suppose there's no harm.' He held out his hand to his wife, who reluctantly handed back the photographs. Her eyes tried to hold on to his, but he kept his own gaze firmly averted. 'This one,' he held up the first of the photographs, 'is of Vince and Betty Harris. They live in Tackley. I'm not sure of the number or the road. It's just off the square though. This one . . .'

Ten minutes later, and they had the names and approximate addresses of all the couples. When he'd finished, Clive Waring leaned back against the armchair, sweating openly. He looked, also, a little puzzled.

Hillary noticed it and felt a familiar tug at her stomach. She was going to have to explore that, later, when she'd got them talking more freely.

'Can you think of any reason why anyone would have taken these photographs?' Hillary asked. 'I mean, of you people, specifically?'

'No!' Dawn Waring almost shouted.

At the same time her husband snorted an unconvincing laugh and said emphatically, 'Of course not!' Their denials were so fierce and unanimous that it was clear, even to themselves, how ridiculous they sounded. Over by the wall, Tommy sighed heavily, and readjusted his weight. When both the Warings looked at him they caught the tail end of amused disbelief on his features.

'How do you know all these people?' Hillary asked flatly.

The Warings exchanged looks. Eventually, Clive said, 'I'm not sure what you mean.'

Hillary shook her head, exasperated. 'Mr and Mrs Waring, would you like me to send for a patrol car? Then we can carry on this conversation back at Thames Valley Police Headquarters. Obviously, you're not taking this interview seriously. Perhaps . . .'

'No, don't do that!' Dawn said at once, clearly appalled. 'The neighbours . . . This is a nice street. Quiet. We've never had any trouble here. We like it here. Please, we don't want to move again.'

Hillary found that very interesting. Not about the neighbours — she'd threatened the Warings with the very visible patrol car precisely because she knew that the last thing either of them would want would be to be seen driving off in the back of a police car.

No, what interested her was that comment about them having to move again. It indicated that the Warings had had to move a lot in the past. Why? Normally, she'd have wondered if one or the other of them had ever been suspected of sexually abusing children. But she'd caught no such whiffs of anything like that in this case.

'Then I suggest you answer my question,' Hillary said smoothly, with no trace of her thoughts showing on her face. 'How come you know these people? It's a simple enough question.'

'We all get together sometimes, that's all,' Dawn said helplessly, in a small voice. 'We meet up, once a fortnight or so, in each other's houses. You know, take it in turns to host a party. Nothing wrong in that is there? We don't play loud music or take drugs or anything! Not like most parties nowadays. We're always very discreet. Nobody's neighbours ever complain.'

Hillary nodded, then caught movement out of the corner of her eye as Janine suddenly jerked in her seat. Suddenly, she began to scribble furiously in her book. Both the Warings had also noticed and were staring at her, fascinated. Hillary decided to let it play out, and said nothing until Janine had finished. Then her sergeant simply handed her the sheet of paper.

Hillary read the following:

GUV — IT'S BLOODY WIFE-SWAPPING, ONLY WITH A TWIST!!!! WHEN I INTERVIEWED JENNY CLEAVER I FELT SOMETHING WAS OFF, BUT I COULDN'T PLACE IT. NOW I KNOW — SHE FANCIED ME! IT WAS THE WAY SHE WATCHED ME CROSS MY LEGS — SHE WAS BLOODY EYEING ME UP. I THINK THESE ARE ALL GAY COUPLES AND GET TOGETHER FOR A BIT OF AN ORGY. I WONDER IF THEY ACTUALLY DO THE CAR KEYS IN A BOWL THING? VERY EIGHTIES IF THEY DO!

Hillary's lips twitched as she read this last comment and quickly turned it into a grimace. Wordlessly she folded the piece of paper in half, then in quarters, and slipped it into her briefcase. She didn't so much as glance at Janine, but when she looked up at the Warings, they looked like rabbits that had been caught in car headlights. Both were clearly desperate to know what Janine had written.

Hillary smiled gently. 'Mr Waring, is there anyone missing from these photographs?' she asked simply. 'Anyone who belongs to your . . . little club . . . who should be amongst these photographs, but isn't?'

On her chair, Janine drew in a sharp breath. Of course! If she was right about this, and the Cleavers were members of these gay swingers, then where were their photos? Why hadn't they found them along with all the others, stashed away in Billy's hiding place?

Damn, the boss was good. She'd seen at once what that meant. Billy had gone to the shed to meet someone — a blackmail victim, presumably. In his cocky arrogance and youthful stupidity, he'd probably brought the photos with him. Oh, he might have had the sense to keep copies stored on Lester's computer, but he'd have taken his set of printed copies with him to show the 'customer.' And his killer would have taken them away with him after killing the boy.

'I don't know what you mean,' Clive Waring said weakly.

Hillary sighed. 'Mr Waring, please believe me, I have no interest in your sexual proclivities, or those of your wife, or the people you choose to mix with.' She ignored Dawn Waring's gasp, and continued to stare levelly at Clive Waring, who was flushing a slow, ugly red. 'Who's missing from this set of photographs?' she snapped sharply. 'Now stop messing me about, or I will snap on the handcuffs and charge you with obstruction of justice.'

'Jenny and Darren,' Dawn Waring blurted out, then burst into tears. 'Oh, why can't you people leave us alone?'

'Homosexuality is no longer a crime, Mrs Waring,' Hillary said gently, making Tommy, who hadn't seen Janine's message, blink in surprise. 'I doubt that anybody nowadays really cares how you choose to live your lives. Surely, there's no need to live in such fear?'

'Huh! Tell that to my brother. Or Clive's mother. It would kill his mother if she knew, and Donald would . . . well, he would disown me!' Dawn Waring said bitterly.

Hillary said nothing. Perhaps she had a point. The Warings were middle-aged and middle-classed, and perhaps they felt that the stigma was still too sharp for either of them to shoulder, even in these so-called enlightened times. Neither Dawn nor Clive were the sort to stick their heads over the parapets and say to the world, 'We don't care what you think of us!'

And who was she to blame them?

'I take it your club consists of married couples?' she asked, just to get things clear. 'Gay men and gay women who enter into marriages of convenience to hide or disguise their real natures?'

Clive Waring nodded. He was still flushed a beetroot red, but at least he was managing to hold her gaze. 'We just meet to socialize. Chat, sometimes. Not everyone, you know, goes off together. Sometimes we pair off. It depends. Mostly, we just like to relax, be ourselves. Cottaging isn't something that suits everyone is it? And for the women, well, lesbian bars and such aren't exactly thick on the ground around here. And if you're in the closet still anyway . . .'

'It just started with Frank and Jane and Pete and Gloria at first,' Dawn Waring explained tearfully. 'Jane and Gloria met and fell for each other, and realised that they were both married to gay men, and then another gay couple began to drop by for drinks and word got around, very discreetly like,' she added, 'and well, we just fell into the habit of holding parties every fortnight or so. On a roster system. You don't really have to talk to them, do you? You don't have to upset everyone! Some of these people would be mortified and maybe even suicidal if they thought people would find out about this.'

Hillary shook her head firmly. 'No,' she said flatly. 'We may have to speak to these people, but we'll be as discreet as possible. Now, can you tell me what you were doing on Tuesday afternoon of this week?'

'Well, we were both at work,' Clive said, and proceeded to give their alibis. They appeared to be sound, but she'd get Frank on to checking them out.

'Thank you, Mr Waring, for your time. Mrs Waring.' She stood up and very carefully shook hands with both of them. They looked unutterably relieved to see them go. They also looked as if they couldn't quite believe that they weren't being arrested.

The moment Clive Waring shut the door behind them, Dawn Waring dived for the telephone.

Outside Janine and Tommy walked to Hillary's car. 'I knew I was right!' Janine hissed triumphantly. 'As soon as they started talking about a private club, I twigged. I wonder how Billy-Boy got on to it?'

Hillary shrugged. 'Doesn't matter now.' She rang the Cleavers' house, but no one answered. Then she tried the dairy, and got through to a production manager who confirmed that the manager was in. He offered to put her through to Darren Cleaver's office, but she told him that wouldn't be necessary.

When she hung up, she turned to Tommy. 'Tommy, go and pick him up. Janine, I want you to go to Jenny Cleaver's Oxford office and bring her back too. I'll get Frank to get a warrant for their bank accounts. If their withdrawals match the pattern in Billy's bank book, we'll have something concrete to go at them with. I somehow can't see either of the Cleavers coming clean with a confession. We've got plenty of hard slog ahead of us yet. Including breaking down their alibis.' And all the gay couples would have to be interviewed and their alibis checked. Some of them had to have been approached by Billy as well. Which of them had coughed up?

'Think the Cleavers did it together, guv?' Janine asked. 'You know, a Bonnie and Clyde job?'

'Don't know,' Hillary said shortly. And at that point, she didn't much care.

* * *

Janine dropped her off at HQ and roared away again. Hillary winced and hoped she didn't get a speeding ticket. Sometimes, Traffic loved to nab their own.

Halfway into the big open-plan office, she detoured to Danvers's cubicle, hoping he was the sort of boss who liked to go golfing or sailing, or what-the-hell-ever on a weekend, thus leaving the nuts and bolts to their second in command; but he was sat at his desk, and looked up as she tapped on the door and walked in. Of course, he was still the new boy, so he probably felt he had to show willing.

'Hillary. Something up?'

'I think the Davies case just broke, sir,' she said flatly, and quickly outlined her day's work. When she'd finished, Danvers leaned back in his chair and smiled.

'I can see why Chief Superintendent Donleavy and Mel both think you're one of the best detectives on the squad. Well done. Do you need anything from me?'

'No, sir. I think we'll get the arrest warrants easily enough, as well as the warrant for the Cleavers' financial records. Unless you want to sit in on the interview, or take charge?' she added flatly.

'Hell no. This is your show. You're going to try for a confession, I take it?'

Hillary sighed. 'We'll see. Both the Cleavers are intelligent, motivated, capable people, sir. I can't see either of them breaking down just because we ask them some searching questions. They'll probably admit to being gay, once they know their secret little club has been busted, but so what? So far we have no forensic evidence that puts them in that shed, although now we have suspects, SOCO might be able to match up trace evidence with their DNA, fibres from their clothes or what have you. But the trace evidence is a nightmare — that shed was filthy.'

Danvers frowned. 'I see your problem. And we have no witnesses who saw either Jenny or Darren Cleaver that afternoon in Aston Lea? I take it you think one of them lured Billy into the shed to buy and get the photos back?'

Hillary nodded. 'Yes — and killed him and took the photos away.' Hillary sighed. 'But knowing who killed Billy and proving it are going to be two separate things, I'm thinking,' she said gloomily.

Paul nodded. 'Anything I can do, just let me know.'

'Sir,' Hillary said, and hauled herself out of the chair. It was going to be a long evening.

'What is this? Why on earth did you have to bring me here from my office like this? Don't you realise how embarrassing it was?' Darren Cleaver asked angrily the moment Hillary joined him in the interview room twenty-five minutes later.

Ignoring him and his outburst, Hillary turned on the tape and went through the usual spiel, stating time and those present. Beside her, Tommy sat silent and unblinking.

'Mr Cleaver, this is a formal interview concerning the murder of William Davies on the second of this month. Are you sure you don't want the presence of a solicitor?'

'No, I already told you, I don't need a solicitor,' Darren said. It had been one of the first things he'd said when Hillary had cautioned him. And it was the first thing that struck her as being off. She'd have expected a man as savvy as this one to have demanded a legal representative right away. The fact that he hadn't worried her slightly.

Carefully, bit by bit, she took him over the day Billy had been killed. And, once again, Darren Cleaver insisted that he'd been in his office all that afternoon. When Hillary introduced the photographs of the gay swapping club, he looked abruptly uncomfortable.

'We've already interviewed Clive and Dawn Waring, Mr Cleaver,' Hillary said, as he scanned through them. 'And we know all about the private club that you, your wife, and these other people attend.'

Darren's eyes narrowed a little, but he remained silent.

'Nothing to say, Mr Cleaver?'

'Why should I have? There's nothing illegal about it.'

Hillary nodded. 'These photographs were taken by Billy Davies, Mr Cleaver. They were found in a hiding place, not far from where he was killed.'

Darren Cleaver looked stunned.

Hillary stared at him for a second, then abruptly got up. Tommy half-rose too, then returned to his seat, getting no indication from her what she wanted him to do. Hillary knew that Danvers was watching in the observation room, and sure enough, he quickly joined her outside in the corridor as she punched the buttons on her mobile phone.

'What's going on? Why did you stop?' he demanded, and Hillary held up a hand to silence him as she heard a voice speak into her ear.

'Janine? Where are you?' Hillary asked sharply.

'At the PR firm, boss. Jenny Cleaver's not in. Her PA reckons she probably stepped out for a bit of late lunch. She expects her back any minute.'

'Forget it. I think Dawn Waring telephoned her and warned her — maybe they're an item, who knows. I want you to get over to the Cleaver house now. It's her. Not him, just her.' She slammed the phone closed, and began to walk quickly down the corridor. 'Guv, can you take over in there?' Hillary said over her shoulder, without waiting for an answer.

DCI Paul Danvers watched her go and smiled. She looked on fire! Tense and animate and more gorgeous than ever. He was glad he'd bitten the bullet and moved down here from York. And he was glad even more that he'd finagled the position of being Hillary Greene's DCI. Now all he had to do was find some way to breach those walls she'd built up around herself, and things would start to get very interesting indeed.

He pushed open the door and smiled as Darren Cleaver looked up at him, puzzled and nervous. 'Detective Chief Inspector Paul Danvers has just entered the room,' he said, for the tape, and pulled up a chair.

'Now, Mr Cleaver, about your bank accounts . . .'

* * *

Hillary drove more quickly than she was used to, and Puff the Tragic Wagon responded gallantly, but even so, as she indicated on the main road to turn off to Aston Lea, she saw Janine's sporty new Mini disappear down the narrow lane ahead of her. When she pulled up outside the Cleaver residence, Janine was waiting for her.

'Boss, what—?' Janine broke off as Hillary, ignoring her, ran to the door and rang the bell. Inside there was only an ominous silence.

'Boss, I don't think there's anyone in,' Janine said. She was peering through the front window, hands cupped to the side of her face to block out excess light.

Hillary turned and walked quickly around the side of the house, opening the wooden gate and turning the corner, intending to see if the back door was open. But suddenly she yelled, 'Shit!' and started to run. Janine, the adrenaline abruptly pumping into her veins, took off after her and felt her breath catch as she too saw what Hillary had just seen.

Jenny Cleaver, her face blue and congested, her tongue hanging grotesquely out from between her lips, was dangling from a hanging basket of flowers. She was turning slowly, almost elegantly in the slight breeze, as Hillary Greene reached her. She was wearing a pale linen suit and a pair of cream Italian shoes that Janine would have given her eye teeth for. It was funny, the things you noticed, Janine thought, as she watched her boss grab Jenny Cleaver's calves and lift her up.

'Quick! Look for some garden shears, something, to cut the twine,' Hillary yelled, although she knew it was probably already too late. Although Jenny Cleaver didn't weigh much, Hillary could feel her arm muscles already beginning to strain, as she took the woman's weight off the cord cutting into her neck.

It was only when her senior officer spoke that Janine saw that Jenny Cleaver had hanged herself with some green garden twine. The white plastic garden chair that she'd used to climb up on was now overturned on the patio flagstones. The flowers in the basket were scarlet geraniums and some pretty blue flowers. Lobelias maybe.

Janine, tearing her eyes away from the flowers with something of an effort, ran to the greenhouse tucked neatly away in one corner, and came back, not with a pair of secateurs, but with an old, sharp garden knife. Dragging the white plastic garden chair upright again, she got up and hacked desperately at the twine, trying to keep from looking at the once-beautiful woman's face, now so near her own.

Hillary grunted as the full weight of Jenny Cleaver suddenly slumped over her shoulders, and Janine jumped off the chair and helped Hillary lay the woman down flat on the patio.

'Call for an ambulance,' Hillary yelled, and began immediate CPR.

But it was too late.

Jenny Cleaver was dead.

* * *

DI Mike Regis paused in the open doorway of the pub and looked around. It was nine o'clock, and the evening sun was coating everything a mellow yellow. At the bar, he spotted Hillary and her team, chatting with the barmaid.

The Boat was Hillary's local, and just where he expected Hillary to be celebrating after closing her case. Scuttlebutt travelled fast, and as he walked over to congratulate her, he noticed how particularly fine she was looking tonight. She'd changed into a soft, floating blue-and-white skirt and matching powder-blue jacket that left a lot of skin showing under her throat. She was wearing a pair of flat white sandals, and a delicate pearl-drop pendant, which nestled in the valley between her breasts.

'Look out, everybody, it's Vice,' Janine Tyler said sardonically as Mike sidled up beside her and slipped on to the bar stool. Regis nodded across at Mel, who nodded back.

Tommy Lynch sighed over his empty pint of beer as he spotted Mike Regis. He'd always suspected the Vice man had his sights set on Hillary, and now that he was divorced and free, there was nothing to stop him making his move.

But he didn't have to stay around to watch it.

'Guv, I've got to be off,' he said, and when Hillary nodded and turned to smile goodbye, he held up his hand in a general farewell.

In three days' time, he'd be gone. He wondered when he'd see any of them again. Then he thought of Jean, waiting at home for him, probably with a meal cooked and ready, and hurried out into the night.

As he pulled away, he failed to notice DCI Paul Danvers climbing out of his car.

At the bar, Mel and Janine were making eyes at each other, and Hillary wasn't surprised when they, too, slipped off early. Mel met Danvers in the doorway, and for a moment they indulged in a mutual bit of back-slapping. Janine lingered long enough to watch Paul Danvers approach the bar and smiled wickedly. Unless she was very much mistaken, the shit was about to hit the fan. She supposed Hillary Greene would be flattered to have two men fighting over her. She knew she would be.

Hillary, however, saw her boss approaching, and felt her heart sink. 'Sir,' she said, starting to stand and alerting Mike to Danvers's arrival.

'Please, don't get up,' Danvers said, with a smile. 'And I've told you before, call me Paul.'

'Paul,' Hillary said flatly. 'DI Mike Regis. Mike, DCI Paul Danvers. Mike works Vice, guv. You've met?'

Mike Regis held out his hand and the two men briefly shook. 'I was just congratulating Hillary on closing her case,' Mike said, catching the barmaid's eye and ordering a half of shandy.

'Yes, she's got good instincts,' Paul said, taking the bar stool next to her. 'I'm still not sure how she knew it was the wife, not the husband, who'd killed the boy.'

'Heard she killed herself,' Regis said. 'Never good when it ends that way.'

'No. For a start, you never get all the answers,' Paul agreed. 'For instance, why didn't she just keep paying the boy his money? We know from her bank records that she had been paying him regularly.'

'I think I know the reason for that,' Hillary said, and went on to explain about Jenny Cleaver's ambitions for a promotion that would see her heading for New York. 'Thing is, her boss was a very religious woman, a Jehovah's Witness. I think she simply got scared that Billy would tell her, just out of spite. Either that, or perhaps he taunted her about being gay. She probably begged him for the photos and maybe she just snapped when he asked her for more money. I don't think she went there that day to kill him, because she didn't take a weapon with her. The shears were just to hand. She probably struck out wildly and there it was.'

Both men were silent as they pictured the scene. A distraught woman, and a dead boy.

'You told his parents?' Regis asked gently, and Hillary nodded. 'I walked across the moment the ambulance arrived to take her away. Aston Lea's a tiny place. They saw it coming and were watching from the door. I had to tell them why Jenny Cleaver did it, as well.'

Regis saw the tight look of pain cross her face and reached across to take her hand and give it a squeeze.

Danvers, watching, drew in a sharp breath. Until that moment, he hadn't realised he had any real competition. Slowly, he sipped his own drink, a mineral water flavoured with kiwi, and turned on the stool. The movement brought his knee closer to Hillary's.

'I was wondering if you wanted to go out for a drink again sometime,' Danvers said quietly. 'I really enjoyed it, the other night. And now that the case is closed, and the pressure's off, perhaps we could go out for a meal, even?'

Hillary felt Mike Regis tense beside her. She reached for her own drink, a vodka and tonic, and tossed it back in one gulp.

And as Mike Regis and Paul Danvers looked at one another across the top of her chestnut head, Hillary waved her glass in the air. 'Another one,' she told the barmaid grimly. 'Make it a double. And this time, forget the tonic.'

THE END

Thank you for reading this book. If you enjoyed it please leave feedback on Amazon or Goodreads, and if there is anything we missed or you have a question about then please get in touch. The author and publishing team appreciate your feedback and time reading this book.

Our email is office@joffebooks.com

www.joffebooks.com

DI HILLARY GREENE BOOKS

More coming soon!

27698302R00141

Printed in Poland
by Amazon Fulfillm
Poland Sp. z o.o., Wr